A Lovely Reality

A Seneca & Michael Novel

Barbara Cutrera

Published by On My Way Up, LLC

Cover Photography: Sherri Proctor www.SherrisIslandImages.com

This book is a work of fiction. The names, characters, places, and incidents are the result of the author's imagination or are used fictitiously. Any resemblance to actual events, locales, or persons, living or dead, is coincidental.

ISBN: 978-0-9913642-5-1

For Carol. Our friendship has spanned decades, and the priceless gift of her time and input as a beta reader has helped make my lovely dream of becoming an author a lovely reality.

Chapter One

"Being deeply loved by someone gives you strength, while loving someone deeply gives you courage." — Lao Tzu

"Seneca, Michael is gone!"

I turned and saw my husband's short, stocky grandfather, Al, hurrying through the throng of relatives gathered in the family room of his mansion. He looked worried, and the men and women I'd been speaking with quickly asked him where Michael was. My stomach muscles tightened with anxiety. Michael and I had been through a lot in the last eight months, and I wondered what was wrong now.

"Michael and one of his cousins had an argument, and Michael stormed off," Al explained in his thick Italian accent.

I frowned and combed my fingers through my long, black hair. I'd heard Benedetto arguments, and they had all seemed to be good-natured, if lively, debates. I hadn't heard an actual cross word between any of the relatives since I'd been in their presence. What on earth could have made Michael leave the New Year's Eve family gathering?

"What were they arguing about?" I asked, feeling cold in spite of the blue velvet dress I wore.

Al looked uncomfortable but proceeded to tell me that his many grandsons had been standing outside on the terrace admiring the Southwest Florida Gulf waters and talking about what was going on in their lives. One of them was slightly drunk and asked Michael when he and I were going to start a family, joking that Michael had always done everything better than any of the other cousins and would probably father more children than the rest. He pointed out that Michael was thirty-two while I was twenty-eight and suggested we begin making babies as soon as possible in order to have as many

1

children as we wanted. Michael reminded him we'd only been married for five months and told him to give us time. When the man persisted despite the cousins' attempts to change the subject, Michael had lost his temper and announced angrily to him and the other men present that neither he nor his wife could have children then stalked off towards the front of the house. Several cousins followed but came around just in time to see Michael's SUV turning onto the road.

"I am going to talk to my grandson who has caused this problem, since he is very upset that he brought his cousin pain," Al told me. "You must find Michael, my angel. Things have been going smoothly for several weeks. I do not wish to see either of you in distress again."

I assured Al I'd find Michael and headed for the front door. As I walked through the rooms, all eyes turned towards me. News obviously traveled quickly through the Benedetto family. Normally, I would have hated that they knew about our fertility issues and would have cringed at the pitying and concerned looks. This time, I didn't care. They'd have found out sooner or later. Better to get it over with right away and allow them time to digest it and discuss it before the next get-together. I only hoped they wouldn't assail me with questions. I needed to find my husband and didn't have time to stop and talk with anyone.

"Seneca wait!"

I halted and looked towards Diane, Al's lady friend. She was in her seventies like Al and as wealthy as he, but he was gregarious whereas she tended to be downright bossy. With her perfectly arranged frosted hair, stylish pantsuit, manicured nails, and diamond jewelry, she looked regal as always. Just then, she also appeared concerned, held out her car keys, and said, "Michael's taken the SUV, remember? You have no other vehicle here. Take mine, and go find your husband before the others decide to form a search party. That would only make things worse."

I thanked her and retrieved my purse, hurrying out the front door before anyone could stop me. Once I'd located Diane's Mercedes, I wasted no time in starting the engine and leaving Al's driveway. While waiting at a traffic light, I grabbed my iPhone and speed dialed Michael's cell number. Not surprisingly, he didn't answer. I tried our home number and got the voicemail. My final attempt was Michael's office number at John's Place, the non-profit organization he'd founded to help veterans when he'd left the Navy, but he didn't pick up there either.

The person in the car behind me honked, and I jumped in my seat. I hadn't realized the light had changed from red to green. I drove forward, considering where I would go if I were Michael and was feeling angry and frustrated. We may have known one another for less than a year, but we were soul mates. I knew him better than anyone else and understood his feeling of helplessness.

Michael's cousins have no idea that he was a Naval Intelligence operative for ten years before he founded John's Place, I reminded myself. *There's a lot they don't know about him and me. We certainly are an unusual couple, and it's not only because we're so driven to succeed and have exceptionally high I.Q. levels. Michael is a former spy who has travelled the world and now runs a business that helps veterans, while I'm a social worker, who grew up in rural Florida and has only been out of my home state twice in my life. I was raised in poverty by undereducated parents, while Michael was raised by affluent grandparents after his mother and father died. He has a phenomenal eidetic memory, which means he possesses uncanny photographic memory abilities, and speaks English, Spanish, and several Arab dialects, as well as Greek, Italian, and Croatian. I speak English and Spanish and am considered to be a physics genius, despite my lack of formal training. Both of us suffer from PTSD. Interestingly enough, we share so many similarities but have so many differences. Yet we're truly in sync with one another. How did I ever live without him?*

I parked the Mercedes next to Michael's SUV in the lot at John's Place then called Diane and told her where I'd found him. I asked her not to tell anyone except Al where we were. We needed time alone.

"With any luck we'll see you all at the brunch tomorrow before everyone leaves to fly back to their respective homes," I concluded. "Enjoy the fireworks at midnight for me. Happy 2006."

The clock on the dashboard read 8:51. I removed my digital key and walked towards the front door of the building. I was suddenly afraid and found my hand shaking as I tried to slide the card. I felt like someone was watching me and waiting for the right moment to attack me, mug me, rape me, or kill me.

Once I was safely inside and had reset the alarm, I chided myself for being such a fraidy cat. True, it was late and I was in a deserted area of downtown Sarasota on New Year's Eve....

Okay, so maybe I was right to be afraid. At least I'm safely inside now. I know Michael heard me come in and reset the alarm. So, why isn't he coming out to see me?

I headed straight for the physical therapy area of the building, pushed open the door, and stepped inside the workout room. Michael had stripped off all his clothing save for his boxer shorts and was beating the stuffing out of a punching bag. I stood and watched his powerful six-foot frame move gracefully as he pummeled and kicked the defenseless bag. His muscles rippled with his movements, and his black hair was damp with perspiration.

"How'd you know I'd be here?" he asked as he spun and kicked the bag.

"You're my husband. I know you better than anyone."

Michael paused, looked at me with his beautiful blue eyes, nodded then launched himself at the bag once more. I took a seat in a nearby chair and watched the show. It was quite impressive.

"Michael?"

Breathing hard, he asked, "Yes?"

"What's the best way to kill someone?"

He shook his head and smiled very slightly before asking, "Why? Are you thinking about killing someone?"

"Of course not. I figured you wouldn't want to talk about what was really bothering you and decided to come up with something else to discuss for a while."

"Lovely choice."

"Remember when I read that book on espionage you had in your office? People had different opinions on what was the best way to eliminate a target. I wondered what you thought."

"I think it depends on what effect someone is aiming for. If one wants shock value or revenge, then prolonged torture is one's first choice. If you want quick but obvious, then you use a sniper. If you want something that isn't as easily detected, one might use poison." Punching the bag, he said, "Don't confuse spies with assassins. Spies have to kill sometimes, but an assassin is a killer by trade. There's a big difference."

"How many people did you have to kill when you were a spy?"

"I can't tell you that, and you know it. All you need to know is that I never took pleasure in it, which is more than I can say for some other operatives. It's a good thing none of my other family and friends know what I used to be. It might put them in danger. I wish you didn't have to know." He kicked the bag and said, "As for what brought me here, my cousin was drunk and pushed me too far by talking about me fathering a large family. He couldn't know about our situation. I shouldn't have yelled at him and said what I did. I'm sorry I shared it with the cousins. I'm sure everyone in the family knows by now." When I nodded, he dropped his head, rested his hands on his hips, and said, "We can skip the brunch tomorrow if you like."

"No. I want to go."

"Me, too. I just hope the relatives don't kill us with kindness."

"They're all great."

"I'm glad you think so. They love you. They keep saying how happy they are that you're part of the family now."

"It makes me happy, too. I feel like I belong somewhere. My Mommy and Poppy were all I had, and they've been gone for so long. Marrying a Benedetto has given me a big, loving family."

Michael smiled, but I could see that sad look in his eyes. I got to my feet before suggesting he put on his clothes so we could go home.

"I'm not used to wearing high heels, and my feet hurt," I told him. "I want to walk barefoot with you on our beach and ring in the New Year."

"You know I can't resist when you flash me that look with those gorgeous brown eyes. Let's go enjoy some fireworks of our own."

When we arrived home, I parked Diane's Mercedes in the garage next to my Toyota, while Michael left the SUV in the driveway. We took off our shoes and walked to the secluded beach just in time to see the beginning of the fireworks display over the water, orchestrated by those with boats in the area. Michael went for a swim in the freezing waters under the colorful bursts, and I was torn between watching the dazzling light show and his dazzling body.

When the display was finished, Michael emerged from the Gulf and used his shirt to dry off as best he could. We turned to admire the progress on the house. Our expansion project had begun at the end of November and was on schedule. The former lanai, a screened-in back porch that had run the length of the home, had been demolished and the bungalow living space expanded. That area was now enclosed and was part of the inside living area but was unfinished. The frame of the new lanai was up and the entire roof had been extended, but the electrical work had yet to begin on that part.

We walked around to the front door and entered our home. I suddenly sensed that something wasn't right. Michael sensed it before I did and stopped me from switching on the lamp. He took my hand and pulled me close to him then moved to one side of the room and reached for something in the darkness. I wanted to ask him what he was doing but dared not speak.

There came an unearthly screeching noise directly in front of us. I screamed. I couldn't help myself. I heard Michael swear before telling me to turn on the lamp. He wasn't whispering, so I decided there must be no danger and hurried to comply.

My eyes quickly adjusted to the light, and I put a hand to my chest and said, "Oh, my God. You have got to be kidding me."

A tabby cat was plastered against the built-in wall unit. Its hair stood on end, and it hissed at us. Michael was standing a few feet away from it appearing bemused and holding a large, sinister-looking knife. He laid the knife down on the cabinet and crouched in front of the terrified, collarless cat.

"It must have come in through some opening made by the construction workers," he told me as he extended his hand towards the feline intruder. "You scared the shit out of us, kitty."

Still shaking with fear and adrenaline, I forgot to chide him for swearing and asked, "Where did you get that knife?"

"Old habits die hard, but those who become complacent die harder. I have several…tools hidden around the house."

"Where?"

He shook his head. It made me furious.

"If someone came in, I wouldn't have any way to defend myself," I insisted. "I need to know."

Michael stood, walked over to me, and said very quietly, "If someone who was a real threat got in while I wasn't home and intended malice, you'd be dead before you ever reached any of the items I have hidden. You have no idea what malevolent people exist in this world."

I squared my shoulders and announced, "I wouldn't go down without a fight, even if I didn't stand a chance."

"I know you wouldn't. You are so innocent that it's both refreshing and frightening."

He turned back towards the cat, which was now cowering in one corner. The tabby appeared to be young and way too thin. It was also wet on its face and paws.

"Doc!" I cried and raced to the kitchen.

What was left of my Siamese fighting fish lay on the table. I looked away, not wanting to see his little mangled fish body. He'd been a constant presence in my house since before I'd known Michael, and it would seem odd not to have him as the handsome sentinel in the kitchen.

"I'll take care of it," offered Michael. "Would you prefer flushing him or burying him?"

"Burial at sea seems fitting for a fish," I told him. "Could you put him in the Gulf?"

"Sure. You're not going to kill the kitty with my knife while I'm out there, are you?"

"No. It's not the poor cat's fault. The thing looks like he's starving, and cats do love to eat fish anyway."

"You want to keep the cat," Michael stated as realization dawned.

"Would that be terrible if I did? Are you one of those guys who hates cats?"

"I prefer dogs, but having a cat when you live at the beach and have our schedules seems more practical."

"I've never had anything but Doc for a pet. I don't know what to do with a cat."

"Let's call an emergency vet clinic and see what they recommend."

The clinic staff suggested a veterinary service that made house calls. They told us there was no way we were going to be able to get the scared cat to their clinic without a carrier, and it had already been traumatized enough. We called the veterinarian who appeared in his mobile clinic an hour later.

By the time the man arrived, the cat had warmed considerably to us and was curled up in my lap. The vet performed a thorough examination. Amazingly enough, the cat did not object and allowed the stranger to poke, prod, and give it several shots and squirt some medication in its mouth. The vet remarked that he'd never examined a cat as good natured as ours.

"He's probably about four months old. He doesn't have a microchip, but it appears he was well-cared for when he was small and has been neutered. My guess is he belonged to someone who got him as a kitten. When that person moved or got tired of him once he wasn't the fluffy little kitten he'd been when adopted, he was put out of the house. Another scenario I often see is that the owner died, and no one wanted him afterwards. It happens all too frequently."

The vet lifted the cat from my lap, took him to the van, bathed him in some special shampoo, then gave us a list of supplies we would need and a booklet on how to care for felines. He agreed to come back to inject a microchip under the cat's skin. It would include the cat's name – once we had given it one – our address, and phone numbers in case the cat got lost and needed to be returned to us.

Michael left me on the couch with the cat and went outside to pay the vet. When he came back in, I asked him how much the visit had cost. Money wasn't really an issue for us, but I'd been raised in poverty and was very mindful of what I spent. Michael told me I didn't want to know the total bill, but it had been worth every penny. Then he kissed me, petted the cat, and left to go to the twenty-four hour Walmart to buy the basic supplies we needed. By the time he returned, it was 3:00 a.m. He set up the litter box he'd purchased in the guest bedroom but told me he was moving it to the new laundry room the moment it was completed.

After putting down the amount of food the vet had recommended and some water, we watched as the cat greedily ate and drank.

"He's so cute," I said with a smile. "I never thought I'd have a cat."

"Me neither, but I think this will work out well." He put an arm around me and asked, "What do you want to name him, as if I don't already know?"

"Okay, Mister Smarty-pants. What do you think I want to name him?"

"You fancy your great-grandfather was John Henry "Doc" Holliday. You named your fish Doc and the baby you lost in college John Henry. All that's left is Holliday."

I shook my head slightly and said, "No. Even if Holliday was my great-grandfather, he wasn't a sterling example of what a man should be. He did happen to be brilliant, charming, cunning, and a great marksman. He was also reckless, a Southern bigot, and violent. Regardless, we'll never know for sure whether or not he was actually my great-grandfather. I have a new family now and think it's time to let go of that past."

"I'm glad to hear it. So, what do you want to name the cat?"

"I was thinking about Cupcake."

"We're not," he laughed.

"I was," I giggled. "Either Cupcake or Twinkle Toes."

Michael sighed dramatically and asked, "Can't we just call him Cat?"

"How about Houdini, since we have no idea how he got in the house?"

"He doesn't look like a Houdini."

"What does he look like?"

"A cat."

"I'm going to call him Cupcake if you don't come up with something better," I taunted.

"Give the cat some dignity, Seneca. He's already been neutered, and now you want to call him Cupcake?"

"Oh, all right. You name him."

Michael lifted the cat and stared at his face then proclaimed, "I dub thee Sir Buttons."

"Buttons is more dignified than Cupcake?"

"Definitely."

"Whatever you say...."

We showered and then slept in our bed with Buttons curled up in a warm blanket on the floor beside us. When the clock alarm rang at 9:00, I quickly switched it off.

"I want more sleep," I groaned. "Four hours is nowhere near enough. Maybe we can sleep a little longer."

"Not if we're going to make it in time for the brunch," Michael murmured, as he licked the curve of my neck. "Unless you'd rather stay in bed all day."

"I'd love that, but we should go to the brunch. If we don't, the family will really be worried and who knows what rumors will start."

"I know. Plus, I need to talk to my cousin who triggered all this before he leaves. Otherwise, he's going to dwell on it until next Christmas."

I was about to agree with him, but his hand was suddenly around my throat. He tightened his grip slightly, and I brought both my hands to his wrist and tried to pull it away. It was like trying to move a massive piece of concrete that had somehow been compacted into the shape of a man's hand.

Maybe he's snapped, I thought frantically. *He's going to kill me.*

As quickly as he'd grabbed me, Michael released my throat and said resignedly, "You were right."

"Wh-what are you talking about?" I gasped.

"You would be completely defenseless if someone attacked you. I love your softness and your naivety, but I started thinking after what happened last night that you need to learn some self-defense moves and that we should have a security system installed. It wouldn't stop a true professional, but it wouldn't hurt to make things a little more difficult for someone."

"I've been thinking about last night, too," I confided. "When you told me you had things like the knife planted around the house, it made me reconsider our idea about adopting. Before he died of natural causes, Tom told me there were three unsuccessful attempts on his life after he left his career as a spy. What if someone comes after you or me and our children? I don't want to put any child in danger."

Tom had been a dear friend of mine who'd been a spy for thirty years before becoming a college professor. He and Michael had become great friends after I'd introduced them. The two of them shared a bond that none of the rest of us could ever truly understand. I missed my friend terribly because he'd been like a father and mentor to me. Michael missed him terribly because he'd lost a brother-in-arms and confidante.

Michael traced the curve of my cheek with his fingertips and said, "I don't want to put anyone else at risk, but I'm retired from my former career. The longer I'm out of it, the less likely it'll be that anyone will come after me or those I care about."

"But it could happen."

"It could."

"What would you do if someone hurt me or our children?"

"I'd kill them without hesitation," he said matter-of-factly, reminding me of Tom's response to a similar question I'd posed the previous year. "Those in that community have an…understanding."

"What kind of understanding?"

Michael kissed me and said, "I can't, Seneca."

"But –"

"I have to live my life, and so do you. You know if we weren't incapable of having kids, you'd already be pregnant. You'd find a way to justify the risk of my past coming back to haunt us so that you could have our babies."

I sighed and said, "You're right. It still makes me nervous. I do want to learn self-defense. Will you teach me? I wouldn't mind learning how to use a gun, too. An alarm system would be welcome as well."

"I'd be happy to teach you self-defense and how to use a gun and a knife. As for an alarm system, I'll arrange for that."

"You know a man who knows a man?"

He grinned and said, "Something like that."

"Michael?"

"Hm?"

"Will you do something for me before we get ready to go?"

"Anything."

We were late for the brunch.

11

Chapter Two

"I can't take it anymore!" Krystal exclaimed, her blonde ponytail moving back and forth as she shook her head in exasperation. "Maybe Greg and I should just get married in jeans and t-shirts and be done with it!"

"Calm down," I said soothingly. "You and Adiba are my best friends, and we'll work together to help you find the perfect wedding gown."

"It will be fine," Adiba told her as she rearranged the blanket over her daughter, Hadeel, who was sleeping in her stroller. "I am confident you will find the right dress today."

"But what if I don't? We leave for Las Vegas tomorrow!"

Adiba sighed and adjusted her hijab, the traditional head covering she wore in deference to Islamic tradition. The rest of her attire was always Western but always modest. She and her husband, Rakeem, had come to the United States from Iraq two years earlier and were in the process of becoming U.S. citizens. They'd lost a son at birth three years earlier, and Hadeel was not quite a year old. Adiba was in the middle of her last trimester of pregnancy with another son. She and Rakeem had decided to name him Hani, which meant "to be joyful" in Arabic. Hadeel meant "dove," although I thought "prima donna" would have been a better fit. I loved the baby, but she could be quite the drama queen when she didn't get her way.

"Krystal, this would go a lot more quickly if you'd only accept my offer," I pointed out to my friend and former co-worker. "After all, you've been looking at dresses for weeks and haven't found one you liked. Let me do this."

"I don't want to accept charity."

"It's not charity. I want to buy you your wedding dress as a wedding gift. I have the money, so let me do something really over-the-top for you. Please?"

"But the dresses are all too expensive, and Greg and I are already caving by letting Michael pay for our flight out there and back as a wedding present to us and allowing Al and Diane to pay for our hotel as their present."

"That is not caving, if I understand the term correctly," Adiba said. "That is accepting a gift from someone who wants to do something nice for you."

The saleswoman at the bridal shop was very patiently waiting to see how this debate would end. She seemed quite pleased when Krystal agreed to try on dresses that cost more than her budget of five hundred dollars and told us to wait while she collected gowns in Krystal's size.

For the remainder of that Saturday morning, we watched as Krystal paraded in front of us wearing various types of bridal attire. Some made us all laugh hysterically, while we had varying opinions on others. None of them seemed to stand out as The Dress.

"We only have one gown left in your size," the saleswoman told Krystal once we'd all agreed the dress she had on was definitely not meant for her. "I think this one may be more of what you're looking for."

Hadeel, who'd slept through the entire visit to the bridal shop, woke and began to whimper. I told Adiba to stay seated and lifted the baby out of the stroller and gave her a bottle.

"Thank you," Adiba told me as she rested a hand on her ever-growing belly. "I am extra-tired these last few days. I know Hadeel is not yet a year old, but she is heavy for me, especially with baby Hani in-between us."

While we waited for Krystal to appear in the final gown, I took Hadeel to the bathroom to change her diaper. Luckily, they had a baby-changing station that folded down from the wall. When I went to lean her back onto the changing pad, she fought me and began to wail. I was prepared for it. She'd been doing that since she was old enough to realize that her tears often got her what she wanted from her parents.

"No you don't," I said gently but firmly. "This is not optional." When she continued to try to twist off the table, I said more sternly, "Hadeel, you're going to fall. Why don't we talk about something different while I change you?"

I proceeded to tell her about the book I'd been reading regarding the phenomenon of black holes and the physical properties of the universe. Hadeel immediately stopped crying and squirming and listened intently for the next five minutes. I smiled and told her we'd have to talk more about the subject the next time I changed her diaper.

"How was she?" Adiba asked. "Like usual?"

"Actually, no. I found out she likes astrophysics."

"Astrophysics?"

"Well, I've tried cajoling her with every other method I could think of with no success since she's been tiny. This time she stopped screaming and listened to what I was saying."

My friend laughed and said, "Perhaps that is the secret to calming all babies, and you are the first to try it and realize how well it works!"

"We'll see if it works again next time. Maybe she'll be a great astrophysicist someday."

"Well, Rakeem is an engineer, and I am a landscape architect. We want our daughter to follow whatever path she chooses, but we would not be unhappy if she were a great astrophysicist."

"Adiba, may I ask you something I've always wondered about?"

"Certainly."

"How do you do work as a landscape architect wearing long skirts and long sleeves and a hijab? Don't those things get in the way? And wouldn't it make you really hot all the time? Well, maybe not the hijab, since that's just like a scarf that goes around your head...."

"I have always done the designing and working with clients, although I worked with the plantings as well when I was not pregnant. One learns early how to do such things however one dresses. A berka might actually be easier in certain instances, but my family did not believe that women had to dress in one. We were always...how do you say it? Progressive for our area. Rakeem's family, too. I am educated, work, drive, and shop without the need for my husband's permission. I know Rakeem and I have a different type of marriage than you and Michael, but that is part of our culture. It is good for us, especially since there is no one left on either side of our families because of the fighting in Iraq."

I nodded and thanked her for the explanation. Adiba and I heard the rustling of fabric and turned towards the doorway. Krystal walked into the room looking confident and radiant in a one-shouldered gown that had a beaded, fitted bodice and full, fluffy, tiered chiffon skirt. I didn't like it at all, but the dress did flatter Krystal's larger size and her body shape. It obviously made her feel like a queen. That was the important thing.

"I feel like royalty!" Krystal confided. "I never thought I'd ever have a dress like this." Turning to the saleswoman, she asked tentatively, "How much is it?"

"Don't tell her!" I said before the woman could answer. "This is my treat, and I don't ever want her to know."

"But Seneca –"

"No," I insisted. "You go take off the dress while I pay for it. Remember, I didn't have to buy my own wedding dress because it was an antique gown given to me, so I'm spending what I would have on mine and adding it to yours. Therefore, this one really won't be as much, right?"

The dress was three thousand dollars. I had expected as much and gladly paid it. I remembered my high school prom dress search and how hard my mother and I had worked to find a nice dress, shoes, and an evening purse at thrift shops. This time, I was able to help someone I cared about own the gown of her dreams. It felt good.

The saleswoman agreed to pack the dress for transport to Vegas while we ate our lunch. The three of us promised to return in an hour or two and pick up the garment. Then, we walked down the street to a Greek restaurant we all liked and enjoyed our meal while Hadeel played with various toys.

"I wish you and Rakeem could come with us for the wedding," Krystal told Adiba as we walked back to the bridal shop. "We hate that you can't be there."

"We would love to come witness your wedding as we did Seneca and Michael's, but you know what my doctor has said. Since there were complications with my first baby, he does not advise that I travel out of town."

"At least you have only a month and a half to go," she said. "Then we all get to meet Hani!"

"I will worry until he is in my arms and is alive and healthy," Adiba admitted. "At least I will know how to care for him well; since Seneca aided me so much when we hired help from Hearts at Home right after Hadeel was born. We were so fortunate that Seneca decided to take our case herself and teach me how to care for my daughter."

"It was my pleasure," I said emphatically. "You're a great mother."

"Thanks to you."

I smiled and thanked her for the compliment, trying not to think of my own missed opportunity with my baby, John Henry. We picked up Krystal's wedding gown, loaded it into the trunk of her car then Krystal and I hugged Adiba and kissed Hadeel, since we wouldn't be seeing either of them until the next Saturday. I then gave Krystal a brief hug, told her I'd see her in the morning, and walked to my own car.

I drove home, parked in the garage, went into the house, disarmed the security system, reset the security system, walked towards the bedroom, and found that the cat had discovered he could have fun with toilet paper.

"Buttons!" I exclaimed, but I was laughing. The cat was rolling happily in a pile of the pieces.

I heard the front door open and close and listened as the alarm was disarmed and reset. I called out for Michael to come quickly and see what "his" cat had done. When he saw the paper strewn all over the hallway and into the two bedrooms, he burst out laughing and withdrew his iPhone. He then took a picture of the cat tangled in toilet paper, texted something, and forwarded everything to Al, whom Michael called "Nonno." It meant "grandfather" in Italian. Al had recently learned to text and encouraged us to text him as often as we wanted.

"What did you say?"

"That his great-grandchild was into mischief, which proved he was a true Benedetto."

His phone buzzed, and he glanced at the screen before grinning and shaking his head. He held it up, so I could see the OMG! LOL! message.

"I don't know if I should be pleased or saddened by Nonno's new fascination with his phone," Michael told me as he bent to begin collecting the paper. "I guess we're going to have to start putting the toilet paper on upside-down like the vet said so that Buttons won't do this."

"But I hate having the roll like that," I protested.

"It's either that or this."

"We could keep the bathroom doors closed."

"And when we have kids, do you think they're all going to remember to close them every time? Their friends and ours, too?"

"I see your point. Let's clean things up so we can pack."

As we picked up the paper and played with the cat, I told Michael about the wedding gown adventure and how pleased Krystal had been with her dress. He talked of his lunch with Greg and Rakeem. We packed, ate a salad and grilled chicken breasts, and spent an hour reading before going to bed.

"How is my naughty great-grandchild?" was the first thing Al asked when we met him and Diane at the airport.

"Being his naughty self when we left," Michael answered. "Although I think he's going to be very confused this week while we're gone and Rakeem and Adiba go over to take care of him."

Krystal and Greg arrived. Greg's blonde hair had been cropped shorter than we'd ever seen it, and he told us he'd wanted a fresh look as he and Krystal began their life together. We went through the process of checking our bags, following the security protocols, and boarding the plane. We were all seated in First Class, which was a first for me, Krystal, and Greg.

Several hours later, we arrived in Las Vegas and were relieved to find that none of our luggage had been lost en route. We were soon checking in at the luxury hotel and casino. I'd never stayed in such a place and was awed by the architecture and décor. It felt as though I was in a museum or in Italy itself. Al and Diane seemed perfectly at home, as did Michael. Krystal and Greg gawked as I did and allowed the others to guide us to the front desk.

I was amazed at the size of the rooms. Each of our suites had a bedroom with a long dresser, an armoire, an HDTV, a king-sized bed, and a sitting area, plus a large main living room, kitchenette, and dining area. The bathrooms were enormous. The windows throughout the suites afforded spectacular views of the city. Every suite was individually decorated with quality finishes and different furnishings.

"The bathroom's as big as our bedroom!" I exclaimed over dinner. "I've never seen a shower that spacious or a tub that large."

"This whole place is unbelievable," Greg chimed in. "All I can say is thanks so much to Al and Diane. This is more than we ever imagined."

"Tomorrow you'll be married and can enjoy the rest of your trip however you like," Diane proposed, as she smoothed her frosted blonde hair. "You may decide not to leave your rooms all week."

"You will embarrass our young friends," Al admonished.

Krystal was, indeed, blushing, and Greg was smiling.

"So, tonight I sleep with Krystal in her room, and one of the guys takes the fold-out sofa in our room," I explained. "I don't know about the rest of you, but I think I'm going to go to bed early tonight. After all, the wedding's at 10:00."

"It has been a long day of travel," Al conceded. "And you want to be rested for the wedding. Diane and I will meet you at 8:45 in the courtyard."

After dinner we three couples parted ways and went to our separate rooms. I had already put my bridesmaid's dress, shoes, jewelry, underwear, make-up, and toiletries in Krystal and Greg's suite and was merely going back to our room to get my pajamas and say goodnight to Michael.

"The hotel staff is going to bring the things I leave in Krystal's room to our room during the wedding," I told Michael, as I removed my make-up and took off my silver hoop earrings. "They told me to leave my stuff on a chair in the sitting area and they'll come in and get it out for me."

"That'll be helpful."

The way he said it gave me pause, and I turned to look at him and asked what was wrong.

"I don't know."

"Are you worried about Buttons?" I teased. "I mean, I'm kind of worried about him, but I know Adiba and Rakeem will take care of him and spend time at the house playing with him while they're there."

"No, it's not that. I don't know what it is. I have a bad feeling about something, but I can't quite pin it down." Taking me in his arms, he said, "I'm sure it's nothing. I probably just don't want to sleep apart from you."

"You and Greg could always share the king-sized bed," I said with saccharine sweetness. "It's big enough for the both of you. Krystal and I are going to sleep together in their bed."

"Men don't do that except in combat or when they're little boys."

"Well, then you'll simply have to miss me and be looking forward to tomorrow night."

"I look forward to every night with you."

It was said with sincerity, but I could tell he was distracted. I wondered what was going on in his mind. He'd been slightly on edge for the past three months since the night we'd entered the house and thought there'd been a human intruder inside. Dr. Forrester, the Naval psychiatrist who worked with both of us, had assured me during our last virtual session that Michael's uneasiness was normal in light of his past experiences and would fade. I hoped he was right.

Michael and I shared a passionate kiss before he escorted me to Krystal and Greg's room. When Greg came to answer the door, it appeared he and Krystal had been sharing a passionate kiss of their own. Greg cleared his throat and gave a flushed Krystal a quick peck on the cheek before wishing us both a good night and leaving with Michael.

"What a kiss!" Krystal breathed. "We've kissed before but never like that. Seneca, if the sex is anything like that kiss, then we may *not* leave the room for the rest of the week!"

I laughed and told her that we'd all understand and wouldn't take it personally. Then we both put on our pajamas and got ready for bed.

"I haven't slept with another girl since I was in high school and went for sleepovers," Krystal told me. "This is kind of neat. It makes me feel like a girl again."

"Me, too. I feel like we should pop some popcorn and watch chick flicks all night, but that probably wouldn't be advisable with your wedding being in the morning."

"Probably not. Another time."

We climbed into bed and turned out the lights. I lay staring up at the ceiling and tried to sleep, but I was wide awake. I sighed and turned towards Krystal then asked if she was sleeping.

"No. I guess I'm too excited to sleep."

"Are you doing okay with this whole Las Vegas thing?"

"You mean not having any of our relatives here? We're fine with it. We've sort of come to the conclusion that if the two of us are going to be successful in our marriage and in our lives, then we need to stay away from our destructive families. It's really sad, but I sort of feel like we're free of them. Gosh, that sounds really bad."

"No, I understand."

"I also can't wait to have sex with Greg. I was used by so many men for that because of my low self-esteem before I started going to the Less of You meetings and beginning to lose weight and gain confidence. The fact that Greg wanted to wait to sleep with me until after we got married helped to prove that he wanted me for *me.*"

"The fact that he lost a hundred and fifty pounds several years ago and has kept it off helped him to understand, just as I do. And I lost only sixty-five!"

"Only! You were the one who inspired me when I heard what you'd done. To know that you'd lost all that weight and never gained it back gave me hope, especially since I'd always been heavy. You'd gained the weight after your mom's death and then your marriage, miscarriage, and divorce."

"I know what you mean, but being overweight has the same effect on most people. You just had to live with it for a lot longer than I did. I'm sorry for that and because your family treated you so badly as a result."

She paused then asked, "How are you doing with everything?"

"Everything?"

"Missing Tom. Healing your body after having that huge mirror fall on you when you had that horrible nightmare about the day you watched your father die. Dealing with Adiba's pregnancy. That sort of everything."

"I still miss Tom terribly, but it's better. My body's great, and pretty much every scar has faded well except the small one on my neck, the one near my lung and, of course, the really bad one on my leg. Those will never go away, but they do look okay."

"And the baby?"

"I wish it were me, but I'm happy for her. I pray that Hani's born safely and is okay."

"Are you going to be jealous when Greg and I have kids?"

"I will, but I'll be happy for you just as I am for Rakeem and Adiba. Besides, Michael and I are going to have our own kids someday, remember? Then it won't hurt so much when other people have babies."

"I can't wait until we all have children," Krystal said in a dreamy tone of voice. "Well, Greg and I plan to wait a while, but you know what I mean."

"I do, and I can't wait either."

"I have to hold off for at least another couple of years before I get pregnant," Krystal informed me.

"Why is that?"

"Because it's the end of March, and I've officially lost fifty-seven pounds. I still have thirty-three to go to reach my weight goal. I don't want to lose it all only to get pregnant right away and gain a ton back."

"Yes, but you'll know how to lose it afterwards."

"True but I want to enjoy being thin for a while before I get a big tummy."

"You do get a really good reward for that type of weight gain though."

"I know. It'll be worth it. I still want to wait a while. By my first anniversary, I want to be the size I've always dreamed of being." Pausing, she said, "If I'd never asked you about losing the weight then we wouldn't be friends, and I never would have gone to the meetings. I would never have met Greg or acknowledged what a beautiful woman I am. Talk about a life-changing experience."

She was asleep before I could comment. I lay awake for a while but soon joined her. I had odd dreams but thankfully no nightmares.

We woke at 6:00. As we waited for Room Service to bring our breakfast, I showered and styled my hair by leaving it loose but using the curling iron to create a few more curls than I normally had. I slipped on a robe and came out after the food had been delivered; then we ate. After she'd put our tray laden with the empty plates and glasses outside the door, Krystal went to shower while I put on my bridesmaid's dress.

The deep red, strapless A-line dress was tea-length and had a black ribbon wrapped around the natural waistline. There was a bow at the back and ribbons that fell just above the hem of the skirt. Made of taffeta, the dress was a very classic style and would definitely be fitting for other occasions in the future. I loved it, and so did Krystal.

Slipping on my pantyhose, I decided to wait to put on the low black heels that went with the dress. I then inserted the black pearl earrings under my diamond studs and donned my heirloom art deco wedding ring before applying my make-up.

"Seneca, you look fantastic!" Krystal exclaimed when she saw me.

"Thanks. *You* are going to look stunning once you're ready."

Grinning, she said, "I am SO ready!"

I had Krystal sit in the chair in front of the vanity but asked her to turn it sideways so I could fix her hair and apply her make-up. She'd asked me to do this for her, knowing my mother, who'd been a hair stylist, had taught me how to do these things from the time I'd been small. At first I'd refused, but she'd insisted. I finally relented, but it made me nervous. I worried about not doing it perfectly and having her be disappointed with the way she looked on one of the most important days of her life.

I remembered Tom telling me once, "You worry way too much, my lovely girl. You're a brilliant, capable, resourceful woman. What you fret over as being merely adequate is far superior to most people's best efforts. I'm so thankful to have you for my very own!"

I smiled to myself and applied Krystal's make-up. I then set about arranging her blonde hair in an up-do that left a few ringlets framing her face. Once I was finished, I asked her not to look at herself in the mirror until after she'd put on her dress.

Fifteen minutes later, she was completely ready. I bit my lip as she stepped in front of the mirror. I prayed that she didn't hate what I'd done. I didn't know what we were going to do if she was dissatisfied. We only had twenty-five minutes left before we were supposed to meet Al and Diane.

"Oh, my gosh," she said in a hushed voice. "It all looks so perfect."

Breathing a quiet sigh of relief, I hastened to get her shoes and the box that held Greg's wedding band. I slipped on my shoes and helped her with hers; then we left the room and went to the elevator. Everyone we passed wished Krystal congratulations, and she was beaming with pleasure and gratitude. When we reached the lavish courtyard, Al and Diane complimented both of us and introduced us to the photographer who'd been hired to capture the images of the brief ceremony and the time before and afterwards.

Al was wearing a dark gray suit, a white shirt, and a black and gray-patterned tie. Diane wore a short-sleeved, deep purple dress that fell just below her knees and appeared to be made of satin. Krystal and I remarked on how wonderful they looked while we waited.

Neither Krystal nor I had a bouquet to carry. She'd decided she didn't want to follow tradition in that fashion. She and Greg were going to hold hands for the entire ceremony, and I was going to do…something with mine. I still had no idea what, but I would figure it out.

The photographer took pictures of Krystal by herself in various poses. Then he snapped photos of the two of us together. Finally, he took some group shots of me, Krystal, Al, and Diane.

The Justice of the Peace, who was to perform the wedding ceremony, appeared and introduced himself. As Krystal and Greg had requested, he was also a minister and was an affable man about my age. He led our little group to an area near the terrace where the ceremony would be held. The man explained that he'd already reviewed the nuptial process with Greg but wanted to discuss it with Krystal as well. The two of them stepped aside and talked, while Al, Diane, and I stood at the ready.

"What is it, my angel?" Al asked gently. "You look concerned about something."

"Just hoping everything goes smoothly for the wedding."

"You are a terrible liar," Al told me. "You are worrying about Michael, are you not?"

"A little. Was there a problem this morning when you saw him?"

"No, but I have noticed a change in him since New Year's Eve. It is very small, but he seems…."

"On edge," Diane finished for him.

"It is as if his guard is up every moment," said Al. "Others probably do not even notice, but we notice, as you have."

I nodded slightly and was about to say that the therapist had assured me this would eventually pass, but Krystal came back over to us then. She once again thanked Al and Diane profusely for acting as family by coming with all of us to Las Vegas for the wedding and for their generous gift. They both declared they were more than happy to bear witness to such a wonderful event and wished her and Greg many years of marital bliss. Then they went up to the terrace.

The Justice of the Peace returned and told us it was time. He instructed me to wait for a couple of minutes after he'd walked up the steps then follow. He left, and I waited. The photographer motioned for me to begin my approach. Still uncertain about what to do with my hands, I placed the palm of my right hand over the back of my left and rested that palm against the front of my skirt. While I walked, I listened to the birds chirping and the sound of a nearby fountain and smiled. It was a lovely day for a wedding.

Chapter Three

As I climbed the steps, I thought of my own wedding and of Tom walking beside me, my arm tucked around his. It made me both happy and sad to think of how it felt to be standing next to him. I knew he would always be with me, but I missed hearing his voice and being in his presence. I prayed that Al would live a very long and healthy life. I'd already lost my Poppy and Tom, and I couldn't bear the thought of losing Al, too. I hoped Diane would be around for a long time as well. I needed her.

The Justice of the Peace stood in the center of the terrace underneath an archway. Stone planters filled with beautiful white flowers dotted the setting, as did classical-looking statuary that appeared as though it had been transported straight from Rome. It was an elegant setting for the small wedding party. I knew Krystal would love it.

Greg and Michael stood beside the Justice of the Peace. Both were wearing black suits, black ties, and deep red shirts that matched my dress. Greg looked nervous but was obviously thrilled. Michael looked at me with such love in his expression that I almost tripped over my own two feet. I smiled at him and took my place on the other side of the minister. Al and Diane watched from their position nearby.

When Krystal came into view, I thought Greg might forget to breathe. He was looking at her the same way that Michael had just looked at me. I glanced back to Krystal, who was grinning from ear to ear and gazing adoringly at her blonde Prince Charming. I knew from our past conversations that she'd never dreamed anything like true love would ever happen to her.

Greg and Krystal joined hands. Once the photographer had snapped a couple of pictures, the Justice of the Peace began the ceremony. He talked of love and God and how things that were meant to be always had happy endings. Krystal and Greg exchanged their vows and then their rings. They were pronounced man and wife and directed to share their first kiss as a married couple. They did, and we all smiled and then hugged each other as many pictures were taken of our little group.

When it was all over, the photographer told us the pictures would be ready for review at 2:00 p.m. that afternoon and gave us instructions about where to meet him.

"Will you all come look with us?" Krystal asked. "I know I'm going to have the hardest time picking out which photos to select, and I know they're going to be expensive."

"Krystal, thanks to our friends here, most of our trip has been paid for," Greg reminded her. "The money I've been saving for years plus what you have will let us enjoy ourselves while we're here and get whatever pictures we want. It's our wedding and honeymoon. It's only going to happen once. I want us to have great memories of it all." He kissed her and said, "Now, relax and let's go enjoy our wedding brunch."

The food was delicious, as was the small wedding cake that followed it. We talked, laughed, and had a great time. Michael seemed to truly let go of the underlying tension he'd held within for the past three months. I wondered if this joyous event would be the turning point in his struggle to let down his guard.

When the bill came for our meals and the cake, Greg insisted on paying for everyone. We all protested, but he told us, "Krystal has a good job in payroll at Hearts at Home, and I make a great salary as a department store manager. We'll never be as rich as you guys, and we don't care about that anymore than you do. However, we can definitely afford to do this. Please let us take care of this, so we can show you our appreciation for everything related to our wedding. I don't only mean the wedding dress, flight, and hotel stay. I also mean coming out here and sharing our ceremony with us. It's meant a lot to me and Krystal to know how much you care."

"If it hadn't been for you guys, we'd probably have ended up at whatever wedding chapel we happened upon in Vegas," Krystal added. "It would have been great because it was our wedding, but it wouldn't have been magical as it was today." Tearing up, she said, "Thank you all for being our family."

My own eyes filled with tears. I knew how she felt, but I wondered which one of us had been in the worst predicament. Before I had become part of the Benedetto family, I'd been utterly alone with no living relatives. Krystal and Greg had plenty of living relatives but had been mistreated by them their entire lives. At least when my parents had been alive, they had loved me and told me how special I was, no matter how mixed up their own lives were.

Krystal excused herself from the table, and I began to rise to follow her to the restroom. Diane told me to stay where I was.

"I have this one," she whispered in my ear. "This is more up my alley than yours."

I nodded and sat. Diane's family situation did parallel Krystal's in more ways than mine, and it would help for my "sister" to have a little heart-to-heart with our atypical fairy godmother. I dabbed at my eyes with a tissue and resumed conversation with the men.

When Krystal and Diane returned to the table, all of Krystal's make-up had been washed off. I was sorry she'd been crying but relieved to see that none of her make-up had ended up on her wedding gown. Diane suggested we all return to our rooms, change into our regular clothing, then meet to view the photographs before parting ways for the remainder of the day.

By the time we reached our room, Michael and I had an hour to change and go downstairs. Michael slid the digital key into the lock and held the door open for me then followed me inside. Within seconds, his powerful body was pressing against mine as my back was pressed against the wall. His mouth was on mine, and my arms encircled his neck.

"You look so beautiful," he murmured when he moved his mouth to my throat.

"Michael, we don't have time," I protested weakly.

"Like hell we don't."

"But we'll have to shower before we go downstairs," I pointed out in a feeble attempt at resisting what I always wanted when it came to Michael.

He stopped and straightened, and I was torn. I looked up into his bright blue eyes and knew I had no reason to wonder what we should do. We *were* going to have sex. The animal inside of him was pulling hard on the leash.

We were both naked in under a minute. He led me to the bathroom. While I washed my face, Michael punched buttons into a panel on the wall and rock music with a driving beat poured into the bathroom from speakers I couldn't seem to locate. He stepped into the enormous shower and started the showerheads going on some sort of mist setting on the three sides. When I stepped in, he immediately pulled me to him. I always adored the sensation of his wet skin against mine, and he knew it.

"You're not playing fair."

"A writer once said all's fair in love and war. I think he might have been onto something."

"We can't have sex in here."

"Why not? We have sex in the Gulf or the shower at home, and it's never been a problem."

I blushed and said, "You know I like to scream. I can stop myself if we're in a bed if I have to but can't seem to stop myself when we're in the water. Other guests will hear me."

He nipped at one of my nipples with his teeth then asked, "Would it bother you if they heard you?"

"This reminds me of the conversation we had in the limo on the way home from our honeymoon, but this is different."

"How so?"

"It's not just the limo driver who might hear. There could be children around."

"That's why I put the music on. Scream all you want."

I did, and we were five minutes late meeting the others. Our hair was still wet, and I hadn't had time to put on any make-up. We'd barely had time to slip on our jeans, shirts, and shoes. No one else commented on our appearance, and we headed to view the pictures. They were all wonderful, and we spent quite a while reviewing the selections and making purchases.

Al and Diane were going to an opera performance that evening, and Krystal and Greg returned to their room. Michael escorted me downstairs and took me on a cab ride around Las Vegas. Our taxi driver was a fount of information regarding the city and its history and was eager to answer any questions we had. The ride lasted for over three hours and proved to be quite entertaining.

After the driver took us back to the hotel, Michael suggested we go to the casino before heading up to our room. I froze and started to feel sick.

"What?" Michael prodded.

"I can't go in the casino."

"Why not? Do you have a gambling problem you've been hiding from me this past year?" he asked playfully. When that didn't elicit a smile, he grew serious and asked, "What's the matter, Seneca?"

"Mommy always told me it was bad to gamble."

His eyes narrowed, and he asked, "Was your father a gambler?"

"I – I don't know. I guess I always wondered. There were big cock-fighting rings in the area of central Florida where I grew up. My parents didn't make a lot, but we should have had enough to eat and have electricity all the time. When my parents would fight, it was usually because my father thought my mother was cheating on him or she thought he was blowing what money we had. He didn't seem to be an alcoholic, so I wondered if he gambled."

"Did they ever resolve any of these arguments or was it all shouting and slamming of doors?"

I half-smiled and said, "We didn't have many doors to slam in our little trailer, and they always resolved their arguments."

"How?"

I looked away and didn't reply.

Michael sighed and asked, "How often did they fight?"

"Almost every night."

"So, you've got your parents screaming at each other every night while you're lying in your little room right next to where they are, and you're scared by that. Then they go off and have sex as a way to deal with not dealing with things, and you get to hear that, too. Did you even understand what they were doing?"

"Not until I was about seven."

"What happened when you were seven?"

"Can we not do this here?" I asked him nervously. "I'd rather be in our room."

"No one gives a damn, Seneca."

"Michael –"

"Stop trying to change the subject by telling me not to swear. You like to do that, you know?"

"I know."

"You admit it? I better write that down somewhere."

"Michael –"

"What happened when you were seven that made you understand what your parents were doing after they fought?"

29

I sat on the edge of a fountain and said quietly, "I was spending the night at a friend's house, and her family had a TV and a VCR. We got up during the night and were going to watch a movie. We thought it would be so cool to do that while the rest of the family was asleep."

"And?"

"And her older brother was up and said we could watch a special movie with him."

"How old was the brother?"

"At least twice our age."

"And he watched a porn movie with his friggin' seven-year-old sister and her friend." When I nodded, he said angrily, "The son of a bitch! Un-fucking-believable." Sitting next to me, he asked, "Did you tell anyone?"

"No, but I never went back to her house."

"Did he try to touch you while you watched the movie together? If he did, I'll find the bastard and beat the shit out of him."

"He didn't try to touch either of us. We all just watched together."

Putting his arms around me, Michael said, "So, your first introduction to sex was some cheesy porn movie. That's how you figured out what your parents were doing after their arguments, but you didn't tell your parents."

"No. I went to the library and found a book about sex and read it one afternoon. I stuck it in another book so no one would see what I was reading. It was a pretty good book that talked about the physical and emotional components of sex. I felt better after I read it. I understood more.

"When I was ten, Mommy talked to me about sex. She had no idea I knew all about it. She told me no one should have sex until they were married. Of course, after she died, I did have sex when I wasn't married and accidentally got pregnant. I should have obeyed her. If I had, then I wouldn't have married the father, lost my baby, or had to get divorced."

"Jesus, you blame yourself for that, too?" Michael didn't speak for a long time. Finally, he said, "We don't have to go to the casino, but I don't want it to be because you're afraid of going. Will you at least walk through with me and see what it's like? I know how to

30

play every game, but I don't really like to gamble myself, so you don't have to worry about that ever. Okay?"

"I don't want to go today."

"Then we won't. We can do it later."

I nodded against his chest. After a while, we rose and went to our room. I brushed my teeth while Michael slipped off everything he wore save for his boxers, then he brushed his teeth while I put on my nightgown. We lay in bed and watched TV for a while before I fell asleep in Michael's arms.

"Seneca! Seneca, wake up."

I woke with my heart pounding and Michael's arms around me. I was crying but not screaming, and I was on my hands and knees on the bed. The sheets were bunched together on one side of the mattress. I crumpled against Michael and brought my hand up to my mouth to muffle my sobs. Michael gently pushed the hand away, and I buried my face against his shoulder.

"It wasn't the one about your dad," he stated. When I didn't answer, he said, "It was about your baby, wasn't it?"

"Y-yes."

"What were you doing in your dream?" he asked softly.

I cried and clung to him as I said, "There was all this blood and…and…and the baby, and there was no one there to help me. So, I had to take off the sheets and…and…throw them away. I had to…I had…I….had to…."

"You had to throw your baby away," he said, his voice tinged with sadness. "Even if you'd lost him in a hospital, you wouldn't have been able to bury him because he came so early, but the hospital people would have helped you and taken care of things for you. They wouldn't have forced you to suffer alone, see it all, and have to…clean up afterwards."

"We were young, poor college students. My husband didn't even know until he got home from school and work that night that I'd spent the day…that I'd lost the baby."

Kissing my head and pulling me closer to him, Michael said, "There's so much life needs to make up for when it comes to you. You don't know how much I wish it was possible to undo it all. I want to make it better."

"You do, and I love you for it more than you can comprehend."

Chapter Four

"I hope Adiba and Rakeem like the thank-you present Michael and I bought them for taking care of Buttons while we were in Las Vegas," I told Krystal, as she and I headed over to the Saleh house. "Hadeel should be happy with the stuffed tiger we picked out for her."

"I'm sure she will, and Rakeem and Adiba will love the art piece you chose for them. It looks really Middle Eastern. It should fit great with their other artwork."

"I wish Michael and Greg could have come with us."

"They'll see them when everyone comes over to our place tomorrow for lunch. I'm thinking we were lucky that the department store waited until after the plane landed to call Greg to come in. They really did great about not disturbing us on our honeymoon."

"They did, and the staff at John's Place kept their calls to a minimum, although Michael did get texts or e-mails throughout the trip. It was fine. That's what happens when you run a business and leave for several days without your savvy grandfather staying behind to mind the store, so to speak."

"I do hate to show up unannounced at Adiba's," Krystal declared. "We usually call each other first."

"I called, and they didn't answer. They might have been playing with Hadeel in the backyard. They may not even be home. If they aren't, then we'll just go have dinner somewhere then I'll drop you at your place and go back to my house and unpack."

"That sounds good. I am really excited to show them the wedding pictures. I mean, I know you and I talked to Adiba during the week, but it'll be so much cooler to talk face-to-face."

I pulled my car into the driveway of the Saleh home and parked it behind Adiba's. Getting out of the Corolla, I was preparing to retrieve the artwork and toy from the backseat when I noticed that the front door to the house was slightly ajar and heard Hadeel crying piteously from inside.

"Krystal, stop."

She looked across the roof of the car at me and asked, "What is it?"

"I don't know. Something's wrong. Look. The front door's open. Listen to Hadeel screaming."

Krystal glanced around nervously and put her wedding album back on the seat before asking, "You think someone's broken in? We should call 911."

I knew we should, but something told me not to – yet.

"What if it's a false alarm? Let's check it out first. I'll lock the car, so leave your purse and the rest. We can just bring our phones."

"Seneca, I don't know about this."

"Me neither, but my intuition is telling me to wait."

She nodded, although I could tell she had reservations about going into the house by ourselves. So did I. That wasn't going to stop me. The family might be in trouble and need immediate help.

"You could wait outside and call 911 while I go in," I told her, my heart pounding.

"No, I think it would be better if we went in together."

As we walked towards the door, I said with false bravado, "I'm sure it's nothing, and we're being silly by worrying."

"I'm sure you're right."

Neither of us sounded sure of anything, and I took Krystal's hand as we neared the front door. We glanced at one another then stepped inside.

Nothing seemed out of place, except the open door and the sound of Hadeel's continuous crying. Krystal and I called out Adiba's and Rakeem's names, but we got no response.

We moved slowly through the living room towards the kitchen area of the house. When we turned the corner, Krystal screamed and I struggled to breathe. Rakeem was kneeling on the floor with his hands bound behind him. His forehead was touching the tile, which was covered in blood. He had been shot execution-style in the back of the head.

I heard Krystal throw up behind me. For a few seconds, all I could do was stare at Rakeem. Then I took off and ran for the nursery. Hadeel was obviously alive, but what about her mother?

Hadeel was standing holding onto the side of her crib looking distressed and exhausted. Adiba lay on her side in a puddle of blood with blood spattered on her chest, one arm draped protectively across her rounded belly. She moaned.

I yelled for Krystal, who came quickly into the room and screamed again.

"Call 911!" I cried. "Adiba's still alive, but she's been shot in the chest. Get Hadeel and go outside to wait for the paramedics and police!"

"But Seneca –"

"Do it!" I yelled frantically. "I know Hadeel's only a baby, but I don't want her to see her mother –"

I had been about to say "die" but stopped myself. Adiba was still alive and might make it. I doubted it but didn't want to give up on her until I had no choice. I wondered if baby Hani was already dead.

Krystal scooped Hadeel out of the crib and ran. Adiba moaned again and opened her eyes, which appeared slightly glazed over. She reached for me. I took her hand and stroked her hair, all the while telling her Hadeel was safe.

"I must tell you quickly how it was," she mumbled. "There were four men, and they were not from…they were Dutch or German or something like that. They knocked at the front door. When Rakeem opened it, they grabbed him and then…said he was to die as punishment…punishment for Michael."

"Michael?" I echoed in disbelief.

"Yes. Rakeem said he did not understand, and I told them they must have made a mistake. Hadeel was asleep, and I prayed to Allah that she would not wake as the men tied Rakeem's hands and brought him to our kitchen then told him to kneel. He said to kill him but to let his family live.

"One of the men took me into the hall. There was a shot, and I screamed. Hadeel woke, and she began to cry. I broke away and went to protect her. The man shot me in the back, and I fell. They did…something…something I could not see. Then one man said someone was coming, and they ran." Looking up at me, she said, "You have saved my daughter. I can never thank you enough."

"You can thank me by holding on until the ambulance comes."

"Those papers we signed….I am glad we took care of that," she said, sounding as though she was speaking from somewhere far away. "You will raise my children for me, and they will be good to themselves and others. Hani will live, even though I will not."

"Don't say that," I pleaded.

"Rakeem is already dead, is he not?"

Unable to lie to her, I nodded.

"I want you to tell Michael not to blame himself for this. It is not his fault that there are evil men who wish for vengeance. Make him swear to keep my children safe and lead happy, normal lives. Promise me, my sweet friend."

I promised as sirens wailed in the distance.

I lifted my head and froze. On the wall above where Adiba lay was a symbol that had been drawn using her blood. It looked like a heart with a dagger driven through it. The previous November, I'd come across a piece of paper in one of Michael's books on the history of espionage that had the same symbol drawn on it. I'd meant to ask him about it. I'd kept putting it off until I'd forgotten it existed.

With a trembling hand, I withdrew my iPhone and snapped a picture of the bloody symbol before stuffing the phone back into the pocket of my jeans. Then I leaned forward, kissed Adiba on the forehead, and told her that I loved her like a sister and wasn't going to leave her.

The police and paramedics had other ideas. They forced me to exit the house so Adiba could be prepared for transport to the hospital, and the scene could be secured. When I stepped outside, I saw Krystal still crying and holding Hadeel, who had stopped screaming but appeared frightened and agitated. I wanted to go to her, but there was something I had to do first.

A middle-aged policewoman approached me and said, "Ma'am, we need to get a statement from you and your friend. I know this is a very traumatic thing, but we may be able to apprehend those responsible if we can get vital information from either of you."

"We found them like they were when you arrived, and we need...we need to be there at the hospital. Please. Can we give our statements there?"

She nodded sympathetically and said, "We'll drive you." She leaned around me and called out to a fellow cop to get the baby's car seat out of the Saleh's vehicle before asking me, "Do you have purses or other things you might want to bring with you?"

I nodded and quickly unlocked my car and grabbed both of our purses plus the stuffed tiger before relocking the Corolla and going over to Hadeel and kissing her wet cheeks. She immediately reached for me, and I took her in my arms and gave in to my tears. Krystal and I hugged each other and walked with the policewoman to the squad car. We waited while Hadeel's car seat was fastened into the backseat, and I sat beside her and used what few reserves of strength I had left to force myself to cease crying. I couldn't stop the tears altogether, but I needed to be able to speak if I was going to call Michael.

My heart racing, I withdrew my iPhone. I was dreading the call. I knew what he was going to believe about what had happened to Adiba and Rakeem, and I would be inclined to agree with him. I said a prayer as the phone rang.

"Hello, beautiful," Michael said with obvious pleasure in his voice. "I should be wrapping things up here at the office in an hour or two. You want to go out for some Spanish food, or I could stop by Whole Foods to buy steaks and vegetables to grill tonight?"

"M-Michael."

There was a brief pause before he said, "You're crying. What's wrong? Where are you? Are you hurt?"

"N-no. I'm – we're with the police. We're headed for Blake Hospital. How soon can you be there?"

"Tell me what's going on," he demanded. "Why are you with the police? Why are you heading for the hospital?"

Hadeel began to cry and squirm in her car seat.

"Hadeel is with you and the police?"

"And Krystal." As the child continued to fuss, I offered her the stuffed toy and said as soothingly as I could, "It's okay. We'll be there soon."

Temporarily distracted by the tiger, Hadeel settled down and began to suck on the thing's tail.

"Seneca, I've told you before that you're a terrible liar, so don't try to lie to me," Michael said before asking, "Is Rakeem alive?"

"N-no."

He inhaled sharply, and it sounded like he choked back a sob before asking, "Adiba?"

"I – I hope she makes it to the hospital so they can take Hani before...before..." I broke down and said, "Michael, I think –"

"Seneca, stop!" he barked, shocking me into silence. "Stop right there before you get yourself, Krystal, and Hadeel killed as well. You tell the police what they need to know and nothing more. Do you understand me?" He sounded angry and desperate as he repeated more forcefully, "Do you understand me?"

"Yes."

"You and I will talk in more detail later. Now's not the time."

"Please call Al and tell him about this and have him phone the lawyer's office after he calls Diane."

"Adiba could survive," Michael said hopefully.

"She was shot in the back, and the bullet exited through her chest! She begged me to make sure that we took care of the children."

"She knew Rakeem was dead?"

"They had her watch while they tied his hands behind his back, made him kneel on the floor, then took her in the hall while they shot him in the head."

Michael cried out something in Arabic. It was grief, rage, and guilt released through words I didn't understand. It was pain and a call for revenge. I said Michael's name, but he hung up the phone without answering me.

Krystal, who was sitting beside me, squeezed my hand and told me Michael would be okay before dialing Greg's cell number. I decided she was about as poor a liar as I was. I listened to her conversation with her husband as I comforted Hadeel, whom I knew was upset, wet, and probably hungry and thirsty.

I relayed my concerns to the policewoman, who was riding in the front passenger seat of the squad car. She reminded me that the hospital staff would have diapers, baby food, formula, and apple juice available for the baby.

When we arrived, we were led to the Emergency Room. The police escorted Krystal to the waiting room for the surgical unit, while I stayed in the children's area of the E.R. with the baby. A pediatrician examined Hadeel to make certain she hadn't been injured in any way. Once he'd determined she was physically fine, the nurses brought me the supplies I needed. The baby was soon changed, wearing a fresh diaper, and was drinking a bottle of her usual formula. When the bottle had been almost completely drained, she quickly fell asleep in my arms.

Michael appeared beside me as I placed the empty bottle on a tray next to the stuffed tiger. He seemed slightly shell-shocked but was in control of himself. When I looked into his eyes, I thought of what this must be doing to him and to me. There was going to be enormous emotional impact for both of us from this tragedy.

"Mrs. Benedetto?"

It was the nice policewoman from earlier. She introduced herself to Michael, who introduced himself to her. She pulled up a chair and apologized but told me she had to take my statement so the police could begin their investigation. She asked me to tell her exactly what had transpired from the moment Krystal and I had arrived at the Saleh home until the paramedics and authorities had gotten to the scene. Feeling as though I was all cried out, I wearily reviewed the events step-by-step as Michael held me and I held Hadeel. I omitted Adiba's remark that the attack was some sort of retribution against Michael and her plea that Michael not blame himself for their deaths. I also left out the fact that I'd seen and taken a picture of the bloody symbol on the wall.

When I'd finished, the woman thanked me and got our contact information before escorting us to the waiting room for the surgical unit. Krystal, Greg, Al, and Diane were waiting for us there. I could tell that everyone had been crying profusely. Michael and I were informed that Adiba was in surgery. There had been no news, yet.

Our lawyer appeared and explained he'd brought with him all of the documentation we would need if it was required, although he remarked that he certainly hoped it wouldn't be necessary. The older man was wearing a tuxedo and looked as though he'd been called away from a formal event. Michael thanked him for coming and assured him we would compensate him for his after-hours work.

"Mr. Saleh's been killed, and Mrs. Saleh's life is in jeopardy," the man said soberly. "There'll be no charge for my services tonight. I hope I came out here for nothing and that Mrs. Saleh recovers. I'm a human being who happens to be a lawyer, not the other way around."

We thanked him, and he joined our vigil. We waited for what seemed like hours. Finally, two men in scrubs emerged from the restricted surgical area and stopped to talk with the policewoman and two policemen. Michael bowed his head, and I understood that somehow he knew Adiba was dead.

The cops and doctors came over to our little corner of the waiting room. The surgeons explained that Adiba had been conscious when she'd arrived at the hospital and had asked them to make certain to save her baby and not to focus on her. Of course, they'd attempted to save both, but Adiba hadn't survived. The baby, who was approximately a month early, had suffered trauma before birth because of his mother's condition and was being cared for in the Neo-natal Intensive Care Unit.

"Mrs. Saleh said something about her husband and someone named Tom right before she lost consciousness, but we couldn't make that part out," one of the doctors told us as we sat in stunned silence. "Before that, she also said that people named Michael and Seneca had legal papers that would grant them custody of her daughter and the baby. She spoke something in Arabic, and one of the nurses wrote it down the way it sounded. We don't know what it means."

Michael asked them to repeat what they'd heard. The two doctors removed a sheet of paper and struggled with pronunciation but painstakingly told us the words Adiba had uttered. Michael nodded.

"You speak Arabic?" the policewoman asked.

"I'm a Navy veteran who worked in the Middle East for years."

"So, could you tell us what Mrs. Saleh said? And could you write it correctly for our files?"

"I can, but you could find it on the Internet just as easily."

"The Internet? What did she say?"

Michael spoke the words properly in Arabic. They sounded beautiful and melodic as he said them. He then translated them into English and said, "The grief you cry out from draws you towards union."

"What does that mean?" Krystal asked through her tears.

"It's from a poem called *Love Dogs* by the religious mystic, Rumi." He paused before admitting, "I don't think I can recite it just now without...." Michael's voice trailed off, and I knew he was struggling not to break down. After a moment, he explained, "The poem speaks of our desire to be one with God. It talks of how that longing is like the whining of a dog for its master, of how the longing provides the connection. It's a beautiful analogy."

I stared at Hadeel, who was sleeping peacefully in my arms. She had no idea that her parents were gone forever and her life was about to be completely changed. I vowed to buy a collection of Rumi's poems as soon as possible and start reading one to her every night. Then we would move on to other Arab poets, scholars, writers, etcetera. Michael would teach her how to speak Arabic and about her heritage from an insider's perspective, but I would learn at the same time and never let her forget her parents' culture. Hani either.

A social worker appeared, and the lawyer produced the documents Rakeem and Adiba had asked us to sign two months after our marriage. We'd readily agreed to their request in order to put their minds at ease, never dreaming that the day would actually come to pass, especially so soon.

The social worker scanned the documents and asked if she could make copies. The lawyer handed her duplicates along with his card and told her to contact his office so we could proceed. She nodded and reached for Hadeel.

"No!" I cried and got to my feet turning sideways in a protective gesture. "You can't take her! She'll be terrified! We have papers!"

"A judge still has to grant you temporary custody until the legalities are finalized," the woman said gently. "It usually only takes twenty-four hours. She'll be in good hands until then."

"Not a chance," Michael said in his most intimidating voice. "Her parents have just been murdered, and no one knows who did it or why. What foster family is going to keep her under those circumstances? Are you going to hire a guard to protect her in case the killers come back to finish what they started? If she's murdered, then are you going to take the blame?"

The social worker certainly seemed affected by his words and stopped her advance. The lawyer took one look at Michael and immediately stepped in and said he'd have the temporary order from a judge within the next two hours. Michael, Hadeel, and I were not going to leave the hospital until the order had been delivered to the social worker. The woman quickly assessed the situation and agreed to remain in the vicinity until the matter was sorted out. Then she handed the lawyer her card and walked away.

"They can't take her!" I repeated after the woman had left the room. "She's already so scared and if they put her in a strange place with strange people –"

"Nobody's going to take her anywhere," Michael declared, as he put his arms around me and Hadeel. "She's staying with us from now on."

"When can we see the baby?" I asked one of the surgeons.

"His new parents can see him now, but everyone else will have to wait."

I passed the sleeping Hadeel to Krystal, as the lawyer excused himself to make the necessary call to a judge friend of his. He promised to return to the hospital as soon as possible with the required document. We thanked him again before walking with one of the surgeons and the policewoman to the NICU. The other two policemen stayed with our friends and family in the waiting room.

Michael and I were led to a small enclosed area where we were instructed on how to properly disinfect our hands and arms and on what we could and couldn't do in the unit. We were required to don surgical gowns on top of our regular clothing. The policewoman agreed to wait in the anteroom.

Adiba's surgeon introduced us to the young neonatologist who was responsible for Hani's care. He assured us that the baby was stable but would be kept indefinitely in the NICU so he could be closely monitored.

"Here he is. Did his parents already have a name picked out for him?"

"Hani," Michael said thickly, as he stared down at the tiny baby boy. "H-A-N-I. It means 'full of joy' in Arabic."

The pediatrician nodded somberly and excused himself for a moment, returning with an index card that had "Hani" printed under the *It's a boy!* announcement at the top next to pictures of rattles and booties. I began to cry again, and another couple who were with their own child in its incubator looked quizzically in our direction.

Michael hugged and kissed me, then he urged me to forget about my tears for a while and focus on the baby. I allowed him to wipe my cheeks with a tissue and turned towards the incubator. We reached through the openings on the sides and touched the baby. He was so small and smooth. Michael looked worried and asked the pediatrician why Hani's breathing appeared labored and why he had tubes inserted in his nose and mouth and an IV. The doctor explained that his lungs weren't quite as developed as they should have been and that he needed help getting fluids, nutrition, and the oxygen required, at least for the first few days. I told Michael I would explain the particulars to him later and asked the doctor how much Hani weighed.

"Four pounds, one ounce. Small for his gestational age but not a bad weight compared to the truly premature infants we see in here all the time."

"Was he deprived of oxygen before delivery?" I asked nervously.

"You're a doctor, too?"

"Social worker. I've worked with every age group from preemies to centenarians. I have varied medical experience as well as counseling skills."

He nodded appreciatively and admitted, "Hani was blue by the time we got him out. We had to resuscitate him."

"What sort of consequences will that have for him?" Michael asked.

"Possibly none," I said without much confidence. "Or he could be brain-damaged, visually impaired, or have cerebral palsy amongst other things."

"Or he could be perfectly fine," the doctor countered. "The younger the baby when it suffers trauma, the greater the recovery much of the time. I'd recommend his development continue to be closely monitored by his regular pediatrician once he's released from the hospital."

"How often can we see Hani?"

"Anytime between 2:00 and 9:00. Only the two of you will be allowed in though, since he has no other close relatives besides his sister."

"He has great-grandparents," Michael offered. "Can they come in, too?"

"I'll allow it. You'll have to give us their names. They'll be the only exceptions though. We want to keep germs to a minimum and not over-stimulate babies at this point."

"Could they see him now?" I asked. "Just for a few minutes?"

"Of course. For this first visit, why don't you take turns bringing them in?"

We returned to the waiting room. While Michael took Al to the NICU, I explained to Diane that I was going to take her next.

"But I'm not his great-grandmother," she protested. "Al and I aren't married."

"So what? You might as well be married, and Michael and I want you to be Hani and Hadeel's great-grandmother. They need you, just like the rest of us do."

"And just as I need you," she said and leaned forward to hug me. I was so surprised that I almost fell out of my chair, but I gladly hugged back. Diane was not usually enthusiastic about hugs, unless she was hugging Al.

Michael returned with Al, who looked both pleased and grim. I brought Diane up to see the baby and was touched by how gentle and kind she was as she lightly ran her fingers over his small head and body. By the time we got back to the waiting room, Hadeel was awake, and our lawyer had returned with the temporary custody order.

"The hearing will be Monday morning at 9:00," he told us. "This will be quicker than usual. These children have no living relatives, and their parents arranged for you to have their daughter and any other children they might have in the event of their deaths. Michael's a decorated veteran, and Seneca's a social worker. You obviously have philanthropic interests through your business, and both of you have a lot more money than most. I have a feeling the judge will grant you permanent custody and allow you to adopt both children when you go to court. Especially since their parents' murders will probably be perceived as a hate crime, I doubt if anyone will cause us problems. If they do, we'll fight them."

After he was gone, I glanced at the clock. It was only 8:00 p.m.

"What happens now?" Michael was asking the policewoman?"

"Our investigation continues. We'll update you if there's any progress."

"What about the baby?" Greg asked. "He could still be in danger, couldn't he?"

"We'll post a guard outside the NICU for now until we know more," the cop replied. "We'll make a determination after twenty-four hours whether or not to maintain a police presence there."

"What do you need from us?" Al asked, once the police were gone from the waiting room. "Do you wish for us to spend the night at your house?"

I so wanted to say "yes," but knew I couldn't. As much as I loathed the thought, I had to talk to Michael alone about the pieces of this terrible puzzle I hadn't shared with the police. I had an idea as to how he was going to react although I knew he wasn't going to take off on some quest for vengeance and leave me and the children unprotected so soon. He also wouldn't miss the court hearing on Monday. He might, however, start thinking about retaliation regarding those responsible for Adiba and Rakeem's murders.

I would have the dream about my father that night and wasn't sure how I'd be affected. Would I cope better than the last time or would this ghastly experience set me back in my PTSD recovery? Hadeel had heard enough screaming for one day, and I didn't want to traumatize her any further.

One thing I knew for certain was that we needed to connect with the psychiatrist as soon as possible. I'd suggest to Michael that he call him on our way home. If he wouldn't, then I would.

"I think we need to be alone with Hadeel tonight," Michael told his grandfather. "We'll call you during the night if we need help."

I kissed Hadeel's temple and said, "We could use help tomorrow turning our old bedroom into Hadeel's room and the old guest room into Hani's room. I know we won't be able to bring Hani home for a while, but I want him to have everything waiting for him when he gets there."

"Will the police let you take the nursery furniture from Adiba and Rakeem's house?" Krystal asked.

"No, and I don't want to," Michael declared. "When they allow us to go in, I'll have movers pack everything and put it in storage to go through later. I can't look at any of it now. We can sort all of the family's things whenever we can deal with it. Until then, it can sit in an air-conditioned unit somewhere and wait. They leased the house, so we won't have to worry about selling it. I don't want to do anything rash so early after…this."

"That's a wise move," Diane agreed. "Give yourselves time."

I told Krystal and Diane I'd call them in the morning, so we could go shopping for the things Hadeel and Hani would need. Both women said they'd help me whenever I was ready. I assured them it would not be before noon.

"We'll have to stop by Target or Walmart on the way home and get a playpen or something for Hadeel to sleep in," I pointed out. "Plus we can get some diapers, wipes, bottles, baby food, formula, blankets, baby shampoo and soap, some clothing, and toys. The rest can wait until tomorrow."

Chapter Five

Michael secured the car seat in the SUV then I buckled Hadeel in and gave her the stuffed tiger before going around and sitting in the passenger seat. Michael got in and started the engine. He drove straight to Target, where we ended up buying the supplies we needed to make it through the night with our new almost-one-year-old daughter. Neither of us spoke unless it was to comfort Hadeel or to remark on items needed. I decided to wait to bring up the psychiatrist until we were at our house.

When we arrived home, we spent time petting Buttons and letting him rub all over us. As always, Hadeel was intrigued by the cat and watched him with fascination as Michael set up the playpen in our old room. That room was devoid of furniture since we'd recently moved everything into our newly finished master bedroom, which had been painted the same deep blue color as the old one. Our old room was now a silvery gray. That was where Hadeel had slept when she'd taken naps at our house during past visits. She had even spent the night in that room twice when we'd babysat so that her parents could have some time alone.

I gave Hadeel a nice, long bath. Afterwards, Michael held her in his lap while I fed her some baby food, then gave her a bottle filled with water. Her eyelids drooped, and she was quickly asleep. I carried her to the playpen, lowered her into it, and covered her with a blanket. As I switched off the overhead light, the nightlight we'd purchased automatically came on.

When I returned to the kitchen, Michael was seated at the table staring at the empty baby bottle. I knew that both of us needed to eat, but neither of us felt like it. I took a seat in the chair beside his and reached for his hand, but he got to his feet before I could touch it. He walked over to the sink and put the bottle in the basin then asked quietly, "What didn't you tell the police?"

"Michael, I think we should call Dr. Forrester and —"

"Later. I need to know this first. Tell me."

Knowing I had no choice, I explained, "Adiba said the men told her that what they were doing was punishment for you. She told me to tell you not to blame yourself because there were bad men in the world who wanted revenge. She made me promise to get you to swear that you and I would raise her children right. She wanted them to lead happy, normal lives." I sighed heavily and said, "Those may not have been her exact words, but they're pretty close."

He stared at the darkness through the window in front of him and asked, "What else? There's something else you're not telling me."

"There was a…a symbol on the wall that had been drawn in Adiba's blood. I didn't tell the police I saw it. I figured they'd think I was too upset to have noticed it, but I did."

He glanced at me sharply and asked, "What kind of symbol? Describe it."

Reaching into my jeans pocket, I said, "I don't have to. I took a picture of it. It was one of the hardest things I've ever had to do, but I knew it was important."

He came back to the table and sat beside me once more. Accepting the iPhone, he pulled up the picture and stared at it for a long time. Then he forwarded it to his phone, deleted it from mine, and handed me my iPhone back.

"You're not done," he commented. "What else?"

"I saw that symbol on a piece of paper in one of your books several months ago. I was going to ask you what it meant, but I never did."

"What paper? Which book?"

"The one on the history of espionage. It's in the living room on the bookshelf. I never did bring it back to your office."

He nodded but didn't rise as I'd expected.

"If I'd told you about the paper, would it have made a difference today? Would it have saved Rakeem and Adiba?"

"I have no way of knowing. I don't know what it means, yet. I'll get the paper soon and get it to some friends. We'll see."

We were silent and still for several minutes.

"Michael? Please talk to me. Tell me what you're thinking."

"I'm thinking that none of this makes sense. I was a damn good spy who was in deep for years. I really wasn't worried at all when I got out because I was so certain no one could locate me. I'm thinking that I have to find this person who did and eliminate him or else everyone I care about will be in danger of being hurt or killed. You, the children, Nonno, Diane, Krystal, Greg, my aunts, uncles, cousins, nieces, nephews…even my staff at John's Place…anyone I know and love could be a target." Running his fingers through his hair, he said, "God, I wish Tom were still alive. I'd really like to talk to him and –"

He stopped mid-sentence and grimaced.

"And what?" I asked.

"Tom died last August."

"Yes, he did."

"In his kitchen. They shot Rakeem in the kitchen."

"Michael, I know where you're going with this, and that's ridiculous. Tom was old and sick and wasn't shot in the head or the back."

"He could have been poisoned. Because he was old and sick, I doubt if they did a tox screen. Fuck it all!"

"I think you're letting your imagination run away with you."

He impulsively kissed me then pulled me against him before saying, "You have *no* idea what kind of people I'm talking about or what kind of world I lived in for ten years."

"I caught a pretty good glimpse today," I said and began to cry quietly. "It was so horrible to see Rakeem like that and Adiba and then Hani. What are we going to do?"

Kissing the top of my head, he stroked my hair and told me we were going to figure it out.

"I'll call in every person I can to work on this. Protecting my real identity is vital to protecting that of other past and current operatives as well."

"I know you're right, but I'm so…."

"Lost?"

I nodded against his chest and said, "You know I'm going to have the dream about my Poppy tonight."

"If you do, we'll deal with it."

"The children –"

"We'll talk about the children and their future in the morning. They're ours to love and protect now. That's all we need to know for tonight. Okay?"

"Okay."

"Seneca?"

"Hm?"

"Which way was Rakeem kneeling when you found him?"

"Towards the stove."

"Towards the East," he murmured. "Towards Mecca." Michael released me and stood then announced, "I'm going to swim for a while."

"What?!?" I got quickly to my feet and asked, "Are you crazy? After what happened today, you're going to leave me and Hadeel alone –"

"With the alarm set."

"-with the alarm set to go out alone and swim in the Gulf where men could be waiting to kill you?"

"No one will kill me tonight."

"How do you know?"

"Because I know."

"But it's March! The water's freezing."

"You're well aware that doesn't bother me." Michael took me by the shoulders and suggested, "How about if we call the therapist, and you can talk to him while I swim? I won't stay out long. I'll talk to him when I come in, and you can shower and get ready for bed."

"What about dinner?"

"I'm not hungry. You?"

I admitted that the thought of eating nauseated me at that moment. I added that the thought of rehashing my experience at the Saleh house with the psychiatrist was also making me queasy.

"I phoned the psychiatrist's emergency number immediately after you called me on your way to the hospital. I told him what little I knew, and he said he'd be available any time after 10:00 p.m. tonight. He knows it's bad."

While Michael swam, I sat in front of the laptop in our new home office, talked to Dr. Forrester, and cried. The virtual session was extremely helpful, and I did feel better as we wrapped up our time together.

"One more thing, Seneca," Forrester said as I dried my eyes. "Under no circumstances are you to have sex with Michael right now."

"Why not?"

49

"Because at this time he's compartmentalizing the events of today so he can move forward. At the same time, he's grieving deeply and suffering great guilt. He'll want to kill the man who's behind all of this."

"What does that have to do with us having sex?"

"We know that Michael inadvertently hurt you during sex once in the past when he's been distraught, and all of this is overwhelmingly distressing to him. If he was hurting you and you told him to stop, he may not be able to this time if he gets carried away with his emotions."

"Is he…is he dangerous?"

The therapist sat back in his chair and said, "Michael's always been dangerous but only to those who were evil and threatened the lives of innocent people."

"He's going to go after this man, isn't he?"

"Eventually."

"Will you try to talk him out of it?"

"That's not my job. The plain truth is that he may *have* to track and kill this man in order to protect the persons he loves and his own future. He'll have to make that decision in conjunction with others who are more qualified than I am to make determinations like that. Regardless, he won't be leaving anytime soon. Try to put that worry aside for now and work on making it through the next few weeks. Do you want to resume the lunchtime sessions instead of our monthly ones?"

"Yes."

"Good. I'm going to be talking to Michael every night like before as well. You're both in the middle of a major crisis. You have my emergency number in case you need to reach me at any other time."

There was a slight knock on the door. I thanked the psychiatrist and told Michael he could come in. He had obviously already showered and wore pajama bottoms and a t-shirt. I gave him a quick kiss then went to shower and brush my teeth while he talked to Forrester.

Like our new bedroom, the new bathroom was larger than our old one. It was painted a dark brown and had a sunken tub and a separate shower stall with two showerheads. There was ample storage space in the cabinet under the vessel sink. A large mirror had been hung above the basin. Everything in the bathroom from the toilet to the towel racks was white. The white tile floor was heated from underneath. All of the white provided a perfect contrast for the dark brown. It felt like a spa bathroom to me, and it had been wonderful to enjoy the space when Michael and I had wanted to unwind after a long day at work. It was not going to help me relax that night, so I quickly showered and got ready for bed.

After checking on Hadeel, I went to the master bedroom and tried to read the biography of Confucius I'd started during our trip to Las Vegas. I couldn't concentrate, so I put it aside and stared at the wall while waiting for Michael. He finally came to bed an hour later. I was still awake.

"I won't be sleeping tonight," he told me. "You can sleep."

"I'm afraid to."

"I know. I'll be here when you wake up from the nightmare."

"Michael –"

He cut me off and said, "Do you want me to hold you while you sleep?"

I nodded and asked him to take off his shirt. He hesitated before telling me he couldn't make love to me for a while. Not wanting to explain to him that the therapist and I had discussed this during my session, I told him I wasn't thinking about making love to him that night. I simply needed the comfort that came with feeling his warm flesh against my exposed skin. He slipped off his shirt and embraced me.

The feel of his muscular arms around me, his hard belly beneath my arms and hands, and his chest underneath my cheek was infinitely soothing. I quickly fell asleep and dreamed.

In my dream, I was eight years old and was playing at recess with a bunch of other little girls. We were skipping rope and having fun singing the rhymes. One of the girls suggested we jump rope Double Dutch for the next rhyme. Another agreed and declared I was the best jumper, so should go first.

"I have the greatest song for Seneca!" one of the girls announced excitedly. "My sister taught it to me last week, and it's an old song about a ballerina. Everyone knows Seneca's the best ballerina at the dance school!"

"Her Mommy cuts the teacher's hair and does her nails and stuff for free so Seneca can have lessons," one of the not-so-nice girls put in.

"Who cares?" asked another girl in Spanish. "We're all poor. She's the best ballerina, and that's the important thing, not how she gets to have lessons. You're just jealous."

"Let's jump rope to the new song!" another girl cried, also in Spanish.

All of us were excited about the possibility of learning a new rhyme. Everyone took their positions, and the ropes began their dance. The little girl told me she would nod when it was time for me to jump in, and the chanting started. The other girls clapped as she sang out:

A sailor went to sea-sea-sea
To see what he could see-see-see
But all that he could see-see-see
Was the bottom of the deep blue sea-sea-sea.

She nodded, and I jumped in and began to skip as she went on:

Not last night but the night before
Twenty-four robbers came knocking at my door;
When I went out to let them in,
This is what they said to me:

Ballerina, ballerina, turn around,
Ballerina, ballerina, touch the ground.
Ballerina, ballerina, go upstairs,
Ballerina, ballerina, say your prayers.
Ballerina, ballerina, turn out the light,
Ballerina, ballerina, say goodnight.

I jumped out of the swinging ropes as she finished. Everyone cheered for me and for the singing girl. They were all giggling and clapping and happy. I, on the other hand, felt fearful and alone. None of them comprehended that the rhyme was a catchy chant about terrible things happening to people. I wished that someone else besides me understood.

"Seneca!"

I looked up at my Poppy standing with the other farmhands in the bed of the truck. He was so alive and strong. He asked me to toss him his hat, and I told him I could bring it to him. After all, I was fourteen. He shook his head and motioned for me to throw it. The wind was blowing, and I tried to adjust my aim so it would carry the hat towards him. It didn't, and he leaned out to grab for it and fell into the wood chipper.

I watched him die horribly then ran screaming, racing through the hot field near the barn. I struggled to breathe. Mommy and some men were suddenly there and were making me go with them, and I was telling them no, that I wanted them to leave me there to die.

"Seneca?"

Mommy was calling my name, but she was so weakened by the cancer that she could barely speak. I took her hand and kissed her forehead as she said, "My little girl is all grown up. Eighteen years old and going to college. Promise me you'll never forget you're the sweetest, smartest, prettiest girl in the world."

I looked down at her hand and blinked in surprise. Her skin was a different color. When I raised my eyes, it was Adiba's face I saw. She smiled at me, despite the blood that covered her chest and belly. I stood immobilized by horror as Rakeem walked over to her and kissed her tenderly on the lips, the back of his head blown apart and dripping blood.

"Seneca?"

I whirled and saw my elderly friend, Tom, standing across the room. He was cupping his hands together and holding them out to me as if making an offering. He moved slowly towards me, his arms outstretched. I ended up backed into a corner and was trying not to look down at what he held in his palms. Finally, I realized he wouldn't let me go until I'd acknowledged what was waiting for me there. Feeling as though I was suffocating, I looked. It was my tiny baby, John Henry. I screamed and screamed and screamed.

I felt a hand on my mouth and heard Michael saying calmly but firmly, "Seneca, wake up." I opened my eyes and found myself pinned beneath him on the mattress. I could tell I'd been crying and must have been screaming, but he'd covered my mouth with one hand in order to muffle the noise so as not to wake Hadeel. There were scratches all over his chest from my fingernails. His blue eyes were shimmering with tears.

"Can you stay quiet if I lift my hand?"

When I nodded, he slowly removed his palm from my mouth. I was able to refrain from screaming, drew in a great gulp of air, and felt tears slide from the corners of my eyes as I apologized for scratching him and kissed some of the marks I'd made on his flesh.

Michael stopped me and said, "I didn't take it personally." Resting his forehead against mine, he confided, "I didn't really know what to do with you until you started screaming. I should have asked the therapist whether it was better to wake you during a nightmare or let it play itself out. I wanted so badly to stop it but didn't want to make things worse for you." Rolling off me, he declared, "Shit, that was terrible."

"What did I do?"

"Cried. Made little distressed noises. Tried to move away from me." Rubbing his face with one hand, he said, "You sang some sort of sadistic song about a sailor and a ballerina. You sounded…different, and it was…unnerving. You screamed at the end of it all, but I knew it was coming and was ready for that."

"Is that when I scratched you?"

"No, that was after the song. You were…." He searched for the right words before saying, "You were crying for me to let you go and not to take you home. You begged your mother to make me stop and to leave you where you were." Wiping at his eyes with the heel of one hand, he admitted, "You asked me to leave you to die and said there wasn't any point in going on. It broke my heart." As I snuggled against him, he said, "That dream wasn't only about your father."

"No. Not this time."

"You want to talk about it?"

"Not right now. I'm just…I'm happy that this time was better. The dream was bad, but look at me. I'm not a basket case. I'm talking normally and don't feel like I have to go back to sleep to get away from the pain." Hugging him, I asked, "Do you ever have nightmares about things you saw or did while you were in the military?"

"All the time."

Propping myself up on one elbow, I said, "But I never hear you."

"That's because I wake myself up before I can cry out and wake anyone else. I learned how to do it years ago. It's very helpful."

"Helpful to whom?"

"Other people."

"What about you? Who comforts you if you never tell anyone when you've had a bad dream?"

"I talk to the therapist about my nightmares."

"And does he put his arms around you through the laptop screen?" I asked sarcastically. "Does he kiss you and tell you you're okay?"

Michael was silent.

"Will you tell me next time you have a nightmare so I can do those things for you? Love is about reciprocity."

"I know. All right."

"And Michael?"

"Yes?"

"Don't just disappear and go off looking for this man who had Adiba and Rakeem killed. I need you and so do the children. I understand you have to find him and will need to go after him or have someone else do it, but I don't want you to leave us now and don't want anything to happen to you ever. Got it?"

"I got it," he said with a sad smile. "I never want to leave you either. You know that."

"I do. I also know that when I went to see Esmeralda, the old Mexican woman I knew who had premonitions and discussed my future with her, she said you would save my life and I would save yours. You saved my life when the mirror fell on me, and I haven't had my turn to save you. She also said you'd be gone from me for a while but not by choice. If anything happens to you, I don't want you to give up. Maybe I'm meant to save the day."

"If anything happens, you are *not* to come after me," he ordered. "Hadeel and Hani have already lost their biological parents and need at least one of us to be there for them as they grow up."

"I intend for both of us to be there for them as they grow up. So, you'd best make sure you stick around."

"That's the idea."

"Good. And don't order me to do anything because I won't listen. If I think you're in trouble, then I'll find a way to get to you. So there."

That morning, Michael went to John's Place, ostensibly to work. However, I knew he'd actually be working on contacting those he needed to reach in order to set things in motion regarding finding the killers and protecting us. I took Hadeel with me and met Krystal and Diane at a local high-end baby shop; then we went by the hospital so I could spend time with Hani before returning home.

"I hated spending so much on the same things I could have gotten more reasonably somewhere else," I grumbled. "But that store was the only one that would guarantee everything could be delivered and put together tomorrow."

"It's worth spending the extra in emergency situations like this one," commented Diane. "Yesterday was a living nightmare, and being in court tomorrow will be difficult for you and Michael."

"Greg and I wish we could be there," Krystal said. "There's no way we can miss work after being off for the honeymoon for a week."

"We know. We'll call and update you. Al and Diane will be there. The lawyer says it should all be fine, but I won't relax until everything's finalized."

"What are you going to do?" asked Krystal. "This is all so sudden, and you have to make such big decisions on such short notice."

"Most of it is pretty straightforward for us. I'm going to quit work and be a stay-at-home mom. Hadeel is obviously confused and wondering where her parents are." I began to tear up again and reached for a tissue before saying, "And I think Hani is going to have physical and mental challenges. I know the doctors won't have a real idea of what's going on with him for a while, but if we get him with an occupational therapist early, then it will help with everything. I can't imagine that there won't be any issues if he was blue when they got him out. Hopefully it won't be too bad, and he can catch up."

"What if he's developmentally delayed or has autism or cerebral palsy?" Diane asked.

"Then we'll deal with it. He's our son, and we'll do whatever we have to in order to take care of him."

"Only the best for my great-grandson."

I smiled tiredly and nodded. The front door opened, and Michael, Al, and Greg entered and reset the alarm before coming to sit with us. Michael kissed me; Greg kissed Krystal; and Al kissed Diane. I reflected that Rakeem and Adiba should be with us.

"How was Hani?" I asked Michael, who looked exhausted.

"The same. The police are keeping a guard on duty until after we go to court in the morning and will then decide what to do about continued security."

"If they discontinue it, should we hire someone?"

"Probably," he said distractedly. "We'll see."

"We should go," Greg suggested. "It's almost 10:00, and everyone looks wiped out. The four of you have to be up early and in court in the morning. I wish Krystal and I could be there."

"And we appreciate it," Michael told him. "We'll call you as soon as we're out."

We said our goodbyes to Krystal and Greg then told Al and Diane that we'd meet them at the courthouse at 8:00 the next morning. Once everyone had left, Michael took me in his arms and held me for a long time.

"I'm going to cry about Rakeem and Adiba when we go to court," I said suddenly.

"Anyone would think something was wrong with us if we didn't get emotional while talking about them. It will only have been two days."

"So, you're going to actually let someone else besides me and Al see how you really feel?"

"I have no choice."

I kissed him and said that being able to show the depth of his emotions would be good for him as well as our case. He agreed but said he wasn't looking forward to it. Concealing his inner turmoil was a learned trait that was difficult for him to disregard.

"How did the shopping go?" he asked as we sat on the couch and stroked Buttons' fur.

"I brought home the stroller, two new car seats for us, and a few other things. Everything else will be delivered tomorrow at 4:00."

"I'll be here with you when the deliverymen come."

"I'm glad. I – we need you all day tomorrow. Maybe we can get in more time with Hani. I know we can't really do anything with him at this stage, but the more he hears our voices and feels us touch him, the better."

"Are you okay with not working? We could hire a nanny and –"

"You know that neither of us would want a nanny for our children. Being a mom *is* work, especially if Hani turns out to be a special needs child. I'm fine with not working outside the home indefinitely. I wish the way we'd gotten our first children was different, but we've talked about how we can't have kids and want them from the beginning of our relationship. Now we have two." Rubbing tiredly at my eyes with my knuckles, I went on, "I promised Adiba we'd raise them right. I'll gladly be a full-time mom. I'll take them to activities and work with Hani in whatever ways he needs."

"What if –" Michael began then was overcome by emotion and started to cry.

I wrapped my arms around his neck, wove my fingers through his hair, and asked him what was wrong.

"What if he's in a vegetative state?" he cried. "What if he's severely brain-damaged because of what those sons of bitches did to his mother in order to get to me?"

"Then we will need help once he gets bigger. We'll need an aide to help care for him or else Hadeel will resent him. I wouldn't be able to lift him once he reached a certain size and weight anyway." Kissing him on the temple, I said, "I'm not thinking that far ahead, and you shouldn't either. As the doctor said, he might be fine. If he's not, then we'll see what he needs."

"You're not worried?"

"I'm worried, but I know we can handle anything. We'll do whatever it takes for our kids, right?"

He nodded, buried his face against my neck and confided, "I miss Rakeem and Adiba. Their absence makes me think about my best friend John's death and the other friends I've lost. It makes me feel pain and rage all the time, and I hate it. I can't live like this. I won't. I *will* find the bastard who did this, and he *will* pay."

Chapter Six

Michael, Hadeel, and I arrived at the courthouse at 7:50 the following morning. Michael was wearing a dark blue suit, and I wore a plum-colored, long-sleeved dress and had French-braided my hair. I'd put Hadeel in a white, long-sleeved shirt and a pink corduroy dress with white tights and black shoes. I had the diaper bag filled with wipes, diapers, bottles, baby food, toys, and a change of clothes just in case. We sat Hadeel in the stroller and proceeded to go through security when the doors opened. Within minutes, we were standing with our lawyer, Al, and Diane.

The lawyer reviewed what was to happen with Michael and me while Al and Diane watched Hadeel. When we were called into the courtroom, our little group entered and took our seats. Hadeel immediately began to wail.

I lifted her out of the stroller and asked Michael to hand me a bottle. He did so, and the baby was soon drinking contently in my arms. The judge reviewed the circumstances of the case with us as Hadeel finished her bottle. She sat up, looked at Michael, and reached out for him to take her. He did so, as tears slid down his cheeks. She was quickly asleep on his shoulder.

We were asked questions about our lifestyle, our work histories, our financial background, our marriage, our family histories, Michael's military service, my experience as a social worker, and our religious beliefs. Our lawyer pointed out Michael's first-hand experience with living in the Middle East and being intimately familiar with the cultures and languages of the areas, including that of the now-deceased parents of the two children involved. I tearfully told the judge we would raise the children in such a way that they'd know their parents' ethnic background and tell them about what wonderful people they'd been.

"Will you raise them Muslim?"

"No, but we will raise them with an understanding of the Muslim tradition, so they can decide what religion they want to be when they're old enough to choose," Michael said. "We'd discussed this with Adiba and Rakeem when we signed the papers."

The judge nodded and said, "From what I've been told by your lawyer, the newborn may have severe physical and mental disabilities. Are you prepared for that?"

"I'm going to be a full-time mother," I told the judge. "As a social worker, I've dealt with preemies and children with limitations. We'll get him whatever help he needs."

The man nodded thoughtfully and said, "I also understand that both of you have been in therapy for Post-Traumatic Stress Disorder. Is this correct?" When we admitted that this was true and that we were currently receiving treatment, he asked, "Could you elaborate somewhat? I have to make certain the two children are in a stable home environment."

Telling myself to remain calm and knowing I was a terrible liar, I said, "I watched my father die in a farming accident that was covered up by the owners of the farm and by the workers who were afraid of losing their jobs and being deported. I've been getting counseling that I should have gotten at the time of the accident."

His curiosity obviously piqued, the judge asked, "How old were you when this accident happened?"

"Fourteen."

"What was the name of the farm?"

My throat constricted when I tried to answer him. Michael put his free arm around my shoulders and told the judge my mother and I had been threatened if we told about the accident and that I still had trouble revealing where it actually took place. The judge then asked Michael if he knew where the death had occurred. Michael told him he did, but that the farm was now shut down. He explained that I had asked him to take me there in November and had revisited the scene of my father's accident. The man then asked Michael to elucidate regarding his own PTSD.

"I worked for the Navy for ten years in various locations around the world. I saw a lot of violence and lost both friends and co-workers. When I started to have problems because of it, I decided it was time to leave the military. I began counseling before I got out and continued it afterwards. I have a great therapist, and Seneca sees the same doctor."

The judge thanked both of us for our candor and said, "It's evident that the children's parents wanted you to have custody of them in the event of their deaths. You're…uniquely qualified. The paperwork is all in order, and I'm more than satisfied with your responses. It's clear to me you'll love and care for Hadeel and Hani and that their welfare will be your top priority. I believe your past and current experiences make you more than capable of being excellent parents to these two children. Therefore, I'm granting you permanent custody of Hadeel Saleh and Hani Saleh and giving you the opportunity to adopt them. Is that what you want?" When we told him it was, he said, "I have one final question." Looking back and forth between me and Michael he continued, "I'm sure you'll want to change the children's last name to yours. Will you be changing their given names as well?"

"We want to keep their first names as they are and add their parents' first names as middle names and our last name," Michael answered.

"That would be fine. Please tell the court what the legal names will be for these two minors. After saying the names, please spell them out for the record."

"Our son will be Hani Rakeem Benedetto," Michael said then spelled out the name. "Our daughter will be Hadeel Adiba Benedetto." He spelled her name for the court reporter, who nodded her thanks.

Once all of the necessary paperwork had been signed, we left the courthouse. Hadeel was still asleep on Michael's shoulder, and he excused himself for a few moments to talk alone with the lawyer. I watched them conversing and inexplicably began to cry. Both Diane and Al hugged me and assured me that everything would be all right as Michael returned to where we stood and put his free arm around me. I could tell by the tension in his body that he was struggling not to break down. Once I'd regained control of myself, I asked him what he and the lawyer had been talking about.

"Krystal and Greg. We need to draw up papers with them just as Adiba and Rakeem did with us. That way, if anything happens to us, they get the kids and the money they'd need to take care of them."

"But what about Al and Diane?"

"We are old, my angel," Al said gently. "Even if we live to be a hundred, we cannot physically care for the children. They require young parents who can give them what they need for most of their lives."

"Even if, God forbid, anything happened to the two of you I'd want to continue to be great-grandmother to Hadeel and Hani," Diane volunteered.

"You'll always be their great-grandmother," Michael assured her. "You know Krystal and Greg would never deny the two of you access to the kids if something were to happen to us. *They* don't have any family they want to acknowledge and think of you as their family."

"But Al and I aren't married," Diane pointed out.

"I think it is about time we changed that," Al announced. "I loved my wife, and you loved your husband. They have both been dead for many years. I love you now and am certain that you love me. We should marry."

"Are you serious?"

"I have never been more serious in all my life." Taking her hand, he asked, "Diane, will you marry me?"

She smiled and said, "I'll have to think about it."

"You wound me, my *bella* Diane!" he exclaimed dramatically.

"Oh, all right," she laughed. "I would never want to wound you. I *do* love you, Alfredo Benedetto."

Michael and I congratulated the couple and hugged them. We parted ways, agreeing to meet them at the hospital at 2:00 so we could take our respective turns with our new son.

When we got into the car, I quickly called Krystal and updated her on the court proceedings and on the surprise engagement while Michael did the same with Greg. We were all talking at once and were relieved and happy about something for the first time since our real-life nightmare had begun the previous Saturday. Both agreed to come to the house that evening to see the babies' rooms and have dinner with us, Diane, and Al.

"We can talk with them about the legal papers then, Michael suggested. "I'd rather broach the subject right away and make certain everything is in order."

"But they're newly married and may not want to make the commitment," I speculated. "What if they say no?"

"You think they're going to say no?" Michael asked. "When I met up with Greg yesterday before we joined Nonno at the hospital, the two of us sat and talked and cried for an hour. Rakeem was our closest friend, and Greg feels the loss almost as much as I do."

"What would it take for him to feel it as much as you?"

Michael shut his eyes and admitted, "Rakeem and I shared experiences that could only be comprehended if one lived in the Middle East. Greg can never truly understand that world anymore than you or Krystal can. With Rakeem and Adiba, I felt that connection that's almost lost to me here in the States. I know there are other veterans I can talk to, but I lived it for a lot longer and on a different level than your average soldier. When Rakeem and I were alone, we…we could really talk about things."

"You're blaming yourself, aren't you?"

"They wouldn't be dead and the baby wouldn't be in such bad shape if someone wasn't out to torment me."

"That's the someone's fault, not yours. Weren't you fighting against bad people? How can you blame yourself for what one of them does in retaliation? You were protecting good people and their lives against evil people and their ulterior motives. This is not your fault, Michael."

"Logically, I know that. Emotionally, I feel like I'm responsible."

"Make sure you talk to Dr. Forrester about this tonight."

"I will." He started the engine of the SUV and said, "We also need to make sure we give the lawyer a nice bonus when we pay him for his work on all this."

"I thought he said he didn't want compensation for coming to the hospital Saturday."

"It has nothing to do with that."

"What then?"

"This morning. I don't know how he did it."

"What?"

"Got the custody and adoption pushed through so quickly. I suspect he and the judge are *very* good friends. Normally, this kind of stuff takes time. When Nonno and Nonnie took me in, there were social workers checking in on us quarterly for the first year. Nothing was finalized until they were completely satisfied. Yet, we managed to adopt these children the Monday after their parents' deaths with not even one home visit by a social services worker, and that's with both of us receiving treatment for PTSD. Pretty freakin' unusual, wouldn't you say? I don't know how, and I don't want to know. I'm just glad it's done."

At 2:00, we went up to the NICU to see Hani. The police decided to remove their guard, and I asked Michael if we should hire private security. He told me no and said he would explain later.

I was dismayed to note that Hani didn't appear to have made any progress and discussed this with the neonatologist while Michael was with the baby. The doctor reminded me it had been less than forty-eight hours since Hani's birth. He urged me not to be too eager for drastic improvements at this early stage. I relayed this to Michael and Diane while Al was in the NICU with the newborn.

Tears filled my eyes as I wondered where Hadeel thought her parents were and when they'd return for her. Sadly, she would forget them soon. Hani would never know them.

Michael and I were at the house at 3:45, and the delivery truck was already there. We put Buttons in the home office, so he wouldn't accidentally get stepped on or sneak out. Michael took Hadeel for a walk on the beach while I directed the deliverymen as to where to put everything. They were gone by 5:30, and our dinner guests arrived at 6:00.

"Oh, my goodness!" Krystal exclaimed, as she and the others caught their first glimpse of Hadeel's room. "It looks like it's been this way for months."

"How perfect," Diane said with approval. "You did a lovely job, Seneca. Hadeel will love growing up here."

"You have done a beautiful job," remarked Al.

Knowing we wouldn't have time to paint either of the children's rooms, I'd decorated accordingly. In Hadeel's silvery gray room, the crib, which could eventually be converted into a toddler bed, was white and matched the crown molding and baseboards. The dresser, nightstand, changing table, and chest of drawers were white as well. The curtains were pink, as was the bedding and the pad on the changing table. Four framed prints of ballerinas in various poses hung in a row on one wall, and HADEEL was spelled out in large purple letters over the crib. A patterned pink and purple rug had been placed in the center of the floor, and a white rocker was positioned catty-corner on one side of the room. Its pink and purple cushions matched the rug. A white dove plaque hung on the outside of her door.

"The dove decoration is very appropriate," Michael remarked.

"I thought so," I replied.

"Why is that?" asked Diane.

"Because Hadeel means dove in Arabic," I told her. "She's our little dove now."

Everyone moved to Hani's room. I'd decided to choose primary and secondary colors to accent the tan walls. This had been partially because I thought it would help Hani with visual stimulation and partially because I thought it would be cute. His crib and matching furniture were black. The curtains and bedding were red, while the rug was striped with red, blue, yellow, green, orange, and purple. The cushions of his black rocker matched the rug in a similar fashion to that of his sister's. Colorful prints of balloons were arranged in a zigzag pattern on one wall, and HANI had been spelled out in the same bright colors above his changing table. A black-and-white mobile hung above the crib.

"I probably should have gone with all black and white," I muttered. "That would be more stimulating for Hani but how boring!"

"I think it's the coolest nursery I've ever seen," Krystal declared. "I was wondering how it'd all look put together. It's great!"

I thanked everyone for their compliments and asked Michael if he liked the rooms as I took Hadeel from his arms. While he looked around Hani's nursery, he said, "I can't believe you coordinated all this in one afternoon."

"I didn't have much choice," I told him. Putting Hadeel down on the rug, I said, "It was kind of a challenge."

Hadeel crawled over to the crib, stopped, sat down then looked up at all of us. Then she crawled in our direction, stopped, sat down, and looked at us again. Finally, she crawled towards the doorway and out into the hall. Diane said what we were all thinking, that the child was looking for her parents.

I bit my lip and blinked back tears. We stood clustered at one end of the hall and watched the baby explore the house. Buttons came out of one room and rubbed against Hadeel's back, and she giggled before resuming her search.

Michael said furiously in Spanish, "Whoever the fuck did this is going to regret he was ever born!"

He stalked out of the room and left the house. We heard the engine of the SUV start, and Michael drove off.

"What was that all about?" Diane asked as Hadeel crawled in Michael's wake.

Al shook his head and said, "My Michael…." Looking to me, he asked, "He was not a Navy SEAL, was he?" When I didn't answer, he confided, "I prayed that he would not join the Navy as his parents had, but he did not listen to me. He said he needed some connection to them, since he was small when they died in the subway accident and remembered the strict, uncaring parents they were. He longed to understand, I think. His father was the only child of mine who disappointed me.

"I knew that what Michael would get out of his military service would be something he had never expected. With his intelligence, drive, and extraordinary eidetic memory capacity, I was certain he would not be relegated to some traditional position. I often wonder what sort of world he truly lived in for those ten years."

I couldn't comment, and there was silence among us for a while.

"Did Michael say where he was going?" Krystal asked me. "I wasn't raised to speak Spanish like you."

"No, but I'm betting it's the hospital. Would you all mind staying with Hadeel while I go to him? We picked up a giant Caesar salad with grilled steak strips and some bread on the way home. The salad's in the fridge."

"Of course we'll stay," Krystal told me. "Go help your husband."

I found Michael in the NICU. As I approached him from behind, I heard him talking softly in Arabic to Hani. I knew he was aware of my presence although he never paused or turned to greet me. Even when I came around to stand on the other side of the incubator, Michael continued to talk to the baby and refused to look at me. I stared across at him and watched as he gently ran his large hand over the tiny infant's head and torso.

"He's breathing easier tonight," Michael said suddenly. "He seems more comfortable."

I studied the baby and nodded. His breathing did seem to be less labored than it had been previously.

"What were you telling him?"

"How I wished I could bury his parents according to their custom and traditions. If we were in Iraq, I'd see to it that they were bathed, shrouded, and buried without a casket in a certain way. I can't do that here, and it saddens me. I'm meeting with the religious leader of the mosque tomorrow to discuss Rakeem and Adiba's funerals. I have no idea how the meeting will go. I'm going to have to be very diplomatic and respectful but show my conviction that what we're doing by adopting the children is right.

"I don't want to cause a serious break with the Islamic community. Hadeel and Hani need to be accepted there. I'm walking a cultural tightrope and can only hope that my background living in the Middle East will give me enough clout to gain acceptance."

"You'll do a flawless job," I told him. "You always do."

He smiled darkly at me and said, "I was well-trained."

"Have you heard from your friends at your…old job?"

"I got a call from someone on my way over here. I'll tell you about it when we're alone."

We left the hospital an hour later. Michael suggested we go to the café at Holmes Beach and have some food and take a walk so he could talk with me in private. We drove the two vehicles there, shared a club sandwich and fries, and set out holding hands and carrying our shoes. Since it was a cold March evening, the beach was practically deserted. I shivered, and Michael didn't hesitate to stop, remove his shirt, and drape it around my shoulders. I didn't bother pointing out that he would be cold. I knew he would dismiss my concerns and tell me not to worry about him, so I kept quiet.

When we reached a truly isolated area of the beach, Michael stopped, pulled me close to him, and kissed me deeply. I felt the electric spark I always experienced when we touched. I forgot for a few moments about the horrible murders, the baby fighting to live, and everything else. I could feel Michael's erection as we pressed our bodies close together and wanted him in me.

After a time, Michael moved his mouth from mine to my neck then up to my ear. I could hear the arousal in his voice, but I knew he had an ulterior motive for our current embrace. As he held me and caressed my back, he quietly told me that the four men who had been responsible for Adiba and Rakeem's deaths had been found by some former co-workers of his. When I began to ask him where, he kissed me on the mouth then drew back slightly and told me not to say anything.

"Just listen," he directed. "Can you do that?"

There was sarcasm in his voice, and my temper flared. I heard laughter rumble deep in his chest, and he kissed me once more before I could speak. He then brought his lips to my ear again and said, "The men had all been killed before our people got to them. I'm not sorry about their murders, but I am sorry they weren't able to be interrogated. I'm thinking whoever hired them silenced them before we could get any answers."

"So, are we all in danger?"

"No. You, me, the children, Nonno, Diane, Greg, and Krystal will all have guardian angels until this is settled."

"What if that's years?"

"Then it will be years."

I stiffened as I realized the implications of what he'd just told me. For the government to put that much time, money, and effort into Michael and his life he had to have been extremely important to them. Or, rather, he had to *be* extremely important to them.

"Your role as an operative in the field was that crucial?"

I couldn't see the smile since his lips were against my neck. I sensed it, felt it, and understood it as he said, "You have no idea how crucial I was in the scheme of things. What I did and my almost supernatural photographic memory capabilities will keep me and mine safe for the rest of our lives."

"But what if they kill you to silence you?"

"You mean our government? They would never do that."

"How can you be so certain?"

"Because I'm a damn smart operative with an extraordinary eidetic memory. I did and saw things over the course of a decade that are still being dissected by the higher ups. I may not be in the Navy anymore, but I continue to do my part to help with Intelligence when contacted. I'm very valuable as an ally to the military. Hell, I'm a goddamn national resource."

"Michael —"

He chuckled and said, "I know. I shouldn't swear. Are you still going to be telling me that after we've been married for fifty years?"

"Probably."

"Tell me to fuck you," he urged playfully.

"I can't. It goes against everything my mother taught me."

"You will."

"Will not."

"Will, too."

Refusing to get caught up in a childish argument, I went on by asking, "What do we tell the others about how the murders relate to you and the security and everything else?"

"Nothing. They're never to know what I was. Ever. If any of them finds out, then our lives are at greater risk. We might all have to disappear and start over with new identities. I don't want that."

"You mean like the Witness Protection Program?"

"Something similar, but it might have to be in another country. We may not be able to stay together as a group if that happened. I don't want to be separated from our family or our friends."

"I won't say anything to anyone ever."

"You never know what will happen in the future. I hope you never have to talk to anybody about it, but if you do, then make certain the ramifications are worth the risk."

Michael and I returned home before 9:00, thanked the others for babysitting, and eventually bid them goodnight. We played with Hadeel before I bathed her and put her to sleep in her new crib. As usual, she was a sound sleeper, and I knew from past experience that she wouldn't wake until the following morning. I reflected that we should make certain to enjoy this undisturbed sleep time since Hani would probably wake more frequently when we brought him home. Premature babies tended to eat more often, because their small stomachs couldn't take in enough to allow them to sleep for long periods. I might be up every hour with him for a while. We would simply have to see.

When Michael had his nightly session with Dr. Forrester, I went to bed and instantly fell asleep. I dreamed of Tom, but he was a younger Tom, a Tom I'd only seen in pictures. He was slender and muscular like Michael, but he was different, of course. He was equally as handsome in his own way and had those eyes that sparkled with intelligence and wit. He came over to me, took my hand, and said, "Seneca. My lovely Seneca. How could you forget?"

Confused, I asked him what he meant.

"I left you a gift, and you forgot."

My eyes snapped open as I woke and remembered the box Tom had given me the month before he died. I'd tucked it away in the secret hiding place in the built-in unit located in the living room and had completely forgotten about it after Tom's death due to my own near-death experience and PTSD breakdown. Now that I'd remembered it, the only thing I wanted to do was rise, go to the cabinet, and remove my hidden treasure. Sighing, I resigned myself to the knowledge that I'd have to wait until no one was home besides me and Hadeel. Tom had told me the contents of the box were meant for my eyes only, and I wanted to respect his wishes.

The following morning after Michael had gone for his run, eaten breakfast, and left for the gym and work; I played with Hadeel and realized we'd neglected to buy the children toy boxes and items to put in them. We had few toys in the house, and I decided Hadeel and I would remedy that after an early lunch.

Diane and Al were meeting me at the hospital at 2:00, so we could take turns watching Hadeel and interacting with Hani. Michael would go directly there after work and spend time with the baby. Krystal and Greg had agreed to babysit Hadeel after she was put down for the night so that Michael and I could make another joint trip to the NICU.

I placed Hadeel in her playpen with the toys she did have and found the Disney Channel on TV. She happily entertained herself while I withdrew the large books from the bottom section of the built-in unit and opened the secret compartment. I removed the box and sat on the floor staring at it for a moment before following the directions Tom had given me and using his birth date as the combination to unlock the box.

Inside there were several items, including an envelope with my name on it, a man's ring that had what appeared to be a raven stamped into the top, and a smaller box that had a glass lid emblazoned with the words "In case of emergency, break glass." There was also a tiny hammer. I smiled.

I opened the envelope, removed a letter, and prepared to cry. I surprised myself by not shedding a tear as I read:

My lovely Seneca,

I've told you many times how much I admire your intellect, your grace, and your determination. Not to sound like a smart ass, but you remind me of myself, only prettier and less able to deceive. You would have made a goddamn terrible spy, but you've made a beautiful, brilliant, kind woman. I'm so proud of you.

You've found a real keeper in Michael. He's just as smart as you and I, but he was probably a better spy than I was, and that's saying a lot. He's better-looking than I, so that's a plus, too. Ha! You're both extraordinarily fortunate to have found one another. Don't take your relationship for granted. It's too important.

Michael may never be able to tell you about that time in his life when he was an operative. I can't tell you about what he did either. What I can share with you is what I did, and that may give you a better understanding of Michael. You'll have to decide after you read this.

I joined the military in an effort to escape my memories of childhood abuse, not to become a spy. I could've been a grunt on the front lines of some war for all I cared. I was looking for redemption from what I thought was my shame. The military men saw my potential and put me in a special program. I became different men for different tasks. I lived different lives for different missions. I played spy games and won the majority of the time. I killed when I had to and learned more about human beings and politics than I could ever document in one lifetime. I also became jaded, lonely, and a little whacko towards the end of my career.

I, Thomas Edison Langston, was a good man. I was also a very dangerous man. I was a powerful tool in a subculture that was both necessary and terrible in order to protect the majority of humanity. With the combination of my brains, ingenuity, and focus, I was superb as an agent for the Powers That Be.

This may or may not come as a shock to you, but I continued to work as a "consultant" for the Intelligence community long after I quit being an operative. Someone has to help safeguard the world, and we spies are gifted and burdened with a desire to be the best. Pride or duty – both can be the catalyst for service.

Michael is all that I was plus more. He would die for you, and he would kill for you. Never underestimate him or those who might wish to do him good or ill. Never underestimate how much he keeps contained inside himself and the few failures that gnaw at his heart.

Take care of yourself, him, and the children you'll have one day. If he or you are ever in mortal danger, then I want you to break the glass of the little box I've included in here. The ring is important and might help you in a pinch. Please remember that you should only use the ring and what's inside the box if your life or Michael's is in jeopardy and you have nowhere else to turn. They may save your life or may get you killed. If the situation is that drastic, you'll have to take the chance.

I love you, Seneca. I love you like you're my very own, even though you're not. Never, ever forget that you are the epitome of what I feel a true woman should be.

Burn this letter after you read it, but keep the ring and the box hidden in case of disaster. Think of me now and again as the old, romantic fool I was. Maybe in death I've finally gotten the peace I've been searching for most of my life.

Your very own,
Tom

I read the letter several times before taking it to the kitchen, getting the matches out of a drawer, and striking one. I set the letter on fire, and it burned quickly and left only a small pile of ashes on the plate I'd placed underneath it. I left the plate on the counter and went back to the living room where I slipped the small box, hammer, and ring into the larger box Tom had given me and put it back in its hidey-hole. Once the books had been returned to the cabinet, I threw out the ashes, rinsed the plate and loaded it into the dishwasher. The only evidence that the letter had existed was what remained in my head.

Chapter Seven

When I went in to visit Hani that afternoon, it was evident he'd made great improvements overnight. I was thrilled to see that the breathing tube had been removed. The nurse told me his condition had stabilized so dramatically that they'd had three pediatricians examine him that morning. Although he still had the feeding tube and I.V., they were extremely pleased with his progress.

I called Michael to relay this good news while his grandfather was in with the baby, and Diane read a Richard Scarry book to Hadeel. He was ecstatic although I could tell he was tense. His appointment at the mosque would be in thirty minutes. I was encouraging and told him to call me once the meeting was over.

Hadeel was taking a nap in her crib at home by the time my iPhone rang. I'd been getting more and more concerned as the minutes had passed and was pacing the house when Michael finally called.

"Well?" I asked nervously. "How did it go?"

"It was…acceptable. There's no problem with the funeral arrangements, but there was definite displeasure that the children wouldn't be raised in a Muslim household."

"But we're not really any religion."

"Also not what a devoutly religious person wants to hear when you're talking about raising children."

"I see your point. What about the rest of the discussion?"

"There was relief that I had such an intimate knowledge of Islam and Middle Eastern culture, but I got the impression there was still disapproval. I can understand. Imagine if you had a Baptist or Catholic family and those kids were adopted by a Muslim family. The Christian pastor wouldn't be very happy about that."

Sighing, I said, "At least it's done now."

"Yes."

"So, you're going to see Hani after work then come home?"

"That was my plan. What do you want for dinner?"

"I think I'll order pizza. Once things settle down, I have to start cooking again."

"I know it's too soon, but we need to develop a routine with the kids and for ourselves. I think it's important that you and I still go to Ceviche with the group on Fridays for dinner and dancing and have other nights out. I know the children need us, but we won't be good parents if we're not a good couple."

"Were your parents a good couple?"

"I doubt it. Yours?"

"You know the answer to that."

"Which is why I think we need to make sure we stay connected."

"Michael, I have a really silly question for you."

"Your questions are never silly. What?"

"What are we going to do about sex?"

"I'm hoping we'll be having some again soon. Why?"

I blushed even though I knew no one was there to see me and said, "You know I like to scream."

I could hear the smile in his voice as he said, "I know. What's the problem?"

"The problem is the children. Before, it didn't matter how much I screamed or how loudly because it was only the two of us here. Now that we have the kids...and Hadeel heard her mother screaming and then Krystal...and I don't...I..."

"Seneca, calm down," Michael said abruptly. "Listen to yourself. You sound afraid, and I don't think it has to do with the kids. It has to do with hearing your parents fight then have sex, not understanding, and having that teenaged pervert watch the porn movie with you and his sister when you were seven. Take a deep breath for me and let it go."

"But –"

"We're not going to scare the children when we have sex. Admittedly, we can't make love anywhere in the house whenever we want to like before, but we can still have sex every day if we want without them hearing."

"How?"

"You remember the particulars of the construction of the addition?"

"Since it was just completed last month, I think I can recall that far back," I said wryly. "What about the addition?"

"Remember when we talked about the building materials? What did I specifically request for the walls and ceilings?"

As it came back to me, I said slowly, "Soundproofing and lots of insulation." Shaking my head in disbelief and appreciation, I said, "You anticipated this!"

"Of course I did. I know how you respond to me, and I've told you many times that I love it. I also knew that we planned on adopting kids at some point and knew you wouldn't want them to hear us have sex or listen to you scream if you had a nightmare. So, what better way to take care of that then to make it a non-issue?"

"But how will we hear the babies if they need us?"

"What about baby monitors?"

"Baby monitors would be perfect."

"Good. I'll stop by the store and pick up two sets on my way home tonight so that your mind will be at ease. How's that? Better?"

"Better."

"Great. See you and Hadeel tonight."

Michael was home by 7:30. I was sitting on the nursery floor playing with Hadeel, who had already been fed, bathed, and dressed in nightclothes.

"How is she?" Michael asked after kissing her on the top of her head and kissing me on the mouth.

"She's done beautifully today. She had another one of those episodes where it seemed like she was looking for Adiba and Rakeem, and that made me cry for a while. The rest of the time, she was happy and playful. She didn't even scream when I'd lay her back on the changing table to change her diaper."

"Did you talk physics to her again?"

I smiled and admitted I had.

"Maybe she's looking forward to it and that's why she's not screaming anymore. You're entertaining her with science."

Michael went to the kitchen, got two slices of vegetarian pizza, and brought his plate and a glass of water back to the nursery. He ate while Hadeel and I interacted with plastic blocks and circles and laughed out loud as she got frustrated and made a little growling noise before throwing one of the circles across the floor when it wouldn't fit where she wanted it.

Once he'd finished eating, Michael asked if he could play. I sat back and sipped some of his water and enjoyed seeing him play with the baby. He'd always been good with her, but now that she was *his* daughter he was totally relaxed and was allowing himself to act sillier than I'd ever seen him. It was heartening.

By 8:20, Hadeel began to look sleepy. I suggested that Michael read her a story and stayed where I was on the floor while he sat in the rocker with her and read her some of a Beatrix Potter book. She fell asleep in his arms, and I got to my feet and went over to take the book from his hands.

"I wish my parents had read to me when I was little," I said, as I laid the book on the dresser. "Did yours read to you?"

"I can't remember."

"I don't believe you," I said frankly. "What's your first memory? Your birth?"

He flashed a quick smile and said, "No, thank God. I'd imagine that would be quite an unpleasant memory."

"So, what is the first thing you remember?"

"My father and mother disciplining me. They were big on discipline."

"Discipline like what?"

"Spanking and berating. They were stereotypical military types. Most of the time, I got the impression even as a preschooler that I was an inconvenience and that they hadn't wanted to be saddled with children. I interfered with their work."

"You were so little. Maybe you misunderstood."

Shaking his head, he said, "My father used to say I was a *carico*."

"A what?"

"That's Italian for a burden."

"Michael, that's horrible!"

"Yes, it is."

Michael touched Hadeel's cheek and said, "When I was three, I overheard Nonno talking sternly to my father about how he and my mother treated me. Nonno got angry and told him that he didn't know how my father had turned out to be such an inhumane man when he'd been such a sweet boy. My father said it was none of his business and to get out of his apartment. I wasn't allowed to see Nonno or Nonnie again until my parents died and my grandparents got custody of me."

I thought of Tom's letter to me and of how he'd said he'd enlisted in the military to escape the shame he'd felt as the victim of childhood abuse. After hearing Michael's story, his motivations for joining the Navy were becoming clearer to me. It made me extremely sad because I intuited that he'd wanted to escape the shame of existing. I suspected he'd wanted to prove to himself and his grandfather that he could be a good man and a good soldier and retain his humanity – unlike his parents.

What an impetus and a weight and how terribly tragic to be made to feel unwanted by those who gave you life, I thought. *At least I knew love from both of my parents and never doubted their devotion to me.*

Michael stared down at our sleeping daughter and said, "She's so innocent. All I want to do is protect her. I can't ever imagine wanting to spank her or berate her or tell her she's a burden to us. I can't understand anyone's thinking like that, yet that's how my parents felt about me. They would have felt that way about any child they had. I've often thought over the years how cruel that was. Maybe that's the way you have to behave when you kill for a living."

My head snapped up as I asked, "What did you say?"

"I know you heard me, Seneca."

"Your parents were assassins? I thought they worked in Communications."

"Oh, they communicated with their targets all right."

"But the military branches don't use assassins."

"Of course not," he said sarcastically. "That would be wrong."

"I was under the impression your parents were killed in a subway accident."

"They were." He laughed bitterly and said, "Pretty ironic if you ask me. Maybe there is some justice in the scheme of life after all."

"Does Al know his son was an assassin?"

"No. No one outside the Navy knows besides you, and I'd appreciate it if we kept it that way." Standing, he brought Hadeel to her crib and lowered her into it before saying, "You don't know how long I've wanted to share all of that with you."

As I put my arms around his waist, I said, "I'm so glad you felt you could, but I'm so sorry your parents were like that. Thank goodness, you had Al and your grandmother."

"I was very lucky to be blessed with them," he agreed. "It's odd how my parents had such orderly lives and little feeling, and your parents had such disorderly lives and such deep feelings."

"The end result is that you and I are both beautiful people who are damaged emotionally."

"Pretty much."

"Let's not waste our opportunity with our children. I want them to have a loving, stable home with us."

"Me, too."

"Michael?"

"Yes?"

"How did you find out about your parents?"

"You mean discovering they were assassins? I was told by Naval Intelligence. They tried to recruit me for that line of work when I enlisted and cited my parents' excellent reputation in that area. When I flat-out refused, they offered me the chance to work as a different kind of operative."

I was going to ask him to elaborate about his career choice when we heard the knock on the front door. Greg and Krystal had arrived to babysit.

"We'll set up the baby monitors while you're gone," Greg told us before we left. "Don't worry about anything."

I glanced at Krystal, who didn't look well. When I asked her what was the matter, she said she was having trouble coping with the events of the previous Saturday. She had an appointment scheduled with a therapist for the following afternoon.

"I've been having nightmares," she admitted. "I keep seeing the same scenes being replayed over and over in my dreams. It's scaring me."

"I'm glad she's going to talk to someone," Michael told me as we rode to the hospital. "Unlike some other people I know who wait half their lives to get help, she's tackling this head-on."

"At least I finally did it," I retorted. "I may be a genius, but I'm also a slow learner."

He grinned and took my hand before saying, "We're going to make it through this."

"I believe you. It's only that I wonder how long it will take before we're truly safe and sound."

Over the course of the next several weeks, we adjusted to learning our new roles as parents and our new schedules, developing a routine with Hadeel, and trying to deal with the absences of Adiba and Rakeem. It got easier each day, but I knew things would never be right until the unknown threat was eliminated. I was relieved but nervous when we were finally able to bring Hani home from the hospital. That led to an entirely new set of challenges, but we seemed to manage well.

One night, I was on top of Michael with my chest pressed against his and was about to climax when I heard Hani's cry on the baby monitor. My instinctive reaction was to extricate myself from Michael's arms and go to the baby, but Michael held me firmly in place and told me to finish.

"He's safe," Michael murmured. "Sixty seconds of crying won't hurt him. It might actually help to strengthen his lungs."

I wanted to argue with him but couldn't do anything except shudder and cry out as he brushed the pad of his thumb over my clitoris. I felt Michael come just as I finished and worked at recovering myself enough to go to our son. Michael kissed my throat and lay back on the mattress before asking me if I wanted him to see to the baby.

"No, I've got it," I assured him. "Go on to sleep."

He smiled up at me and said, "Not yet. I'll bring you some water in a minute."

I got myself together, put on my nightgown and robe, and went to lift Hani from his crib. It was late July, and he was now four months old. Although still small for his age, he weighed over ten pounds and had had only one upper respiratory infection since we'd brought him home in early May. To our surprise and delight, Hadeel had readily accepted his presence and was excited to "help" me with her little brother whenever possible.

As I sat in the rocker and gave Hani his bottle, Buttons rubbed around my ankles and purred. Michael appeared with a glass of water for me and knelt beside the rocker and watched as the baby gradually drained the bottle. He touched Hani's dark hair and said something to him in Arabic.

"What did you tell him?"

"That he was a good boy and should eat up so he could grow stronger." Pushing my hair away from my face, he asked, "Are you sure you don't want to learn Arabic? What are you going to do when the children and I can all speak it and you can't? It will frustrate you."

"Are we going to teach them Spanish? Are you and Al going to teach them Italian? Are you going to teach them all of the other languages you know?"

"We've already had that conversation. It's enough to bring them up as bilingual. It would just confuse them to try teaching them Arabic, Spanish, Italian, Croatian, Greek, etcetera." Kissing Hani lightly on the head, he said, "I worry that Hani won't even be able to learn to form words."

"Will you try not to obsess about that? Hadeel's saying words, but she's almost a year and a half old. Hani's four months. The occupational therapist says —"

"I know what she says," he grunted. "I read the reports. His motor skills are acceptable, but we don't know what's going on in his brain."

"You're wrong," I countered. "If there were nothing going on in his brain, then his motor skills wouldn't be even close to age-appropriate." As I withdrew the empty bottle from Hani's mouth and lifted him to my shoulder, I purposefully changed the subject and said, "I can't wait for the Benedetto family to descend at Al's tomorrow and meet Hadeel and Hani."

I knew Michael wanted to continue our conversation about Hani's development, but he merely followed my lead and said, "You know the family will love them. Hadeel's feet will never touch the ground when we're with them. She'll probably forget how to walk after they've carried her around for seven days."

I smiled slightly and kissed Hani before I returned him to the crib and hooked him back up to the sleep apnea monitor. We'd been extremely fortunate that it had only sounded twice and that Hani hadn't stopped breathing in his sleep more often than that. It had still terrified me each time, but he'd responded well to our manual stimulation and had immediately resumed breathing afterwards.

We looked in on Hadeel, then we returned to our room and our bed. I snuggled against Michael, who draped one arm around my waist. I was asleep in seconds.

When I woke some time later, Michael's arm was no longer around me. I figured he'd gotten up to make a trip to the bathroom and prepared to turn over in the bed. I opened my eyes slightly and saw his naked back facing me. He was sitting on the edge of the mattress with his elbows resting on his knees.

"Michael?" When there was no answer, I propped myself up on one elbow and repeated, "Michael?"

"I had a bad dream," he told me. "I didn't mean to wake you."

"You're supposed to wake me. You said you'd talk to me when you had a nightmare, and you never have followed through with that."

"I haven't had any nightmares since we discussed it."

"Of course you have. We've been married for almost a year. You don't think I can tell in the mornings when you've had a terrible dream? You're different, quieter, more remote."

"Why didn't you confront me?"

"I figured when you were really ready to talk, you would."

"I can't talk to you about the things I see in my nightmares. I save that for my weekly sessions with Dr. Forrester. There's no need to torment you with images of things I saw or did in wars or…other situations."

"Was that what your nightmare was about tonight? War?"

He shook his head, and I scooted across the mattress and wrapped my arms around his shoulders. I kissed his neck and told him everything would be fine.

"Nothing will be fine until the man who had Adiba and Rakeem killed is dead."

I pressed my forehead against the spot between his shoulder blades and admitted I agreed with him. I asked if there was any new news on the search for this man, to which he replied no.

"Is that what you dreamed of?" I pushed.

"No."

"What then?"

"I thought you were going to wait for me to come to you when I was ready."

"Maybe you need a nudge."

"More like an anvil to the head," he joked, but his voice was devoid of mirth. "I dreamed about the little girl I accidentally killed when I was in the gunfight with her arms-dealing father and she ran out in front of him during the chaos."

"Did you know her name?"

"Of course. I knew everything there was to know about the family, the business, the household, their schedules, their habits, and anything else that pertained to my assignment."

"So, what was the little girl's name?"

He paused, and I supposed he was considering whether or not he could share this information with me. In the end, he said, "Jadranka."

"That's very pretty."

"Yes, she was." He suddenly announced, "I think I'm going out for a swim. Will you reset the alarm after I'm outside?"

"I think I'll bring the baby monitors to the lanai and sit and watch you swim for a while. Unless you don't want me out there."

"No, it's fine. I just need to do something mindless for a while. When I swim, I don't allow myself to think. I simply *am*. It's nice for a change."

I sat in one of the chairs on the lanai and looked out at the Gulf while Michael swam. I thought about Jadranka and Michael's guilt. Had the little girl's father actually been capable of loving her, or had he been like Michael's father and considered her an inconvenience and a burden? Would she have grown up to become as cold-hearted as her father and uncle and sworn to harm American soldiers for the purpose of promoting evil or gaining wealth? Or would she have broken ties with her family and fought against them? Perhaps she would have grown up, married, had children, and died without any knowledge of her family's involvement in arms dealing and murder.

Michael came back to the lanai and dried off before following me inside. I returned to bed, and he showered then joined me there. We both slept until Hadeel's crying roused us the following morning.

I was instantly panicked and told Michael to go to her while I went to Hani. The infant was typically up every two hours to eat and had only eaten once during the night. What if the apnea monitor had failed, and he died?

I got to the edge of the crib and grasped the rail before staring down at the baby. Normally, he slept on his stomach, although this was not conventionally accepted by pediatricians. He simply refused to sleep in any other position, and the doctors had informed us that we could allow him to continue this practice as long as he was hooked up to the apnea monitor. As I looked at Hani, he was lying on his back contentedly staring up at the mobile above him. Michael hurried in with Hadeel in his arms and came to stand beside me. When he saw that the baby was fine, he said, "Hani, you scared the shit out of us!"

"Don't say that in front of the children!" I rebuked, but I was trembling with relief. I kissed Hadeel and looked down at Hani before saying, "You are such a good little man. How did you manage to roll over onto your back?"

"You're not supposed to be that strong, yet," Michael added.

Hani turned his head towards us, looked up, and smiled while excitedly waving his little hands and feet. Michael and I both began to laugh and cry tears of happiness. Not only had the baby responded to our voices and presence, but he also recognized us. It was a huge milestone, especially for his age and developmental level. We hugged each other and a confused Hadeel before I unhooked Hani from his monitor and lifted him up to join us.

The next seven days were filled with the typical Benedetto family reunion chaos. On the last day, Krystal and Greg joined us at Al's house where Al and Diane were married by one of Al's sons, the priest who'd married us. Diane was not Catholic, and the ceremony was even shorter than our wedding and Krystal and Greg's. For two people who adored dressing up, going out to dinner, and attending highbrow social functions on a regular basis, the couple's wedding was remarkably casual.

Al and Diane stood in front of the infinity pool behind Al's house that overlooked the Gulf of Mexico. Al wore khaki shorts and a blue knit Polo shirt, while Diane had on a tan pair of Capri pants and a rose-colored cotton top. Of course, she also had on fashionable backless shoes and simple, yet elegant expensive gold jewelry. To this, she added her new wedding ring, which was a two-carat solitaire diamond that had a band of diamonds extending down and around from it. Al's wedding band was a plain gold circle.

The rest of us were dressed as casually as the wedding couple. The men all wore shorts and t-shirts, while the women were either similarly dressed or had on sundresses. Al and Diane had announced that they wanted the entire affair to be as relaxed as possible, and everyone had readily complied with their wishes. Relatives were snapping pictures with their digital cameras or phones.

The catered food for the backyard reception held behind Al's enormous home was all Italian and all fantastic. Krystal rolled her eyes and shook her head as if to say, "There goes my weight loss for the week!"

"You're still doing fabulously and keep losing weight most weeks," I told her as we sat at one of the outdoor tables that had been set up under tents for the reception. "This one meal isn't going to derail your overall weight loss."

"I know, but I've been doing so well and hate to backslide."

"It'll be fine," I assured her as I spooned some risotto into Hadeel's mouth. "You think *I'm* not going to gain something after this?"

Once I was certain Hadeel had chewed and swallowed her food, I offered her some juice. She shook her head and said clearly, "No, Mama." Pointing to the rice and pasta mixture, she demanded, "I want more of that."

I gave her another spoonful before looking at Krystal, who looked as surprised as I felt. Krystal waited until the toddler had finished chewing and had taken a sip of juice before asking, "Hadeel, who is that over there?"

After looking across to where Krystal was pointing, she said, "Daddy and Hani."

"What is Daddy doing?"

"Feeding the baby," she replied before reaching for the risotto and saying, "I want more, Mama."

I gestured to Krystal and asked, "Who is this?"

"It's Kry-stal!" Hadeel said then giggled before indicating she wanted more risotto. I gave her another spoonful and asked Krystal to get Michael, who was giving Hani a bottle while talking to a male cousin. I watched as Krystal interrupted the discussion and motioned for Michael to follow her. He walked over with Hani in his arms.

"What's wrong?" Michael asked worriedly as he sat on the other side of Hadeel's highchair.

"Hadeel, tell Daddy what you want."

"I want more!" she exclaimed and indicated the rice and pasta. "I like *that*."

Michael looked stunned then amused. I recounted the other sentences Hadeel had uttered and wondered aloud how many others she knew and just hadn't shared with us, yet. A few moments later, she dropped the stuffed Winnie the Pooh toy she'd been holding and exclaimed, "Oh, fuck! Pooh fell down."

I was horrified. Michael exploded with laughter and couldn't seem to stop. Krystal snickered beside me. The relatives in our vicinity asked what was so funny. Michael was laughing so hard he was crying and couldn't catch his breath.

"I guess you were right," he said, once he'd regained enough control over himself to speak again. "I suppose I shouldn't swear in front of the children." He burst out laughing again, saw my expression, and said, "Sorry. It's too funny."

"It won't be funny when we go to Mommy and Me exercise class and she says that word in front of the other mothers and children," I declared angrily.

Michael got up, came around the highchair, bent down, and kissed me. Depositing Hani into my arms, he turned to Hadeel and said something to her in Arabic. She answered – in Arabic. Michael turned to me with a huge grin on his face and said, "By Jove, I think she's got it!"

My anger dissipated in an instant. Michael seemed exuberant. He looked carefree and totally happy. I caught a glimpse of Al out of the corner of my eye and saw him as he intently watched Michael. He himself was grinning madly, and I knew how happy it made him to see his grandson so relaxed and overjoyed.

"Was he like that as a boy?" I asked Al later when we were alone in one corner of the living room.

"After his parents were gone, he became like that. My wife and I worked hard at playing with him and encouraging him to have fun. His father and mother were...." Al sighed and said, "I hate to say this of my own child, but that son became a man I did not recognize or respect. He and his wife were not good parents to my Michael. They were not like the rest of the family. I used to wonder where I went wrong with Michael's father, but I stopped blaming myself for his choices long ago." Glancing across the room at Michael, he added, "During the years Michael was away, I worried he would become like his parents. I am so relieved to know it did not happen." Taking my hand, Al said, "He has a fulfilling life and is an excellent man, husband, and father. That is all I ever wanted for him, my angel."

Chapter Eight

"We'll fly to New York in the morning then catch a flight bound for Heathrow," Diane was telling me the next evening when we were discussing the honeymoon trip that she and Al were preparing to take. "We should be in Paris by midnight our time tomorrow. We'll fly back in two weeks. It will be lovely in France this time of year, although it will be crowded with tourists." Looking down at Hani, who was in her arms, she said, "We'll have to bring back something extra-special for our great-grandchildren."

"They'll just be happy to see you when you come back," I told her. "Look, Hani's smiling at you now."

He was, and she nodded with satisfaction and said, "He knows his great-grandmother when he sees her. I never had children and never imagined that being around little ones would be so rewarding."

Hadeel toddled over to me and reached her arms out before saying, "I want up, Mama!" I lifted her into my lap and kissed her cheek before nodding to Diane and asking, "Who is this?"

"Diane!" she exclaimed. She looked around the room until she located Al and said, "Nonno!"

"I like that she calls me by name," Diane declared. "It sounds a lot better than *Grandma* or *MawMaw*."

"Then *Diane* it is. Hani should be able to pick up on that one once he starts talking."

"Quite. How is Michael handling his concern about Hani's progress?"

"It varies. He really stresses over it."

"And you don't?"

I thought for a moment before saying, "I have no control over it. I can't do any more than I already am."

"Michael seems to blame himself for the children's being orphaned," Diane observed. "Why do you think that is?"

You're not a good liar, I reminded myself. *Tell the truth as much as you can.*

"Michael wants to make everything better for everybody. That's why he's so good at so many things. John's Place has flourished since he opened it, and it's become a real hub for the veterans in our community. I know it makes him feel like he's doing something to right wrongs he didn't even create. It's evident that he wants to do the same with our children."

She gave me a look of appreciation that told me I'd given her a satisfactory answer but hadn't answered her question. I speculated as to how much she and Al really suspected when it came to Rakeem and Adiba's murders. Although Michael had told me his grandfather hadn't known that his son and daughter-in-law were assassins, I sensed he did and was greatly concerned that Michael had followed in his parents' professional footsteps. I couldn't reassure Al without telling him Michael had been a spy, and I'd sworn never to do that with anyone unless it was a life-or-death instance.

"Mama, where's Daddy?" Hadeel rubbed tiredly at her eyes and said, "I want to go night-night."

"I believe Chatty Cathy is ready for bed," Diane said with a slight smile. "Hani appears to be falling asleep in my arms."

"Yes, we should probably go. These two need their baths, books, and bed." I gave Diane a brief hug and said, "Have a safe and wonderful honeymoon."

"We plan to. I'm sure Al will be texting you the entire time we're there. I'm glad he's enjoying that phone of his, but I personally don't see the fascination with texting. At least one of us is interested in such things. I'll simply call if I want to talk to you while we're gone."

"We'll be looking forward to hearing all about it."

Michael came over to us, hugged Diane, and took Hani from her arms and placed him in his infant carrier. Then he picked it up and hoisted Hadeel into his free arm. We said our goodbyes to Al and Diane before leaving and walking to the SUV.

"I hope they have a great honeymoon," I said, as we rode home.

"Me, too. It's got me thinking about our upcoming anniversary. What do you want to do to celebrate? Before Adiba and Rakeem…." He sobered and said, "Before we got the kids, I was thinking we could take a long weekend trip somewhere. I don't think either of us would feel comfortable with that at this point, but I'd like for our anniversary to be special. So, what do you want to do?"

"We could go to dinner at Michael's on East. After all, we got married in the atrium next to the restaurant and had our reception in the hall."

"It's a start, but I want it to be more than that."

"Then surprise me. No overnight trips though. I know Greg and Krystal are always willing to babysit when they're available, but I still think it's not a good idea to leave Hani overnight until we're sure he's past the sleep apnea issue."

Michael agreed and said he would surprise me with something special.

"I don't need anything material," I told him. "Just having some alone time would be nice."

"Same here. I'll work on it."

The following Saturday, Michael and I went to Michael's on East for an early dinner. He'd chosen to wear a dark blue suit, while I'd purchased a green cocktail dress with spaghetti straps specifically for the occasion. Everyone who worked for the restaurant made a special effort to wish us a happy anniversary, so I knew Michael had informed them when he'd made the reservation that we were celebrating. I was brought a dozen orange roses when we received the bill, and I admired them greatly and thanked Michael for his gift.

"They made me think of the orange dress you have, the one you wore the first time we went to Ceviche for dinner and dancing. I love that dress."

"Maybe I should have worn it tonight."

"No, I think the one you have on is beautiful, but that's probably because you're in it," he told me. "It will work better for what I have planned for after dinner."

"Hm. My man of mystery and his plans."

As we walked out of the restaurant, I asked, "Did Al text you twenty times today?"

Chuckling, he said, "More like twenty-five. He said Monet's Garden in Giverny was spectacular and that you and I were going to have to go there with the children sometime. He was awed, and so was Diane."

"I'm so glad they're having fun." Once Michael had paid the valet and we were seated in the car, I asked, "Are your friends watching Al and Diane while they're in France?"

"Yes."

"Good." Pausing, I inquired, "If I ask you something about your former job, will you get upset?"

"Depends on what it is, I guess."

"All of these guardian angels who watch us, the children, Al, Diane, Krystal, and Greg are professionals." I hesitated and said, "I know you told me I had no idea how valuable you were and are to the Intelligence community. Do you still do…consulting work with them?"

He tensed and asked, "What would make you think that?"

"Tom did after he retired. If the Intelligence community is throwing a lot of money into safeguarding us, then you must be still working with them, and I don't' mean only to sift through your past assignments. It makes sense that you're still involved, even though you're not in the Navy anymore."

"Would you be freaked out if I said I was a consultant?"

"Not unless it puts us and our family and friends in danger."

"What happened to Adiba and Rakeem has nothing to do with my current consulting work. You can trust me on that. If I thought I was endangering anyone because of my occasional review of materials, then I'd end my involvement."

"You promised me once you'd never go back to the Navy or be a spy again."

"And I never will. What I do is different but necessary. It involves information only and is extremely high security."

"I think Tom's was, too. Yet, there were three attempts on his life after he retired."

"Those all had to do with earlier jobs."

"What happened to the people who tried to kill him?" I asked, emboldened by his openness.

Michael's blue eyes left the road and glanced at me. When he looked back, he asked, "You really want to know?"

"Yes."

"Fine. The first attack happened shortly after Tom left the military. It was a physical attack, and he and the assailants struggled. He broke one man's neck and stabbed the other."

I tried to imagine my elderly tender-hearted friend breaking someone's neck and stabbing another man. Unnerving as it might be, I was able to envision it.

"The second attack came three years after his retirement. Someone tried to poison Tom, but he caught wind of the scheme. Another professional eliminated that threat, so Tom didn't have to."

"And the third?"

We were sitting at a red light, and I saw a muscle tighten in Michael's jaw before he admitted, "Someone tampered with his car, and it cost him his daughter."

"You mean the daughter he was closest to?"

"Yes."

"So, her death wasn't an accident?"

"No."

"And Tom knew this?"

"Yes. *He* was supposed to be in the car that day, but she'd borrowed it because the battery in hers died. He went after the woman responsible. When he found her, she tried to have her thugs take care of him. He got through all of them and took care of her as well. Then he had his breakdown." As the light changed and he drove forward, Michael said, "You wondered why Tom's kids weren't close to him. Partly, it was because of his absences while they were growing up. Partly, it was because he purposely distanced himself from them after his one daughter was killed. He didn't want to see another one of his children die because of him."

I nodded thoughtfully and asked, "Did you...did he tell you about his childhood?"

"Some."

"Was it as bad as I think it was?"

"Probably worse."

I shook my head and thought of my friend. I wondered aloud why he hadn't become an assassin instead of a spy. Michael asked me what made me think he hadn't been both, and I was speechless for a while.

"Tom? The man who cried at *Romeo and Juliet* even though he knew how it was going to end because it was so tragic?"

"Seneca, you think assassins don't have feelings?"

"Your parents didn't."

He smiled wanly and said, "Oh, they had very strong feelings. One of them was that they shouldn't have had children."

"But you said they were stereotypical strict military types in their daily lives."

"They were, because they couldn't handle their feelings. That's my supposition anyway." While I considered this, he said, "Most assassins have deeply rooted psychological problems, as you can imagine. They probably *feel* more than most. Their feelings are abnormal is all. They derive pleasure, some sort of satisfaction, or even sexual gratification from killing."

"And Tom?"

"I'm no psychiatrist," Michael reminded me.

"No, but you obviously worked with assassins being a spy, and you said you killed people when you had to in the line of duty. If Tom was a spy *and* an assassin, what do you think his motivation was for killing?"

"Tom was your friend."

"Tom was your friend, too," I countered.

"Ours was a different kind of friendship from yours."

"I want to know."

Michael said quietly, "I don't even know if Tom understood why he killed."

"But you think you know."

"Seneca –"

"This is important!" I said angrily. "What you're familiar with as acceptable is so foreign to me sometimes. I'm not going to judge Tom because of what you say or even what he did. He was a dear friend and I know there had to be a reason for him to do that kind of work. I only want to understand *why*!"

Michael growled, "It's not always in your best interest to know *why*!"

"I don't care!"

For some reason, I *needed* to have an answer to my question. It was vital to my own emotional well-being, even though I didn't know *why*.

Michael pulled the car over to the side of the road, took me by the shoulders, and said calmly, "Tom was abused for years. He couldn't kill his abuser, so he found release in killing other bad people. Is that what you wanted to know?"

I nodded and asked, "And your parents?"

"I never really knew them and never understood why they killed. Their files were officially closed to me. I got access through other means, but from what I uncovered, I didn't really get the insight I was looking for. I eventually resigned myself to the fact that I would never figure them out." He released me and asked, "Do you mind if we stop talking about my parents, spies, and assassins? I want to enjoy our anniversary and not think about all of this other shit tonight."

I nodded and thanked him for sharing what he had with me. I reflected on what he'd told me as we drove towards wherever it was we were heading. My iPhone rang, and the Caller I.D. showed up as our home number. My heart sank.

"It's okay," Krystal said immediately when I answered. "The kids are fine, and so is Buttons."

"Thank goodness. So, what's up? I hear Hadeel pitching a fit."

"She wants to watch her favorite *Thomas the Tank Engine* DVD, and we can't find it. She's throwing a tantrum."

"The DVD is on the top shelf in the little bookcase we put in her room. Tell her she can't watch it until she stops screaming, and she'll settle down right away."

"Great. Thanks." After she relayed what I'd told her to Greg, she asked, "Are you having a nice anniversary?"

"So far. We're headed for the surprise part now."

"Enjoy it, and don't worry about us. I won't call again unless it's a true emergency. We'll see you two later tonight."

"Everything okay?" Michael asked once I'd put the phone back in my purse.

"Thomas the Tank Engine crisis."

"Ah. At least you were able to avert disaster." He frowned and asked, "Seneca, do you miss working outside the home?"

"I'm too busy to miss it. Between the activities with Hadeel and the occupational therapy with Hani, I don't have time to think about much of anything else. When they sleep, I clean, cook, or take a few minutes to read. Krystal and I have lunch or shop with the kids whenever we can, just like you and Greg go fishing when you can. It's…it's life. I like it. It feels right, at least for now. I am kind of starved for adult conversation during the day. When I had my monthly session with Dr. Forrester, he suggested I try to connect with someone I could talk to regarding something I was passionate about."

"Have you considered Rob?"

"Who?"

"Rob Kilmer. Remember my friend, the one we had lunch and dinner with when we were on our honeymoon in D.C.? He still works for NASA. I'm sure he'd love to talk science with you. He's probably one of the few people who actually *can* talk science with you, genius girl."

"Hm. That's not a bad idea. The only problem is that he'd have to do it when the kids are napping. Could he do that?"

"You still have his card in the home office. Call him and see."

"I think I will." Resting a hand on his thigh, I asked playfully, "You're not going to be jealous if I'm talking to another man?"

"As long as you stick to things like the effects of cosmic radiation on deep sea creatures, then I'll be fine with it." He turned the car onto a narrow dirt road, and we wound our way down it for almost two miles until we arrived at what appeared to be a dome home. I looked quizzically at Michael, who grinned and said, "It's an associate's house. I asked if we could have exclusive use of it until midnight tonight, and he said sure.

"An associate? Let me guess. He's a retired spy."

As he reached for the door handle and pulled it, Michael said, "Florida is a great place for all sorts of people to retire."

I got out of the car and looked at the house. I was fascinated. I had heard of dome houses but had never seen one in person. I loved the geometry at work and wondered if the house was truly as energy-efficient as dome homes were advertised to be.

Knowing that they would die if I left them in the heat of the car, I brought my orange roses with us as we walked to the front door of the house. Michael typed in a code, and the door unlocked itself. I stepped inside and said, "Wow."

The entire home was one large room. Everything inside was made of natural wood, stone, and fabrics. There was a living area with a couch, a chair, and an ottoman. A small dining table was positioned in the area beside it. The kitchen was behind that. On the other side of the living area was a king-sized bed with two nightstands and lamps. The bathroom part of the house was beside the bedroom portion. There were no walls separating any of the areas.

I laid the roses on the table and followed Michael as he led me through the house to the back door. When we stepped out onto the porch, I was unable to even say, "Wow." The entire back area of the property had been turned into a beautiful garden with native Florida plants and a small pond with a waterfall that had been created in the center of the yard. I was going to make a snide comment about the energy needed to run a waterfall but stopped myself when I saw the solar panels tucked away on one side. Michael informed me the pond was actually a natural spring and that rainwater was collected to help take care of the plants.

"My friend is very concerned about sustainable resources here," he told me. "That's become his passion."

"How long did it take him to do this?"

"I honestly don't know. I've only been here once, and that was before I met you. I never asked him what was involved. I just thought it was cool and that you'd like it."

"I love it."

"So, are you ready to tear down our house and have a dome home?"

"No one is taking down our house ever," I replied. "Well, unless it gets blown down by a hurricane."

"Let's hope that never happens."

Michael pulled me to him and kissed me. As he did so, his hands caressed my back then moved lower. He drew up the material of my short skirt and groaned as he touched my bare backside and pressed against me. He was hard and ready, as usual.

He slid his fingers between my legs and caressed me inside and out. I came, and he supported me until my climax had ebbed. Once I was finished, he unzipped my dress. He turned me around and slipped the spaghetti straps from my shoulders then gradually lowered the dress, kissing me along my spine as he did so. The dress was soon neatly draped on a nearby bench.

I slowly undressed him and placed his clothing with mine. As I turned back to face him, I said, "Something just occurred to me."

He waited, looking suspicious but interested.

"Our guardian angels are always watching us except when we're in the house."

"Right."

"So, they're watching us now?"

A small smile played on his lips as he said, "Would it bother you if they were?"

I thought of our infamous interlude in the limousine on our way home from our honeymoon and said, "I don't know. Do all of our guardian angels look like you, or are they a bunch of unattractive old men with big bellies and thinning hair?"

He laughed and said, "They're with us to protect us in case our lives are in danger. What do you think?"

"You want this," I said in a rather outdone tone of voice. "Just like you wanted the limo driver to hear us."

"What I want is irrelevant. What do *you* want?"

"Michael, I'm only going to say this once, so I'd like for you to listen very closely."

He narrowed his eyes before commanding, "Don't say it."

"How do you know what I'm going to say?"

"You're going to ask me to fuck you. I don't want to hear you say it."

"But why not? You always tell me you want me to say it."

"I like that you don't swear and that you call me on it when I do. I find it…refreshing. When I tell you I want you to tell me to fuck you, it's because I know you won't. It reminds me even more of your femininity. Does that make sense?"

"And men say women like to complicate things!" I cried. I reached out my hand and took his then led him to the pond before stepping in and saying, "Michael, I want you to make love to me."

He did, and I did not make any attempts to stifle my screams. Our sexual encounters were usually high-intensity. As we made love several times in various positions in the pond, neither of us was disappointed. By the time we emerged from the water, the sun had set and I was happy and only slightly sore. We gathered our clothing and went into the house and headed for the shower. It felt odd to shower in the main living area, but I supposed one would adjust to this, especially if one lived alone.

"That was phenomenal," I told Michael on our way home. "Thank you for my anniversary present and the roses."

"And thank you for mine."

"But you didn't let me say it," I reminded him.

"But you would have, even though you really didn't want to. 'A' for effort."

We rode in companionable silence for a time before I asked, "So, are you going to stop swearing?"

"In front of the kids." He reached across and touched my cheek with the back of his hand before saying in Spanish, "My beautiful wife. We have a sacred love, you and I."

"A sacred love," I repeated. "I like the way that sounds. Tom told me once that you had a sacred love for me, and I didn't really understand it. I think I do now."

"What do you think it means?"

"A love which is meaningful, passionate, and transcends everything else. That's the way I feel about our love, and I hope that you do, too."

"I do. I always will until I take my last breath," he vowed. "You are The One for me. There has never been and never will be anyone else in my heart but you."

"That's lovely," I said with a contented sigh. "I'm glad we feel the same. If anything ever changes that, then promise me we'll get counseling or something. I don't want to lose what we have."

"We never will," he said with conviction. "Our love is forever."

Chapter Nine

"Mama! Mama, come see!" Hadeel cried from her room.

"Hang on just a minute!"

I added the leeks to the pot of *Estofado de Ternera a la Catalana*, a Spanish beef stew I was preparing for dinner. It was a pleasant May afternoon, and we were going to be eating outside with the family that evening. Michael would be home from a business trip any minute.

"Mama!"

"Coming! Is it an emergency?"

"Yes!"

I smiled. Lately, everything had been an emergency for our now three year-old daughter. I turned down the heat on the stove burner so that the stew would simmer and headed for Hadeel's room. I expected to see something like a tower of stacked blocks, a doll dressed in a new outfit, or a picture drawn on the erasable slate she loved so much. Instead, all I saw was Hadeel and two year-old Hani sitting on the rug with various toys and books scattered around them.

Hadeel was slim and tall for her age with shoulder-length black hair, brown eyes, and olive-colored skin. Two year-old Hani was small and wiry with short black hair, dark eyes, and skin the same color as his sister. Even though neither child resembled Michael or me, I was glad that at least he and I had dark hair. Michael's blue eyes did set him apart from the rest of us, but it would have been extremely odd-looking if he and I had blonde hair like Krystal and Greg and our children looked like Middle Easterners, which, of course, they did. It might have made things harder for the kids.

"What's the emergency?" I asked Hadeel as I scanned the room.

"Watch!" she ordered with a grin. Looking at Hani, she commanded happily, "Show Mama what you can do!"

Hani pointed to his chest and said, "Hani. H-A-N-I."

I smiled broadly and sat on the floor with my children and hugged both of them. When I inquired, Hadeel admitted she'd taught Hani how to spell his name and had been working on it with him "for all the days." This was one of her favorite expressions, and Michael and I had quickly learned that it could mean anywhere from an hour earlier to weeks or months in the past. Although she was an extremely bright child, the concept of time eluded her.

Hani, on the other hand, was acutely aware of time. He enjoyed the routine of a schedule. I could set my clock by when he woke, ate, napped, and went to bed. It didn't matter where we were or what we were doing. His internal clock was fixed.

"Mama?"

"Yes, Hani?"

"Daddy?"

"Daddy had to take a trip in an airplane," I told him. "Remember? He went bye-bye a few days ago. He'll be back today. Nonno, Diane, Krystal, and Greg are coming over for dinner. We'll all eat together out on the lanai."

"Lanai," Hani repeated. "Hani lanai."

"Not yet. Mama has to go check the stew."

My son looked at me, stuck out his lower lip, and said, "No!"

It was extremely difficult for me not to giggle. He looked so cute. I managed to control myself and said, "No lanai until I check the stew."

Hadeel said, "I can take him, Mama."

"Okay, but stay on the lanai with him. I'll be right out."

The two children got to their feet, and Hadeel took her little brother's hand and led him to the back door. I picked up Buttons and kissed him as I walked back to the kitchen to stir the contents of the pot. I had just put the cat down and lifted the ladle when I heard the front door open and close.

I bent back slightly and peered through the archway, as Michael left his rolling suitcase in the living room and came towards me with a big grin on his face. The sight of him still thrilled me every time, and I felt that electric spark between us as he took me in his arms and kissed me deeply. I also felt the hardness of him pressing against me and wished the children were taking their naps so that he and I could go to the bedroom for a while.

As if he was reading my mind, he asked, "Where are the kids? Do we have time to –"

"Daddy!" Hadeel cried as she ran into the kitchen. "Daddy, there's an emergency!" Turning to Hani, who was following closely behind her, she said, "Hani will tell you!"

Michael scooped up both children in his arms and kissed them before asking, "What's the emergency, Hani?"

The boy pointed to his chest and repeated, "Hani. H-A-N-I."

"Great job!" Michael exclaimed. "Who taught you to spell your name?"

"Hadeel," Hani replied. "H-A-D-E-L."

"No, silly," our daughter said seriously. "H-A-D-E-E-L."

Hani repeated this and said, "Hadeel."

"Right," she told him. Wriggling out of her father's arms, she said, "Daddy, put Hani down so I can take him to my room and show him my name on the wall again. Then I'm going to read him the book about spelling and letters. I'm a good teacher like Mama!"

We both agreed that she was, and the two children darted off towards Hadeel's room. Once they'd disappeared from sight, Michael turned back to me and kissed me again, his hands finding their way to the front of my dress.

"Michael, we don't have time."

"I have time to touch you," he murmured. "God, I missed you this past week. I bet I can make you come before they get back."

I was prepared to protest but he slanted his mouth over mine and wedged me in one corner of the kitchen. His body completely blocked me in, and his hand was suddenly underneath my skirt. I felt his fingers slide in through the top of my panties, and I came within thirty seconds. I cried out, but the sound was muffled by his mouth, just as he'd intended.

He quickly withdrew his hand and steadied me. Putting his lips to my ear, he whispered, "Later we'll do this again but in our favorite way."

"Which favorite way?" I asked, as he drew his tongue along my neck.

"You decide," he said with a wicked grin and stepped away from me. He walked over to the sink and casually washed his hands then got himself a glass of water.

The children came back into the room, and I had to work hard at collecting my thoughts. I managed to ask Michael how his meeting earlier that day had gone, and he told me everything had been great.

A new branch of John's Place would be opening in Washington, D.C. within the next two years.

"They love the business model and our success," he said with a satisfied smile. "We're starting to talk about putting more facilities in other locations across the nation."

I beamed and told him how proud I was of him but reminded him that he couldn't be flying off every week to various states all over the country.

"It won't be every week," he promised. "And you and the kids can come with me anytime, especially before they're old enough to start school. Didn't you have a great time when we all went on those trips to Seattle, Denver, and Boise? I got to spend quality time with the family every evening, and you and the kids did a lot during the daytime while I was working."

"Those places were wonderful, and so was Quebec. I just don't want you to become such a workaholic that you lose sight of us."

"That will never happen," he declared angrily. "I'll *never* put my work before my family! You know that."

I thought of his parents and of their views about work and children and forced myself not to snap back at him. He was hurting, would always be hurting when it came to his mother and father and their disregard for him.

"I know we'll always be first," I assured him. "We just miss you when you're gone, but we do understand. The work is important."

"Your work is equally important," he told me as he lifted Hani into his lap. "There's no way this one would be at the physical and intellectual level he's at without all the occupational therapy appointments and the way you've implemented everything outlined by the OT and the doctors. You've done so much with Hadeel and all of the activities like the reading programs, art, and dance classes. You're a great mother, Seneca."

I suddenly thought of my baby, John Henry, and my eyes filled with tears. Michael frowned as I turned back towards the stove and stirred the pot of stew. Hadeel came over to me and asked why I was crying.

"I'm not," I told her.

"Are too. How come?"

"You can't even fool a three year-old," Michael told me in Spanish. "Talk to her."

"She won't understand," I answered in Spanish. "She shouldn't."

"I don't know what you're crying about, so I can't advise you on that," he admitted. "Make it simple, and she'll understand."

I put down the ladle on the spoon rest and came to sit in the chair next to Michael's at the table. Hadeel instantly climbed into my lap and hugged me, which made me cry harder. Michael leaned over and kissed one of my wet cheeks then encouraged me to talk.

"Mama's sad, Hadeel," I said truthfully. "Years ago, Mama was going to...Mama had a baby, but he went to Heaven."

"Where our first Mama and Daddy and brother are?" Hadeel asked soberly. I noticed Michael's eyes shining with tears, as I nodded.

"What was your baby's name?" asked Hadeel.

"John Henry."

"When did he go to Heaven?"

"A long time ago. When Daddy just said I was a great mother, it made me think of John Henry and how much I wish he were here with us."

"Was he Daddy's little boy, too?" the child asked.

"No. It was before I met Daddy."

Hadeel sat looking contemplative for a while then said, "I think that Hani and I are here with you and that John Henry is in Heaven with our first Mama and Daddy and brother. That's why John Henry went to Heaven, so he could be waiting there with our brother, and our first Mama and Daddy wouldn't miss me and Hani so much."

"Wise beyond her years," Michael muttered quietly before saying, "I think you're exactly right, Hadeel. It's okay for Mama to miss her son, but he's safe in Heaven with your first family. That's very smart thinking."

I hugged our daughter tightly against me and allowed Michael to wipe my cheeks with a napkin before he rose from his chair and announced he had something for each of us that would make us all smile.

"From your trip?" Hadeel asked excitedly.

"Yes. I'll be right back."

Michael went to the living room while we sat waiting at the table. He returned with a large bag in one hand and told Hani to close his eyes. The child obeyed and held out his hands, which made us all laugh.

"I think he's used to your trips now," I quipped.

Michael withdrew a wooden toy that was a model of the solar system. The child could push the planets around the sun. It was an extremely simplified version of the planets, sun, moon, and stars but was lovely and required good coordination in order to move the pieces. Michael told Hani to open his eyes and explained what the toy was, even though Hani was too young to truly comprehend.

"He'll get it," Michael said as the child sat on the floor and moved the pieces. "I thought it would help with stimulation and coordination. Plus, I just thought it was cool."

"It is," I agreed. "I may have to play with it myself while he's taking his nap."

"Mine!" Hani declared with a grin.

"Yes, it is yours, but you have to share," Michael said firmly. "With Hadeel, Mama, me, and others."

Hani nodded and continued to play with the unusual toy.

"Where did you get that?" I asked.

"Your friend, Rob, found it for us through some co-worker at NASA."

"*My* friend! He was your friend and your colleague before I ever met him."

"Well, you two talk science every week. You talk to him more than I do."

"I think you're jealous," I teased. "You said you wouldn't be envious if all we did was talk science."

"I'm not jealous. I talk science with you. I'm just not the science genius you are."

"You're a genius in several other categories," I reminded him. "We can talk science in bed later if you like."

He grinned, kissed me then handed me a book with the words, "This is from *me*, not Rob."

It was a book on new research regarding nanostructure fabrication for opto-electronic, electronic, and magneto-optic devices. I was so excited that I immediately opened the front cover and began to read. Michael laughed and asked me if I wanted him to stir the pot of stew. When I told him yes, he laughed again and said he would as soon as Hadeel had her present, which turned out to be a book on great art created specifically for young children. Once she was seated on the floor studying the pages with fascination, Michael got up and stirred the large pot of stew.

Al and Diane were the first to arrive for dinner and brought fruit with them for our dessert. The children were overjoyed to see them and were eager to show them the gifts Michael had brought from D.C. Hadeel was looking at the art book with Diane while Al played with Hani and the wooden toy when Krystal and Greg arrived bringing with them bread to go along with our dinner.

I could tell in an instant that something wasn't right between the couple and asked Krystal if she would join me on the lanai and help me put out the placemats and napkins on the table. Michael, evidently sensing the same tension I was, asked Greg if he would mind stepping outside in the front for a moment so they could discuss something that had come up on his trip. Al and Diane readily agreed to watch the children.

"What's the matter?" I asked Krystal. "You and Greg look miserable."

"We are. The department store Greg manages is closing several locations across the country. If he wants to keep his job, then we have to move to Atlanta so he can manage a store there. Neither of us wants to move, especially since I found out this morning that I'm pregnant!" She burst into tears and said, "You, Michael, Al, Diane, and your kids are our entire family! We want to stay in the Bradenton and Sarasota area, but jobs are so scarce, and there's no way we can make it on my salary alone. Greg is the one who makes a really good income. My job in the business area of Hearts at Home is adequate, but it won't support the two of us, much less the three of us!"

"Okay, calm down," I told her, trying to prevent her from getting hysterical. "First of all, congratulations on the baby. I'm so happy for you." I hugged her and continued, "As for the job thing, I know it's a shock, but try not to panic. I have an idea, and I bet Michael is having the same one and is talking to Greg about it now."

"What kind of idea? We can't move now. We need to be here!"

"We will be," Greg said from behind us, causing both of us to jump. "Krystal, can I talk to you alone for a minute?"

I excused myself and went into the house where Michael was waiting for me. Before he could speak, I said, "I know what you did, so you don't have to say it. Do you think it will work out?"

"Yes, but how do you know what I did?"

"Because I know you and the way you think and what you need."

"So, how do I think and what do I need?"

"Regarding this, you're thinking Greg is a great manager and that he's your best friend. You're also thinking that you're traveling more for work and will be opening other locations of John's place all over the country in the future. Al is a wonderful businessman and is doing well physically and mentally but is getting older and doesn't really want to be tied down on a regular basis. If Greg works with you, then he can run John's Place in your absences. Plus, it keeps him and Krystal near to us, which we both want."

"Damn, you're good," he said with a smile. "What else am I thinking?"

"You're thinking about what you and I are going to do later tonight."

"Right again," he said huskily, as he pressed me against the wall with his body. "You know me too well."

He stepped away as Greg and Krystal came in from the lanai. They told us, as we had known they would, that Greg would love to work at John's Place. They were thrilled to be able to stay put. We all returned to the living room where the good news about Greg's new employment and Krystal's pregnancy was shared with Al, Diane, and the children.

"So, you're going to have a baby?" Hadeel asked curiously.

"I am," Krystal answered as Hadeel sat beside her on the couch.

"Where is your baby?"

"It's in my tummy."

"How did it get there?"

"Um…."

"Mama will explain later," I interjected, saving Krystal from trying to figure out what to say on the spur of the moment. Of course, *I* would now have to think of what I was going to say later.

"Okay. When will we get to see your baby?" Hadeel asked.

"Not for several more months," Krystal told her. Knowing she wouldn't understand the length of time, she added, "The baby has to grow in my tummy for a long time until it's ready to be born."

"Oh. Will it be a boy baby or a girl baby?"

"We won't know until it comes. We want to be surprised."

"What will you name it?"

"We don't know, yet," Greg told her. "We'll have to think about it. Do you have names you like?"

"I like Yasmin and Aladdin!" she stated before saying something to Michael in Arabic. He grew rather stoic and answered her in Arabic then nodded to her before announcing that he was going to put out the plates on the table. I fought the urge to follow him outside.

"We'll have to put Yasmin and Aladdin on our baby name list," Krystal told Hadeel. "We'll tell you once we make up our minds."

I went to stir the stew one last time. Coming up behind me, Michael asked me if I was all right.

"Am *I* all right? Are *you* all right?"

"I had a bad moment, but I'm better now. I'll discuss it with Dr. Forrester during our next session."

Michael's weekly sessions with Dr. Forrester had now become monthly appointments. I was only talking to the therapist on an as-needed basis, which had averaged out to one virtual session every couple of months. I was well aware that both of us would probably need counseling off and on for the rest of our lives and could live with that. In many respects, Michael and I were much different from most people and required someone who was well-trained in dealing with those of us who had above-average intelligence levels, traumatic childhood experiences, traumatic adult experiences, PTSD, and the constant knowledge that someone might come after us because of Michael's former work with the Intelligence community.

Our family gathering was wonderful, which was nothing new. When our little group was together, it really was like having a true old-fashioned family meal, and we chatted, ate, and relaxed. After Greg, Krystal, Al, and Diane had departed and the children were asleep, Michael and I retreated to our room and were quickly naked in the bed. Not surprisingly, the sex was intense and amazing, and we both climaxed more than once before we were done for the night.

I wondered if we would still be as passionate when we were old and gray-haired.

"What are you giggling about?" Michael murmured without lifting his head from my chest.

"I was picturing us as an old, married couple having sex. I don't know if my vision is funny or frightening, but it made me happy."

"Not that I want to dwell on it, but Nonno's told me that he and Diane have always had a great sex life and that good sex doesn't end with aging. I doubt if you and I will have anything to worry about."

Michael moved to one side and spooned his body against mine. I drowsed for a while then floated into a peaceful slumber. I had a lovely dream about the two of us walking on the beach hand-in-hand as octogenarians and of children, grandchildren, and great-grandchildren visiting and crowding our happy house. I woke feeling fabulous and looking forward to my day with the children and the fundraiser Michael and I were attending that evening at the Dali Museum in St. Petersburg. It was going to be an exciting and interesting event, and I couldn't wait.

Chapter Ten

Once Michael had left for work, the children and I had breakfast, then we went to Hani's weekly occupational therapy session. Next, we headed for Hadeel's ballet class and then to the bookstore. As Hadeel and Hani romped in the center of the children's area, I went over to a nearby saleswoman and inquired about an age-appropriate book for Hadeel regarding where babies came from. She asked me to wait for a minute then returned with three selections. I scanned them quickly and decided on the one I thought was the best choice for our daughter.

I allowed each child to pick out a book. Then, I got a novel I'd been wanting to read and paid for everything. After a trip to the grocery store, we returned home, unloaded the groceries, and ate lunch. Hani was quickly asleep as per his schedule, and I sat in the living room with Hadeel and read her the book about men, women, and babies. She listened intently and studied the simplified pictures as I read. She interjected questions periodically. Once I was finished, she asked if we could read it again. We did.

"You and Daddy do this with your bodies?" she asked seriously.

"Yes, we do just like other grown-ups."

"Then why don't you have any babies with Daddy?"

I debated as to how I should answer this question. Recalling that I wasn't even capable of lying to my three year-old, I said, "Mama and Daddy can't make babies together. Sometimes, that happens. That's why we're so blessed to have you and Hani as our babies."

"Will you have more other people's babies someday?"

"Maybe. Would you like that?"

She paused then said, "I kind of like it with just me and Hani, but if a boy or girl needed a new mama and daddy, then they could come and live with us and we could play all the days. They would need love like we do and a house and even a cat like Buttons!"

When she went to take her nap, I retreated to the master bathroom, turned on the tap in the sink, and cried. I wanted to have babies with Michael even now. I was thrilled for Krystal and Greg but sad for us. It was a natural reaction, and the terrible ache would ease again soon. As I washed my face, I thanked God again for the two children we had.

While I dried my forehead and cheeks, I thought of Adiba and Rakeem who had been dead for over two years. We still missed them, although that pain had faded over time to a tolerable level. I hoped they'd be pleased with the way we were raising their son and daughter.

When Michael came home that evening, I waited until the children were occupied, then I gave him the book I'd read to Hadeel. He immediately sat at the table and read it, then he asked me what she'd thought about it. I repeated my conversation with her but left out the part regarding my crying spell in the bathroom afterwards. I didn't have to tell him; he knew. I saw a flash of pain in his own eyes when I told him of the child's question about why he and I hadn't had any babies of our own.

"It's a good book," he remarked as he placed it on the table. "We'll have to tell Krystal and Greg to read it tonight when they get here. That way, they'll know what she's learned and can respond with reinforcing ideas." Glancing at his watch, he asked, "Do you want to go get dressed, and I'll play with the kids then change?"

"Sure. Greg and Krystal should be here in a half hour. I'm running a little behind."

I went to our room and slipped into a strapless evening gown made of orange taffeta ornamented with beading that made it appear as if dozens of tiny blue butterflies and dragonflies had landed on my dress. It was whimsical and fitting for a fundraising gala held at the Dali Museum. I smiled to myself as I stepped into the blue shoes I'd had dyed to match the beading. They were a true tribute to the heart of the Surrealism movement.

I thought of Tom and the glass art piece Salvador Dali had given him decades earlier. Tom had insisted I take possession of it when he died. The blue glass piece had sat on the top of my dresser encased in a special clear box that was lit from the bottom for almost three years. Only Michael, Al, Diane, and I knew that I had the piece, since Tom had told me his children would only want to sell it and not appreciate its intrinsic value or the fact that Dali himself had given it to him. I wished Tom was still alive to join me and Michael at that night's event.

"You look beautiful," Michael said from the doorway of our room. "Where did you find that dress?"

I grinned and admitted, "On the clearance rack at a department store. I guess no one else wanted to be as fanciful as me."

"Tom would have loved it," he said with a hint of sadness in his voice. "Dali would definitely have approved."

"And Frida Kahlo," I added.

He walked over to me, put his arms around my waist, and said, "Speaking of Frida, I have a surprise for you later."

Before I could ask him what, the doorbell rang. Michael went to answer it as I hastily arranged my hair and applied make-up. He reappeared while I was putting on my lipstick and came up behind me and rested his hands on my hips.

"Michael –"

"I know," he said resignedly. "We'll be late."

We arrived on time. As we circulated around the museum, we talked with other businesspeople we knew and were introduced to many we didn't. Michael effortlessly worked the crowd, and I enjoyed watching him and seeing friends and acquaintances and doing my own networking for John's Place. As I did so, I took time to study the art although I'd been to the museum many times. I'd taken the children there only the previous month.

After three hours of walking, talking, and promoting, I was ready to sit for a while. I went to find my favorite Dali work, a piece entitled *Nature Morte Vivente*. The title in English was *Living Still Life*. It had been created during Dali's fascination with DNA and linked science and art, two of my favorite subjects. I relaxed and studied the knife in the center of the table that divided the work into equal sections, the post that looked remarkably like the DNA helix, and all of the other details I knew so well.

"We should buy a print of this one," Michael said as he sat beside me on the bench. "I know it's your favorite. We have the empty wall in our bedroom. What do you think?"

"I'd like that."

Taking my hand, he asked, "Are you ready for your surprise?"

I'd expected him to take me to a part of the museum that was not accessible to the public and make love to me. Therefore, I was caught off guard when he put an arm around my waist and guided me out of the museum. I wanted to ask him what we were doing, but he stopped me by commanding, "Don't say a word. Just come with me."

It was difficult for me, but I complied. We got into the SUV, and he drove to an area of St. Petersburg that I had never before visited. We pulled up at a secured gate, and Michael talked to the man standing in the booth outside of it who then typed in a code. The gate automatically swung open, and Michael drove up to a large mansion and parked in the front.

I walked hand-in-hand with him up the steps to the enormous doors of the mansion. A man in a suit who I assumed was the butler let us in and escorted us through cavernous hallways and rooms and up a winding staircase to a pair of ornately carved doors. He then pressed his finger to an electronic pad, bowed slightly, and excused himself. Once he'd disappeared back down the stairs, Michael opened the door and ushered me inside.

I stepped in and froze. We were in a small room that had special lighting and some sort of filtration system. I could smell the difference in the air quality. The temperature of the room was also evidently well-regulated.

I stared ahead at a wall on which three Frida Kahlo paintings were displayed. Two were simple self-portraits. One was *Roots*, the unusual self-portrait that was our favorite Kahlo piece.

"These are the originals," I said with reverence.

"Yes."

"How?"

"Wealthy people like to have greatness around them. Sometimes, they lend their treasures to others they trust or to those who make sizeable contributions to their business endeavors. I heard through the grapevine that the owner of this house had these pieces on loan, and I wanted you to see them in person. I'll never forget the first time you saw the print of *Roots* when you came to my office and explained about Kahlo and the meaning of the painting. It helped me to understand why John had mailed me the print the week before he died."

Michael's dearest friend, John, supposedly had the gift of premonition like the older Mexican woman I'd met as a young girl. The Navy had studied John because of this just as they'd studied Michael because of his superb eidetic memory and had used the special gifts of both men to perform more challenging assignments. They'd also done a lot of research on them.

I looked at Frida Kahlo lying in her orange dress on the cracked and barren land. The vines coming out of what had been her wounded body were infusing life into a world that was starved for it. John had known that he was going to die when he bought the print and knew of the symbolism of the elements in this particular portrait. He'd predicted my appearance in Michael's life and much of his future before being killed himself. Michael had realized all of this in hindsight, and it made him treasure the print even more.

We spent an hour studying the paintings. When we were ready to leave, we stepped out of the small room, and the butler magically appeared and relocked the doors. Michael thanked the man and gave him a sealed envelope as we left the house.

"What was in the envelope?" I asked as we drove towards home.

"Money."

"How much?"

He smiled that dark smile of his and said, "Don't ask."

"A lot?"

"Enough."

"But that money could have gone towards John's Place or the children or hungry people or –"

Michael reached across the seat and lightly covered my mouth with his right palm. He smiled more gently and said, "We only live once, Seneca. Some things are priceless. We may be here today, but who knows where we'll be tomorrow?"

I hadn't realized how literal that statement was until Michael announced the following evening that he was heading for Charleston, South Carolina in one week. It would be a seven-day trip, and he wanted to know if I wished to bring the children and go with him. Having never been to South Carolina, I agreed.

We arrived early on that Sunday morning and checked into a nice hotel in downtown Charleston. I was instantly in love with the architecture and feel of the city. The four of us spent the entire first day exploring the town and shopping at the old open-air market. For the next three days, Michael was tied up in meetings. So, Hadeel, Hani, and I wandered, visiting local tourist attractions. During the fourth day, Hadeel became whiny, and Hani grew fussy and demanding.

I took our son and daughter back to our room, then texted Michael and asked him to bring a digital thermometer back to the hotel with him. Both children felt abnormally warm but showed no other overt symptoms of illness other than the changes in their normally easy-going personalities. I gave each of them a dose of Children's Tylenol and some apple juice, and the three of us sat on one bed and watched *Sesame Street* until Michael got back to the room.

Hadeel's fever was barely over one hundred degrees Fahrenheit, but Hani's was two degrees higher. We gave them both a cool bath and coaxed them to eat something but to no avail. Hadeel complained her throat hurt every time she swallowed, and Hani continually tugged at one ear.

Michael, who was supposed to attend a business dinner that evening, withdrew his iPhone from his pocket and dialed a number. As I comforted the children, I heard him say, "I apologize, but we'll have to reschedule. My kids are sick, and I'm not leaving them and my wife. I'll have to call you in the morning and will let you know. Thanks. Sorry about that."

I smiled at him as he came over and lifted Hadeel into his lap. "What?"

"That was a really important meeting you just canceled."

"Nothing is as important as our family."

Michael and I ordered soup and sandwiches via Room Service. Again, we tried to coax the children to eat with no success. He and I finally took turns eating. Michael, gentleman that he was, insisted that I eat before him.

The children slept fitfully, and Michael and I lay awake and alternated checking on them. When we took their temperatures at midnight, Hadeel's was a hundred and three. Hani's was over one hundred and four. Michael called the front desk and asked them to have a cab waiting for us when we got downstairs. He and I hastily dressed. I slung my purse over my shoulder and picked up Hani, while he lifted Hadeel from the bed.

We arrived at a hospital a short time later and explained that we had two very sick children running high fevers. The woman behind the desk directed us to the Pediatric E.R. area and told us someone would be waiting there to assist us. Two nurses, one male and one female, came into the waiting room as we walked in. I was relieved to note that there were only two other children waiting to be seen.

"Hey!" a man wearing a baseball cap that bore the name of a farm equipment company called out as the nurses approached us. "My kid's got a hurt arm, and we were here first!"

"And my kids are running high fevers and need more help than yours!" Michael snapped. "If we could wait, we'd gladly let your son go in first."

The man glanced at Hadeel and Hani then at us and asked, "You're going to let these little terrorists in before my red-blooded American boy?"

Had Michael not held Hadeel in his arms I had no doubt that he would've launched himself at the man. Instead, he said through clenched teeth, "My red-blooded American children are not and never will be terrorists. Thank God, they won't grow up to be bigots like you either."

Sensing something bad was about to happen, the nurses hurried us out of the waiting area and into a room that had Disney characters painted on the walls. As we laid the children down on separate gurneys, Michael growled furiously in Spanish, "I'm going to fucking kill that bastard!"

"No, you're not," I said firmly in Spanish. "He's an ignorant jerk. He's not worth it."

He grudgingly agreed. We gave the two nurses the information they needed regarding Hadeel and Hani then waited for the doctor. An Indian woman in scrubs came into the room and introduced herself as Dr. Chopra. She informed us she was the pediatrician on duty and would be caring for our children.

"I heard of your encounter with the Redneck," she told Michael. "You think *you* have it bad. *I* will be the one treating his son. That is, of course, assuming he lets me touch him. Not only am I from India, but I am a woman, too."

The children were quickly examined. Hadeel, in a throw-back to her prima donna days, woke then screamed and cried as the doctor tried to swab her throat. In the end, Michael had to hold Hadeel pinned against his chest while the female nurse assisted the doctor. Once the swab had been obtained, Hadeel vomited juice all over herself and Michael and wailed.

Hani was a much better patient. He simply lay listless and allowed the doctor to do whatever she wanted. It worried me. His eyes seemed glazed over.

"I believe they both have strep throat, and your son has a severe ear infection. We will treat their fevers and start them on antibiotics." Looking back and forth between the two of us, she asked, "Does either of you have a sore throat?" When we shook our heads, she said, "I would still like to take a culture. Strep throat is serious. Will you allow this?"

Michael and I were stunned when our cultures quickly came back positive. Our entire family was given antibiotic injections and began oral antibiotics. One of the nurses brought Michael a clean shirt, and the children were dressed in hospital gowns.

"We can move them to the Pediatric Unit or you can stay in here with them," the doctor told us. "It is a slow night. There are only four other patients here at the moment. If all goes well, you should be able to return to your hotel tomorrow."

We opted to stay where we were. Michael and I sat in uncomfortable chairs and watched over Hadeel and Hani as they were attended to by the hospital staff. By 5:00 a.m., I was ready to drop from exhaustion. Michael urged me to curl up in my chair and put my head in his lap. I didn't hesitate to accept his offer and fell asleep while he stroked my hair. The next time I woke, it was 1:00 in the afternoon.

"The children," I said groggily.

"Are better. Their fevers are down to below a hundred."

"Your meetings," I mumbled, as I struggled to sit up.

"Are postponed."

"But what if you lose business because of that?"

"I wouldn't want to do business with anyone who didn't understand a father's need to be there for his sick children." Kissing me, he said, "You had a nightmare last night. Do you remember?"

I shook my head and asked if it had been bad.

"Not at all. You didn't even scream. You…you whimpered and squirmed a little, but I told you that you were safe and you quieted right away."

"My Poppy," I said, as the dream came back to me. "I had the dream about my Poppy and the field. And I didn't scream?"

"Not once."

I smiled tiredly at him and said, "Now that's real progress."

"I'll say. The therapist will be thrilled. I know I am."

"I'm more than thrilled. I'm ecstatic."

Chapter Eleven

We were able to fly back to Florida on schedule although the children were not completely recovered. One of the men Michael had canceled on did not reschedule their meeting, but the others were eager to meet and told Michael they admired him for putting his young children before his business. He happily forged tighter connections with them.

We were relieved to be home. Over the course of the next few days, the children became their usual rambunctious selves once again. Michael focused on working with Greg, who was doing well in his new position at John's Place. I began to toy with the idea of taking a ballet class for adults but continued to be uncertain as to whether or not I was ready. After all, I hadn't danced ballet since I'd been offered the opportunity to join the Junior Company of the Houston Ballet as a young teenager and had been forced to decline.

The Friday after our return, Michael and I went to Ceviche with our usual group of friends. We danced; we ate; we drank; and we had a wonderful evening. We stopped by John's Place on the way home so Michael could pick up some paperwork he'd left at the office and ended up making love on his desk under the Frida Kahlo print. I felt happy, blessed, and loved, and I prayed that the feeling would never end. Our lives were as close to perfect as they could possibly be.

Three weeks after our return from South Carolina, Michael was once again heading to Washington, D.C. He didn't say that his trip had anything to do with John's Place, and I quickly deduced he was doing some "consulting" work. He didn't ask me if the children and I wanted to go, and I would have said no even if he had. I wanted to keep the kids home for a while.

"I'll be back in a few days," he told me as he prepared to leave on Wednesday. "Greg is still learning the ropes at John's Place, but he'll do fine for that length of time with the staff's help." Kissing my throat, he said, "Maybe Rob will send you a present this time."

"Rob's in Houston this week, not D.C." I reached my hand to the front of his pants and said, "Besides, this is the only present I ever need when you come home from a trip."

He laughed and brought his mouth to mine before going to Hadeel and Hani's rooms to tell them goodbye. Then he loaded his SUV and headed for the airport. He'd only been gone for fifteen minutes when Krystal called.

"Tell me when this morning sickness ends," she groaned. "It's awful!"

"I never had it," I confided. "I felt great the whole time I was pregnant until…until that morning when I started bleeding."

Krystal was silent for a moment then said, "I am so sorry. Here I am complaining, and I wasn't even thinking about anything except myself."

"Don't be sorry. Eat some crackers and drink some ginger ale."

"At the rate I'm going, I'll be *losing* weight during this pregnancy instead of gaining. My doctor says this should end soon, but I don't believe her."

"The hundred pounds you lost in the three years before you got pregnant was plenty. I'm sure the nausea will stop soon. Are you and Greg still coming to dinner tonight?"

"I think we're going to have to pass. I don't feel well, and I know Greg will be wiped out after his first day of being totally in charge at John's Place."

"I understand completely."

"I feel bad because you were expecting us. Michael's away. With Diane and Al on that Antarctic cruise, *they* certainly won't be coming to dinner."

"I don't understand why they wanted to go to Antarctica. Brrr! I guess we'll see what they have to say when they get back in a couple of weeks. Anyway, it's no huge deal if we skip the big family meal once in a while. It's okay. Really. Feel better soon."

I hung up and went to put the cooked turkey meatballs and homemade sauce in the Crockpot. Once everything had been added to the ceramic stoneware, I washed some dishes and went to play with the children.

"Hani lanai!" Hani announced after a while. "Hani beach!"

"I don't want to go outside," Hadeel protested. "I want to play dolls."

"Well, how about if I take Hani outside on the lanai for a while, and you can play in here with your dolls?" I suggested. "Then we'll come in and you and I can play dolls while Hani plays with his toys. We'll go down to the beach later today or tomorrow."

Hadeel readily agreed to this. I took Hani on the porch and blew bubbles, which he chased excitedly. I adored hearing his laugh and was grateful that he and his sister were fully recovered from their recent illnesses.

Hadeel ended up being unable to resist the bubbles and soon emerged from the house. For a half hour, the brother and sister took turns chasing bubbles and trying to blow them. They were having a great time.

"I need to go turn down the temperature on the Crockpot," I told them. "Can you stay out here and play with the bubbles for a few minutes while I do that?"

"Yes!" Hani cried.

"Me, too!" Hadeel chimed in. "I'll watch Hani."

I was in the kitchen and had just flipped the Crockpot switch to Low when I heard Hadeel scream. I ran for the lanai, imagining that one of the children had fallen and been hurt. However, when I made it outside, they appeared unharmed. Hadeel was standing in front of her brother with her arms out like she was blocking something from hitting him.

"Hadeel, what is it?"

"A stranger!" she cried. "We don't talk to strangers!"

I whirled around and scanned the screening that surrounded the lanai. I saw no one. That didn't stop me from picking up both children, carrying them inside, and setting the alarm.

Hani, who always seemed to have a delayed reaction to any sudden changes in his environment, started crying. I soothed him and Hadeel, who had obviously been frightened. Once they'd calmed down, I sat them at the table and got them each a cup of milk and some cookies.

"What did the stranger look like?" I asked Hadeel, as she drank her milk.

"Just like Daddy!" she answered. "But he had some lines on his face and no big arms."

"He was older than Daddy and didn't have big muscles," I inferred. "What color was his hair?"

"Black like Daddy's!"

"And his eyes?"

"Blue like Daddy's!"

"Was he tall or short?"

"Just like Daddy!" she insisted, sounding rather impatient.

It finally hit me. She was telling me that the older stranger literally looked exactly like Michael. I reminded myself that this was impossible. No one looked exactly like Michael. Except....

My mind was racing, and I was having very bad thoughts about who might have been standing outside our lanai. I was also wondering how our guardian angel on duty had missed him. Or perhaps our guardian angel on duty was now passing through the Pearly Gates of Heaven.

I was at a loss as to what to do. If I called Michael, he would be frantic and was probably in the middle of the Atlanta airport. Perhaps he could find out if our guardian angel was safe and what had happened. Perhaps not.

I put on a *Barney* DVD to entertain the children while I weighed my options. In the years since Michael and I had been together, he'd taught me how to do basic self-defense moves and how to use a knife as a weapon. He'd taken me to the firing range, so I could learn how to shoot a handgun. Could I really do any of those things and keep our son and daughter safe if we were attacked by a professional assassin? I doubted it.

Almost immediately after Rakeem and Adiba's murders, I'd been forced to memorize various phone numbers and instructions in case something happened to Michael or if I was unable to reach him during an emergency. Under normal circumstances, I would have called Michael first regarding that day's incident and asked him what to do about the stranger on the property. Under current circumstances, there was no way I could call him, yet.

If I dialed the first number available to me, I could quickly find out if the house was still well-protected. However, the person on the other end would certainly contact Michael to alert him, and I didn't want that. How could I explain to him that Hadeel had seen a man whom I assumed was his supposedly long-dead father standing outside the lanai?

Al and Diane were on the cruise to Antarctica. I really didn't want to call any of the Benedetto relatives and ask them if they had a photo of Michael's parents available. They would certainly want to know why I was requesting such a thing.

If I Skyped the psychiatrist to ask for advice, would that be more advantageous or would it cause more problems since the therapist actually worked for the government? If the man Hadeel had seen was truly Michael's father, then was the government aware he wasn't dead? Had Michael's parents' deaths been staged? If so, why? Was his mother still alive, too?

A more sinister notion began to worm its way through my brain. What if Michael's parents were *both* still alive and were behind Adiba and Rakeem's murders? What if they'd had them killed as punishment for Michael...for what? Existing? Being better than them when it came to...what?

Maybe Hadeel imagined that the man looked like an older version of Michael, I thought. *Perhaps she wanted to see him and envisioned him when the stranger appeared outside the porch.*

I hastily dismissed this idea. If our daughter had wanted to see her father, then why would she be afraid? Wouldn't she be excited? The stranger had obviously seemed menacing and had frightened her.

I sighed and walked to the home office. I shut the door, sat in the desk chair, and reached for my iPhone. After dialing the desired number, I waited and listened to the ringing. I prayed it wouldn't go straight to voicemail.

"Hello, fellow science geek."

"Hi, Rob."

"This is an odd time for you to be calling. What happened to talking during the kids' naptimes?"

"I didn't call to talk science like usual. Are you in the middle of something?"

"Sort of, but I can spare a few minutes."

"This will take more than a few minutes. It's urgent, and I don't know where else to turn."

He paused then said, "Are you on your cell phone?"

"Yes."

"Give me a minute to go somewhere private. Stay on the line."

I listened as he excused himself from a room then heard him moving, walking, and climbing stairs. A door opened and closed, and then there was the chirping of birds. Another thirty seconds elapsed. Finally, he said, "What's up?"

"It's…complicated."

"You and I have had more complex scientific discussions than I've had with most colleagues. Whatever you have to say can't be as complicated as our talks."

"It's complicated in a different way." I drew in a deep breath, exhaled, and said, "I think we're in trouble, Rob."

"What kind of trouble? Where's Michael?"

"Headed to D.C. on business."

"John's Place business?"

"No."

Rob paused. As a former operative and co-worker of Michael's during their years in the military, he hastily knew what I meant.

"What's the emergency, and why didn't you call him first about it?"

"Do you know about Michael's parents?"

"Basics. Navy people who weren't good to him. They died in a subway accident when he was a little kid. His grandparents raised him."

"Right. Except I think his father was standing outside our lanai about an hour ago. He scared the children."

"You saw him?"

"No, I'd gone in for a few seconds. Hadeel said he looked exactly like Michael, just older. She's not one to exaggerate and seemed genuinely terrified of this man."

"Have you called in to check on your protection?"

"No."

"Why not?"

"What do you think?" I asked with more than a hint of sarcasm. "If it was Michael's father that Hadeel and Hani saw, then whom am I supposed to trust and how is Michael going to take the news?"

He swore in a language I didn't know then said, "I hate this kind of shit. This is why I went to work for NASA and stopped playing the operative game on a daily basis."

"What do I do? Can you find out if we're safe?"

"Yes. Sit tight, and I'll call you back as soon as possible. We'll figure out where to go from there."

"Thanks, Rob."

"What are friends for?"

I hung up, tucked my iPhone in the pocket of my shorts, and went back to the living room. I announced it was time to eat, and the three of us sat at the table and had our dinner. Since the children had recently had the unexpected snack, they weren't very hungry and didn't eat much. I ate but didn't taste my meatball sandwich at all.

After the table had been cleared, I played with the children for an hour. I bathed Hadeel and Hani, got them ready to go "night-night," then read them each a book and put them to bed. Both children were asleep before 8:15.

I returned to the living room and sat heavily on the couch. Buttons curled up in my lap and rubbed his head against my hand. I stroked his fur and focused on his innocent little cat face.

"It must be nice to be a cat," I told him. "Eat, sleep, play, be petted, and –"

My iPhone rang. I had expected it to be Michael and hadn't been sure of what I was going to tell him. Instead, it was Rob.

"You're safe although your guardian angel wasn't so lucky. You've got a lot more protection for the time being."

"What about Krystal and Greg? Krystal's pregnant, Rob. We've told you what happened to Rakeem and Adiba when Adiba was pregnant with Hani."

"They have the same security upgrades as your family."

"And Al and Diane? They're on a cruise in the Antarctic of all places."

"They'll be safe."

"Good. I've been waiting for Michael to call although I don't know what to say when he does. Have you talked to him?"

Rob said nothing, and I suddenly couldn't breathe. I felt the familiar but almost forgotten heat of the field and reminded myself to breathe through my nose as I waited for my friend to continue.

"Michael never made it to his meeting tonight."

"Oh, God," I whispered. My heart pounding, I asked, "Does anyone know what happened?"

"There are a lot of really pissed operatives scrambling right now. I don't know the whole story, but somebody screwed up big time."

"Where was the last place he was seen?"

"Dulles International Airport. He arrived, but never picked up his luggage. Something happened between the time he got off the plane and the time he was supposed to pick up his suitcase."

"What's the next move?"

"I'm still in Houston, but I'm catching a flight to D.C. as soon as possible. I'm going to use every resource I have to find out what in the hell is happening and to track Michael."

"What can I do?"

"Stay put and keep your kids safe. If you feel as if you're in danger, then make the calls you need to without hesitation."

"Rob, I have a really important question for you, and I want you to promise to be honest with me. You know I can't lie to save my life, but you were a spy. I'm sure you were a very good liar when it was called for, but you have to swear you won't ever lie to me."

"I could, but how would you know I'm not lying?"

"I wouldn't. I'd have to trust you, which I do with Michael's life and with mine and the children's. Promise you'll only be truthful with me."

He angrily swore again in the same language he'd used earlier and said, "I shouldn't make any promises, but I can't seem to say no when it comes to you, Seneca. I won't ever lie to you. That doesn't mean I may not have to withhold information for security purposes."

"I get that."

"Ask your question."

"How expendable is Michael?"

"Not very."

"How expendable are you?"

"Not very. I do my own version of consulting through NASA."

"Will you please tell me what your definition of consulting is? I've never asked Michael because I thought it was better for me to stay out of that world as much as possible. In light of today's events, I think it's important for me to understand the scope of what consulting means to people like you and Michael."

"We interpret data from current operatives and sometimes gather our own data. We just don't work the front lines. Think of it more as corporate management. We have the experience, the intelligence, and the drive to continue to serve our country in a different way than we did when we were in the field." He sighed and said, "You don't have to worry about our own people offing us.

A lot of money was put into our training and work. Michael and I, and others like us, are extremely valuable."

"What are the odds of our finding Michael alive and unharmed?"

"People like Michael and I never play odds. We play to win."

"What if we lose?"

"No operative plans on losing. I intend to find Michael and bring him home."

"Will you call and update me?"

"When and if I can."

"At least once a day, Rob. If I don't hear from you for more than twenty-four hours, I'll be on a plane to D.C."

"You'd be fucking insane to do that."

"Maybe. Love makes people do crazy things."

"Let's hope it doesn't come to that, and I can bring Michael home to you before you go chasing after him. You have no training, no contacts, and absolutely no ability to be deceptive. You'd get yourself killed. Where would that leave your children?"

I thought about this for a few seconds before asking, "Did you know John? Did you work with him like Michael?"

"Yes," Rob answered quietly. "John was a great man and a great operative. He had a sixth sense that no one could understand. He also had a unique personality that made you want to be in his presence."

"Well, I knew a woman who had extrasensory abilities similar to John's. She told me before Michael and I got married that one day the man I loved would save my life and one day I would save his. She also said he would be gone from me for a time but not by his choice. Michael fulfilled the first part of the prophecy when he saved me from dying not long after we were married. I think now it's going to be my turn. I have to trust that she was right, just like you and Michael would have trusted John."

"Maybe this isn't the time or way you were meant to save him, but who am I to say? John proved to us time after time that there was more to this world than what we could perceive."

"Thank you for understanding and helping."

"You and Michael are my friends. I've lost too many friends already to lose the two of you, too. I'll be calling again soon. Try to get some rest."

I lay awake picturing Michael on the plane, arriving at the airport, and taking an elevator or escalator to pick up his luggage. When had he been taken? How? Where? Was he already dead? Was he being tortured? Was he merely imprisoned? How could we find him? The world was an awfully big place to look for one man.

I wanted my mother there with me. I wanted to tell her the entire story and get one of her reassuring hugs and hear her encouraging words. I missed her terribly, more than I had since I'd married Michael and learned to loosen my hold on the past.

I dozed in the early hours of the morning and dreamed. Michael and I were swimming naked in the Gulf waters just off our beach. He playfully caught me in the water and pulled me against him before lowering his mouth to mine. I woke aching with the emptiness of not having Michael with me. As I tossed and turned, I reviewed what I was going to tell the children, Krystal, Greg, Al, and Diane if Michael wasn't found and returned to us in a timely manner. None of my explanations seemed satisfactory, and I sat up in bed and fought the urge to scream with frustration and pure fear.

I turned to look at the Dali print of *Nature Morte Vivente* we'd purchased and framed for our room. There was so much going on in that painting, so many layers of meanings in every detail. I studied the table with its white tablecloth and with the red cloth draped on the right half. I looked at the post, the rail, the knife, the water, the bird, the floating dinnerware and glassware, the food and drink, and the clouds in the patch of sky that was visible. I had read about the significance of every part of the painting and had discussed it at length with Tom who knew it was my favorite Dali work. It was vibrant and complicated and not understood by the average person who would merely admire the pretty colors and interesting composition but not examine it as thoroughly as its creator had intended.

Like Michael, I thought. *There's so much more going on than what most people see when they look at him. They have no idea who or what he really is. I suppose the same could be said about me. What on earth am I going to do?*

Chapter Twelve

I glanced at the clock. It was 5:30 a.m. I put on my robe and went to the living room to move the oversized books from the bottom shelf of the built-in unit. Then I opened the hidden compartment, took out the box Tom had left me, and closed the secret hidey-hole. After putting the books back, I shut the cabinet door and went to the kitchen to retrieve a towel.

I worked the combination on the fireproof box and opened it. I then withdrew the glass-topped box and placed the towel over the lid before using the tiny hammer to break the glass. After carefully removing the shards, I reached inside and withdrew the papers Tom had trapped within.

My lovely Seneca,

I'm sorry you're having to read this, for it means that either you or Michael is in mortal danger. I am pleased that I left you this information though. I hope it proves useful.

Below is the name of one of the most important men in the world. No one in the general populace would even be aware of his existence. Yet, he's more powerful than most heads of state and wealthier than most billionaires. He is also ruthless, cunning, and the smartest man I've ever met. That's saying a lot.

If I were alive, then I could contact this man and ask for his help. As it is, I'm obviously dead. However, I did plan for this. I contacted the man not long ago and told him my days were numbered by my age and health. I asked him for permission to leave you his contact information in case it was needed. He accepted my request without hesitation. I knew he wouldn't refuse although I can't explain how I knew. Should you meet this man, you will understand instantly that his reaction had little to do with me or you.

I'm sure you're asking yourself how I know this man and why he would agree to such a thing. I gave you his wife's necklace, earrings, and ring. He's the man I spoke of when I gave you the gift he presented to me after I saved his life and that of his special needs daughter over forty years ago. One of the things I didn't share with you and Michael is that he also gave me a lifelong pledge of assistance out of gratitude for saving his life and, more importantly to him, the life of his little girl. I told him I would only use it if I had no other choices available to me.

If you do need to contact him, do so through the instructions I have listed on the second page. Make sure you wear his wife's jewelry when you meet with him. It, along with the ring in the box, will be your initial identification and will prove to him that you are my very own child, for that's what you've become to me. He understands that and has sworn to protect you and Michael once I've gone.

Don't for a moment think that he's a good man. He's a dangerous man who has good in his heart. You are one of those rare persons who knows how to bring out the best in people, and I have no doubt he'll be as deeply affected by your grace, brilliance, and beauty as Michael and I have been.

Memorize this information before you hide it again or destroy it. If you give it to anyone else, it will forfeit his debt to me and will probably lead to your death by his order. You cannot ever reveal anything about him to anyone without his permission, not even to Michael.

There will be serious repercussions for Michael if this man is involved. I know you'll only use the information included if you're desperate. Tell Michael I'm very sorry I couldn't talk with him openly about the man. It wasn't my place and didn't seem right.

I love you, my girl. Be safe.

Your very own,
Tom

I read the name of the man then scanned the instruction page that followed. I read everything over and over until I'd memorized it. Some of it was extremely confusing, but the entire Intelligence world seemed confusing to me. I debated about putting the papers back into the fireproof box and returning it all to the hiding place. In the end, I decided it was too risky. If someone else was to get to the information, it would destroy my only chance to save my husband, myself, and our family.

I burned the letter and instructions, then I placed Tom's ring into my jewelry case. I took the iPhone into the bathroom with me while I showered, but no one called. I was full of anxiety, tension, and uncertainty. By the time Hadeel and Hani woke at 7:50, I had baked two loaves of zucchini bread and a dozen banana nut muffins.

"Hani beach!" my son said after finishing a muffin. "Hani swim!"

"I want to swim, too!" Hadeel proclaimed.

I hesitated. Did I really want to take the children to the beach where we would be easy targets? I reminded myself that our protection had been increased but continued to be wary. If I told the children no, then I'd be reneging on a promise and would have to come up with a plausible explanation for my change of heart.

You can't hide in the house with them forever. Act normally, and maybe whoever's behind this won't suspect that you know anything's wrong and will leave you and the kids alone. Besides, if you don't do something to distract yourself from what's happening, then you're going to stroke out from high blood pressure with all this worry.

"We'll go swimming before lunch," I told the children. "That way, your food will have gone down so you don't get a stomachache. When we come back in, we can get clean and eat."

"Now!" Hani demanded. "Hani swim now!"

He stomped one of his little feet, and I had to smile in spite of myself. Was he starting a Terrible Twos phase? Hadeel's had only lasted about a month. Hopefully, his would be as short.

I said firmly, "We'll swim at 10:00. Hadeel, will you show Hani when 10:00 a.m. is in your book about telling time?"

As she led her brother to her room, my phone rang. I almost dropped it in my haste to answer it. I had an irrational thought that maybe Michael was safe and was calling to tell me it had all been a misunderstanding.

"Hi, Seneca."

"Rob? You sound exhausted."

"So do you. I'm sure you didn't get much sleep last night either."

"Not really. Do you have any news?"

"Nothing, yet. I have a meeting this afternoon with someone who might be able to clarify things somewhat. I'll call you right away afterwards."

I started to cry and said, "Thank you so much."

"Please, don't cry," he said gently. "We'll find him."

"But will he be dead or alive?"

"Remember what I told you. We operatives play to win. No matter where Michael is, he's going to fight like hell to stay alive and escape to get back to you. You're his world. You and those kids are his life. He wouldn't give up without a fight."

"That doesn't mean he'll survive," I pointed out tearfully. "He can't die. Our life together isn't meant to end like this. Even John said he'd die a happy old man surrounded by his loved ones."

Rob was silent. I figured he was attempting to think of comforting words or to remind me as kindly as possible that we could all die at any moment in our fragile lives. Maybe he was thinking that John was human and, therefore, fallible in his predictions.

Rob surprised me by saying, "You don't know how much I wish I had someone in my life like you."

"What do you mean? I am in your life. We're close friends."

"I mean a partner. I'm so damned jealous of Michael sometimes that I don't know what to do with myself."

I was stunned. Rob was a handsome, super-intelligent guy, but I had never thought of him in romantic terms. He was my buddy, my fellow science geek. Perhaps if I hadn't already been married to Michael when I'd met Rob, then I would have fallen head over heels for him. Instead, that particular line of thinking had never occurred to me. I didn't want to say this to Rob, of course.

"If things had been different –" I began.

"Yes, but things weren't different. The two of you were meant to be together, and I accept that. I just don't think I'll ever find a woman like you to share my life with, and it saddens me."

"You'll find the right woman someday," I said encouragingly. "I can't be the only woman you've ever been attracted to."

"No, but you're the only *you*."

Before I could say anything, he hung up. I reflected upon his words and on this new revelation and wondered how his frankness would affect our friendship. I liked Rob and didn't want to lose the closeness we had, but I wasn't looking for more. Michael was my soul mate.

At 10:00, I took Hadeel and Hani down to the water. We played in the Gulf and in the sand. Although the children seemed to be having fun, Hadeel kept looking at me with suspicion in her eyes. Finally, she asked, "Mama, what's the matter?"

I started to cry, and both children stopped what they were doing and came over to me. They wrapped their little arms around me and told me it would be all right, just as I did with them when they were sad or upset. It made me cry harder, and I hugged them tightly to me.

Don't lie, I reminded myself. *Just don't tell them everything, and they won't know you're not telling them the whole truth.*

"Daddy might be gone for a while, and I might have to go to where he is," I told them. "Little boys and girls aren't allowed there, so the two of you would have to stay here with Krystal and Greg."

Hadeel said seriously, "Hani and I would be good while you and Daddy were gone."

I nodded and wiped at my cheeks. All I succeeded in doing was getting sand on my face.

"I'm hoping Daddy comes home when he's supposed to. Grown-ups take trips without children sometimes, but this is a trip I don't want to take."

"Sometimes we have to do things we don't like," my daughter informed me.

"You're right. Thank you for reminding me."

"Hani, lunch!" the two year-old declared. "My tummy rumbly!"

We took our towels and toys back to the lanai, and I bathed both children and instructed them to work on wooden puzzles while I showered. Again, I took my iPhone into the bathroom, but, again, no one called.

We ate lunch and read a book before the two children were ready for their naps. They had been asleep for five minutes when my phone rang. Expecting Rob's call, I answered, "What did you find out?"

"Seneca?"

"Michael! Where are you? Are you okay?"

"I don't know."

He had either been drugged or hurt; I couldn't tell which.

"They want me to hear your voice," he mumbled. "The kids…"

"The kids are safe, and so is everyone else. Who has you, Michael?"

"I don't know."

"Everyone's looking for you," I told him. This was partly for his benefit and partly for the benefit of his captors, who were more than likely listening to both sides of the conversation. "Remember what John told you. Remember what Esmeralda told me. You'll be home soon. I love you so much."

I heard him scream and practically lost my hold on the phone. Covering my mouth with my hand, I felt tears slide down my cheeks as he cried out. What were they doing to him? Whatever it was, I was powerless to stop it.

He ceased screaming, but I could hear him breathing hard. After a long silence, he was put back on the phone and said my name again. This time, I could tell that he was struggling simply to talk.

"I…love…you, Seneca. These…bastards won't…fucking…kill me without –"

The line went dead. I went to the living room, got the Cookie Monster doll my parents had somehow managed to purchase for my fifth birthday, walked to the master bedroom, sat on the bed, and sobbed. By the time Rob called a few minutes later, I was still crying.

"Seneca, what is it?"

"They had Michael call a little while ago. Whoever has him is torturing him."

"Tell me everything."

I did.

"At least we know Michael's still alive."

Squeezing Cookie Monster, I asked, "Did you find out anything at your meeting?"

"Whoever's behind this has been planning it for a long time. It would be good to know what they want. If it's information, they'll keep Michael alive indefinitely. If not, then I'm not sure."

I grew calm. I knew now what I had to do and was at peace with my decision. I had no other choice.

"Please call me if you find out more, Rob."

"And you call me if you need anything or if you hear from Michael again."

"I will. I'll have my phone with me all the time from now on."
I hung up and dialed Krystal at work.

"How are you feeling?" I asked when she answered.

"Better today. You don't sound so great though."

"I'm not. I need to talk to you and Greg right now."

"You mean right this minute?"

"I mean as soon as you can get to my house."

"This is about Michael, isn't it?"

"Yes," I said, my voice quavering slightly. "I'll call Greg. Just come."

"I'll be there in thirty minutes."

Greg got to the house first, and Krystal arrived a couple minutes later. I asked them if we could sit at the table in the kitchen so that I could explain but would hear the children when they woke from their naps. We sat.

"Whatever I tell you today, you can't share it with anyone except Al and Diane. Promise me."

Both didn't hesitate to promise.

"Also, please don't ask me a lot of questions. You know I'm not a good liar, and I can't tell you a lot of things or it will put you at risk. Okay?"

They nodded and looked worried.

"Michael's in trouble. I need to leave right away. I need you to stay here with the children." Turning to Krystal, I said, "I'm afraid you'll have to take an indefinite leave of absence from work. We may be home shortly or it may be a while. I have no way of knowing. We'll pay your salary and get you a doctor's excuse or something the office will accept." Looking to Greg, I said, "Tell the people at John's Place that Michael's business trip has been drawn out and that you're in contact with him daily. Keep things running for him."

Greg nodded then startled me by asking, "Was Michael a spy?"

"I can't answer that."

"You just did. Is that what this has to do with?" Krystal asked, one hand on her still-flat stomach. "I'm scared for all of us and the baby."

"I don't know what led to this."

"Are we in danger?" Greg asked.

"You're protected. So are Al and Diane." Combing my fingers through my hair, I said, "I've tried to stay out of Michael's past, but I can't do that anymore. I have to try to save him."

"How?" Greg inquired. "You're not a spy. Is the government aware of whatever is going on?"

"They're working on it."

"So, why do you have to go?" asked Krystal. "You could get killed."

"You would go if it were Greg."

She opened her mouth to argue then nodded slightly and closed it.

"What if you do get killed?" Greg asked pragmatically. "What if neither of you comes back?"

"Greg!" Krystal said with obvious horror in her voice.

"No, it's a valid question," I hastened to say. "If we don't come back then you'll have three children and a ton of money plus our house and the business to run with Al." I smiled tiredly at them and said, "I have every intention of returning with Michael. I'm not sure how, but I know I'm going to be able to save him. We'll both come back, and we won't be in danger anymore."

"How can you know?" Greg asked.

"Call it woman's intuition," I told him. "I sense that we're all going to be fine."

"Have you contacted Al and Diane about any of this?"

"It's virtually impossible to reach them. I'll have to get in touch with them when they get back into this hemisphere."

"Do the kids know anything?"

I reviewed my conversation with the children, which brought Krystal to tears. Both she and Greg swore that they would take care of Hadeel and Hani and told me to be careful and not worry about anything except bringing Michael home safely.

"I need to make my reservation and pack," I told them. "Krystal –"

"The people at work know how poorly I've been feeling. I told them I got to feeling bad again and left saying I was sick. I'll call in sick tomorrow and all next week if I have to and then we'll see."

"I'm going back to John's Place and schedule a staff meeting for tomorrow morning," Greg said. "I'll figure out what I want to say about Michael's absence tonight and present it at the meeting."

I hugged both of them and thanked them for being there for us.

"We're your family and you're ours," Krystal declared. "Real family helps each other through thick and thin."

Krystal departed for the couple's apartment in order to pack enough clothes to last them several days. Greg went back to John's Place. I hurried to the home office and dialed one of the numbers I had memorized on the list Tom had left for me. I was on my way, but was it on my way to rescuing my husband or on my way to my death?

Chapter Thirteen

I arrived at LaGuardia Airport on Friday afternoon in a private jet and was quickly whisked away in a limousine. The ride to our destination lasted over two hours, and I found myself in the heart of Manhattan for the first time in my life. Despite my apprehension and exhaustion, I was fascinated.

The limo pulled into the secluded driveway of a stately apartment building. I was escorted out and greeted by a doorman as the driver brought my luggage in behind me. I insisted upon taking my carry-on bag from him but allowed him to pull my two rolling suitcases. The man led me to the elevator, and we rode up to the twentieth floor. When the doors opened, I waited for direction from the limo driver, who told me that this entire floor belonged to the man I'd come to see and to approach the door directly in front of me. I did so and raised my hand to knock, but a thirty-something, tall, brown-haired, brown-eyed man in a nice suit opened the door before I could do so and ushered me into a wide hallway. He had a lovely British accent and thanked the limo driver before taking all of my luggage in for me.

"My name is James Harrison," the man told me. "I'm your host's personal assistant. You may call me James or Harrison. Which would you prefer?"

"James."

"Very well, Mrs. Benedetto."

"Would you please call me Seneca?"

"No, but thank you for the offer," he said with a polite smile. "Let me show you to the guest quarters."

He opened a door to my left and gestured for me to enter before him. I walked into a sitting room that looked as if it belonged in Versailles. I had expected no less from my host and glanced around at the furnishings and paintings. I suspected almost every period piece was authentic and had been restored for this room.

"This mirror is actually a television, the man told me. "Here is the remote control. If you press this button, the mirror will vanish and you can watch whatever you like. You have eight hundred channels from which to choose, including channels from other countries. There's a guide on that table there." He went over to a large painted cabinet and opened the doors to reveal a mini-fridge and shelves lined with snacks then said, "If you desire something else, please let us know." Closing the doors, he asked, "May I show you your master suite?"

When I accepted his offer, he led me into an enormous master bedroom decorated in the same style. There was another mirror that was actually a television and controls that operated a wireless, hidden stereo system. The bathroom was huge and reminded me of the one Michael and I had shared in Las Vegas, only this one was larger.

"If you need anything at any time of the day or night, simply press the intercom buttons. There's one in each room. Someone is monitoring them at all times." Pausing, he said, "I must ask that you give me any cell phones or other devices such as laptops. These items will be returned to you when you leave."

"I can't," I protested. "My husband...."

"I must insist," the implacable James declared. "If you refuse to comply, then I'll have to call the limousine and make arrangements for you to return to your point of origin."

I withdrew my iPhone and stared at it. What if Michael's captors had him call me again, and I didn't answer? How would I talk to Rob? What about checking in on my children, Krystal, and Greg?

"There's a phone beside your bed with an untraceable line you're welcome to use whenever you like. I will tell you that it's under constant surveillance by certain members of our staff. As for your phone, it will not be turned off and will be monitored twenty-four hours a day."

He waited, knowing that I had no choice but to give him the phone if I wished to remain. I reluctantly handed it over to him along with my charger. He pocketed both articles and thanked me before taking my luggage into the bedroom and asking me if I wished to put away my clothing myself or have a maid come in to do it for me.

"I'll handle it, but thanks."

"Very well. Dinner will be at 6:00 tonight. When you leave your quarters, turn left and walk to the end of the hallway. Someone will be waiting to let you into the main quarters."

Once James had gone, I sat on the side of the bed and wondered what it was about him that seemed familiar. I'd never met the man in my life, so why did I have such a sense of recognition? Could our paths have crossed in Florida somehow? No, that was highly improbable. I decided I'd push the uneasy feeling I had about James to the back of my mind for the time being and concentrate on the here and now.

I forced myself to call Rob. I was not looking forward to the conversation but knew I had to phone him right away. He answered after the first ring.

"Seneca! Where the fuck are you?"

"Rob, calm down. I'm safe. And what is it with you ex-spies and the foul language? I have to get on Michael all the time about that. At least he doesn't swear in front of the kids anymore."

"Goddamn it, this is no joke!"

"I'm not joking. I'm tired and stressed."

"You managed to lose your protection."

"I had help with that and had no choice."

"What the hell is that supposed to mean?"

"You said spies didn't play odds; they played to win. Well, I'm taking a lesson from spies and doing the same. I have one trump card, and I intend to play it."

"Seneca, you're going to get yourself killed."

"I certainly hope not. All I want to do is get Michael back. I think this is my best option. Have your guys come up with anything new since I talked with you last night?"

"Lots of new, but no Michael, yet."

"Can't you trace Michael's call to my cell phone? They do that all the time on TV."

"Our people tried to pinpoint the place of origin, but they hit a dead end. Whoever has him has enough money and wherewithal to hide from us. That's saying a hell of a lot."

"You're not making me feel better."

"You wanted the truth."

"Yes, I did. Make sure everyone else is kept safe."

He sighed and said, "You're on an untraceable line."

"Yes."

"Will you give me a clue as to where you are?"

"I can't. I'll call you again soon. You can call my iPhone anytime, but I won't answer it right away. Leave a message." I glanced at the clock and said, "I have to go."

"Take care of yourself, Seneca."

"You, too."

I hung up and went to put away my things. The representative for my host had been very specific over the phone about what I should and shouldn't pack. I'd followed his directions without deviation. In addition to my personal articles such as jewelry and make-up, I'd brought casual and dress clothes as well as two evening gowns. I also had several pairs of shoes to go along with the clothing. I'd added the man's wife's jewelry and Tom's ring to all of this.

Since I'd been instructed that my first dinner with my host was to be a formal one, it had been strongly recommended that I wear one of the evening gowns. Recalling Tom's instructions about wearing the platinum, sapphire, and diamond jewelry, I welcomed this. I would simply have to carry the ring or tuck it somewhere until the appropriate moment when I would need to present it.

I showered, fixed my hair and make-up, and then slipped into the sleeveless blue satin gown I'd chosen to wear. It was not revealing but had a dipping neckline that flattered the necklace. The skirt was flared and rustled as I walked. The color of the gown made the sapphires in the necklace, earrings, and ring appear even more stunning.

Once I was ready, I put on the jewelry and said into the mirror, "You can do this. You can do whatever it takes to save Michael. Everything will be fine. Just be yourself."

I left the guest quarters at 5:55 and followed James Harrison's instructions. The door at the end of the hall was opened by an attractive young Hispanic maid who welcomed me inside. As she led me into the living room, I scanned my surroundings. I could have been in someplace like Morocco with all of the beautiful colors, exotic furnishings, tiling, and the wall fountains that highlighted one entire side of the room.

I was informed that my host was on an important business call and would be fifteen minutes late. The maid asked me to wait in the living room until I could be summoned to dinner. I sat on the couch and studied the patterns in the gorgeous tiles that had been used in order to create the wall of fountains.

"They're pretty, aren't they?"

I turned and saw a middle-aged woman with a round face, small chin, almond shaped brown eyes, and shoulder-length brown hair. She wore a long, white dress that had brightly-colored polka dots on it. A pink ribbon banded her thick waist. The only jewelry she wore was a pearl bracelet.

"I like the one there," she said in a pleasant British accent. "I like pink!"

It was evident that this woman had Down Syndrome, and I realized this was my host's daughter; the one Tom had saved over forty years earlier. I was surprised she was still alive since the life expectancy of Down Syndrome patients was at most around fifty years old. I reminded myself that her father had enough money to provide her with the best care possible but knew it was unlikely she would live another ten years. It made me sad.

I smiled at her and rose from the couch as I said, "I like pink, too. Purple is my other favorite color, but I like all the colors there are."

"Me, too! We're the same!"

My smile broadened, and I went over to her and said, "We are the same. My name is Seneca. What's yours?"

"Elizabeth!"

"Well, I like your dress, Elizabeth. It has so many pretty colors on it."

She beamed and said, "Yours is so shiny! And you have pretty jewelry like a Barbie doll. I have a Barbie toy that I can do her hair and her nails and put on jewelry. Do you want to see?"

"If it's okay."

"It's okay," she assured me, as she took my hand.

She led me down a corridor to her room. It looked like the room of an eight-year-old girl who had wealthy parents. There was a white, four-poster, queen-sized bed that had a white ruffled bedspread and lots of fluffy, pastel-colored pillows on top. There was a huge, white armoire, large dresser, and a chest of drawers.

The walls were painted a soft pink, and there were toys and dolls all over.

Elizabeth showed me her Barbie head and demonstrated how one could style the hair and apply Barbie make-up. We selected jewelry for the plastic, smiling Barbie and dusted her hair with glitter.

"Doesn't she look pretty?" Elizabeth asked.

"She does, but she's not as pretty as you."

Elizabeth looked shyly at me and said, "I'm not pretty."

"Of course, you are," I told her. "You're beautiful!"

"I'm not like you."

"We're all pretty. Sometimes, we just don't see it."

"What makes me pretty?" she asked seriously.

"What you feel in your heart makes you prettier than most people, but you also have such lovely brown eyes and hair. Plus, you have a beautiful dress and one of the cutest rooms I've ever seen."

"Thank you," she said sweetly. "I think you have a pretty heart and pretty eyes and hair, too. I don't know what your room looks like though. Is it pink?"

"No, but my little girl's room has lots of pink in it, and her furniture is white like yours."

"How old is she?"

"Three years old."

"What's her name?"

"Hadeel. I have a little boy who's two years old. His name is Hani."

"Is his room pink?"

"No, it's tan." When she looked blankly at me, I corrected, "Like a kind of brown, but his furniture is black and there's red and all sorts of other colors in his room."

"It sounds nice."

"He likes it."

"Do you want to see what I got for my birthday last week?"

"Sure."

"You sit on the floor, and I'll get it."

I sat and waited as she'd directed. She went into what I assumed must be her dressing room and emerged with a white rectangular box that had flowers painted on the sides and the lid.

She wound something underneath, then asked if I was ready to see. I told her I was.

She sat on the floor with me and opened the lid of the box. I watched as a tiny ballerina twirled around in front of a mirror as the wind-up music box played Tchaikovsky. I blinked back tears.

"Why are you sad?" Elizabeth asked. "It's pretty."

"It's very pretty. It's so pretty that it makes me cry."

"I don't understand that."

I wiped at my eyes and said, "It's hard to explain."

"You can tell me," she said earnestly. "Papa is on the phone. We can talk until he's ready for dinner."

I bit my lip then said, "When I was a little girl, I was a ballerina. I loved ballet and was very good at it, but I had to stop. It made me very sad."

"Why did you have to stop?"

Struggling to find a way to tell her without making it overly complicated, I said, "My family didn't have any money. My dance teacher had retired from Houston to Florida and opened a dance school to keep herself occupied. She said I was better than any of the other students she'd ever instructed and arranged for me to audition for the Houston Ballet Junior Company. I was accepted, even though I was very young. But I couldn't go. I had to go to school and work from the time I was little to help my family be able to have food to eat. We were very poor."

"Did you have any very pretty things?"

Unable to speak, I shook my head. Elizabeth digested this information then held out the music box to me.

"You should have this," she said. "You should have pretty things, since you didn't have them when you were a little girl."

I was deeply touched but protested, "That's your birthday present! It was bought especially for you. I'm glad you shared it with me though. Could I see it again?"

She quickly wound the knob at the bottom and displayed the dancing girl once more. This time, I was able to admire the box without crying.

The maid came to the door of Elizabeth's room and summoned us to dinner. I took Elizabeth's hand, and we walked down the corridor towards the dining room. As we walked, Elizabeth told me how lovely the dining room was and how it had a long table with shiny wood and lots of green curtains that felt nice when you touched them and nice plates, glasses, and silverware. We arrived to find three places set at one end of the table. Everything was elegant and perfectly balanced.

"Do you want to feel the curtains?" Elizabeth asked.

"I'd love to." As I ran my hand along one length of the fabric, I said, "Oh, velvet. It feels so wonderful."

"I have a red velvet dress! I wear it to dinner sometimes."

"Do you dress up every night for dinner?"

"Only when we have very special people come or it's a day like my birthday." She grinned and said, "Or if I ask Papa if we can dress up for fun! Would you have a tea party with me? We could dress up for that."

"I'd love to, but I've never been to a tea party. You'd have to tell me what to do."

I heard a British male voice say," Elizabeth would be delighted to teach you."

I turned and was instantly paralyzed. There, standing in the doorway, was a man who looked exactly like an older version of Michael dressed in a tuxedo. Whatever I'd been thinking flew out of my head, and my vocal cords refused to work. I was shocked and at a complete loss as to what I should say or do next.

"I'm quite certain you're a bit overwhelmed," the man told me. "Rest assured I'll explain after dinner while Elizabeth is getting ready for bed."

I opened my mouth but found I still couldn't speak. So, I merely nodded as the man approached me. He studied me with keen interest and took my hand. He smiled and lifted it in order to kiss the back.

"You are a vision," he murmured appreciatively. "The jewelry looks quite fitting on you. I know Tom wouldn't have given it to you had he not considered you to be extraordinarily worthy. You can't imagine how much that pleases me."

"I'm aware that we can't really talk until later, but would you mind telling me one thing before we sit down to dinner?" When he arched one dark brow, I asked, "Would you tell me your name?"

"My name is Brian Maggio."

"You're Italian?"

"My father was an Italian banker who married a British heiress."

"Mr. Maggio –"

"You must call me Brian."

"But I –"

"Elizabeth doesn't need to hear any tedious conversations about our current predicament." Pulling out one of the chairs at the table, he gestured for me to take a seat and informed me, "We'll be having Spanish cuisine for dinner." As he went around the table and pulled out a chair for his daughter, he said, "Here, darling. It's time to eat."

"Papa, I like Seneca," she told him with enthusiasm.

"I like Seneca as well. Did you two have a nice talk?"

"We did, and I showed her my room and my toys and my Barbie and my music box. I wanted to give the music box to her, but she said I couldn't because it was my birthday present."

"She's absolutely right, although that was a lovely thing to offer her."

As Brian took his seat at the head of the table, a door swung open and servers appeared. For our appetizers, we had bacon-wrapped dates and *Pollo Rebozado*, a battered chicken tapas with honey and mustard. Our main course consisted of *Guisado De Chorizo Papas*, a delicious sausage-and-vegetable stew. We enjoyed a Basque salad made of greens, hard-boiled egg, and what tasted like an apple cider vinegar dressing. There was Manchego cheese and fruit and then flan for dessert. Everything was fresh and expertly prepared and served with the appropriate libations.

Elizabeth did most of the talking during the meal, and Brian seemed genuinely interested in her comments, no matter what the topic. I was included in the conversation and found it wonderfully relaxing to be a part of such a simple discussion. It reminded me of eating with my children and comforted me since I couldn't be there to share in their dinner.

When the meal was over, we adjourned to the balcony where Elizabeth pointed out various locations of interest in the area of Central Park below us. She was surprised to learn that I had never been to New York or to Central Park and asked if I would go there with her and her nanny during my stay at the apartment. I promised I'd try and said I wanted her to take me to special places she liked in the park.

An older woman appeared and told Elizabeth it was time to get ready for bed. I was introduced to the nanny before Elizabeth said,

"I have to go take a bath and put on my nightgown. Then I'll brush my teeth and say my prayers. What time tomorrow can we go to the park?"

"Seneca and I have business to discuss," her father interjected. "It's very important. I promise you that I'll not keep her all day, my darling. You'll take her to the park at some point. I'll go with you."

I stepped forward, hugged Elizabeth, and told her to have sweet dreams.

"Is that what you tell your little girl and boy?" she asked as she hugged me back.

"Every night."

"You have sweet dreams, too."

I thanked her and released her from my embrace. She went to hug her father, who kissed her tenderly on the cheek and told her he loved her. He and I watched as she obediently followed her nanny into the apartment.

Brian took my elbow and led me inside to his private study. Then he asked me to produce Tom's ring. I handed it to him, and he pocketed it without a second glance.

"Have a seat," he instructed. "This might be a lengthy conversation."

"Before we start, do you mind if I give my children a quick call?"

"By all means. You may use the phone on my desk. Its line is also untraceable."

I dialed my home number and waited for someone to pick up. After four rings, I began to get worried. What if someone had gotten past the guardian angels on duty and hurt my family?

"Hello?"

"Oh, Krystal. Thank God. I was getting panicky."

"Sorry. We were reading bedtime stories to the kids. Any news?"

"Not so far. How are things there?"

"The kids miss you. Greg said everything went smoothly at John's Place today. We've had no problems, except one."

"What?"

"Al and Diane are coming back into town early. They'd left a message on your home phone. They'll be here in the morning."

I sighed and said, "I'll deal with it tomorrow. If they ask you where we are, tell them it was an emergency and what you know."

"They're going to try to phone you and Michael."

"I'll deal with it when I have to. I can't even think that far ahead tonight."

"Hang in there, okay? Don't worry about us."

"That's impossible."

"The kids are ready to talk to you."

"Good night, Krystal. Thanks to you and Greg again and again."

"We love doing it. Good night. Here's Hadeel."

There were muffled noises as the phone was passed from adult to child, then Hadeel said, "Mama! Where are you?"

"Kind of far away. I miss you and Hani. Are you being a good girl for Greg and Krystal?"

"Yes. Krystal took me and Hani to dance and his exercises today. It was cool! I learned a new dance."

"You'll have to show it to me and Daddy when we get home," I told her and wiped at the corners of my eyes. "You have sweet dreams tonight, Hadeel."

"I love you, Mama."

"I love you, too."

The phone was then passed to Hani, who said, "Hani Superman!"

"You were Superman today? Did you fly a long time?"

"Yes!"

"Did you get a prize?"

"Dinosaur. Grrrr!"

I smiled and said, "I'm so proud of you! By the time Daddy and I get home you'll be able to fly even longer. I love you, Hani. Have sweet dreams tonight."

"Love you, Mama."

I hung up the phone and reached for a tissue in the box on the edge of the desk. I wanted to take the entire box and sit in a chair and bawl until all of the tissues were used. I was weary; terrified that Michael was already dead, and worried about the safety of my children. I also knew I'd have to think of something to tell Al and Diane and had little faith in my ability to deceive them.

"You love your children very much," Brian remarked quietly. "Your emotions are almost palpable, which is perhaps why you're such a poor liar."

"How do you know that?"

"I know just about everything there is to know about you, Michael, and your little family." He smiled and said, "We'll get to that in a moment. First, I'm curious about something."

"Yes?"

"Your two year-old flies like Superman?"

"That's part of his occupational therapy. He has to lie on his stomach and extend his arms and legs, lift them off the floor, and hold that position for as long as he can. It's a muscle-strengthening exercise."

"You are quite the woman. You remind me so much of my wife that it's uncanny. So giving, dedicated, beautiful and intelligent...." Sighing, he said, "You're wonderful with my daughter."

"She's so sweet. I've never met anyone with Down Syndrome who's her age."

"She does have some typical health issues related to her chromosomal disorder – a congenital heart defect, ear problems, thyroid trouble, and some gastrointestinal difficulties that flare up periodically. I'm thankful she's made it to forty-five but am no fool. If she lives another few years, she'll most likely develop neurological deterioration as is the case with older Down Syndrome adults. She'll develop something similar to Alzheimer's. I wish for her to be spared that." Looking grim, he clarified, "Rather, I wish to be spared that. My darling Elizabeth wouldn't know what was happening."

"What happens if you die before she does?"

"There's a plan in place should that happen. She would be well cared for during her remaining years." Directing his gaze at me, he said firmly, "I have no intention of dying anytime in the near future. I know life is uncertain and that I'm a dangerous man in a dangerous world. I also know that I'm only sixty-five years old and have much more to accomplish in this lifetime."

"Such as?"

"At the moment, saving the life of a son who doesn't even know I exist."

There were two oversized chairs on one side of the room. I sat in one, and he took a seat in the other. Suddenly, he asked, "Would you prefer if we spoke in Spanish? I know you're fluent in the language."

"English is fine, but thank you. Do you speak many languages?"

"Quite a few."

"Just like Michael."

"More than Michael."

"Do you have superior eidetic memory like Michael, too?"

"Yes."

"And your I.Q.?"

"Close to two hundred. Yes, I know that sounds impossible. Believe me, I've been tested multiple times by multiple professionals. I understand that you refuse to be tested."

"That is so irrelevant at this point. Please just explain all of this to me. I'm so confused and afraid, but I have to know who you really are and how all of this happened. Does it have anything to do with Michael's disappearance? Why did you come to our house Wednesday?"

"I came to your house so you'd find your way to me. I knew you'd begin to question the deaths of Michael's parents and that would lead to a suspicion of the government and everyone's motives. I knew you'd use whatever information Tom gave you to track me down." He stared pointedly at me and said, "I'm a very private man, Seneca. I've gotten used to holding things close in order to stay alive and to advance my ambitions. However, I find I can't seem to resist you and your requests. No wonder Tom found you so delightful. No wonder my son loves you so deeply." Shaking his head, Brian admitted, "Michael is almost exactly like me, yet he's also extremely different in some respects."

He rose and withdrew a brandy snifter and a bottle. He poured himself a glass and drank some before asking, "Would you like some red wine? I know it's your favorite."

"No, thank you."

"Before I begin my tale, I have but one more question for you. I believe it may hold the key to finding Michael alive."

"Whatever you want to know."

"Michael was in Intelligence for years. I have extensive data regarding his career. I have access to his records, but I don't have access to his heart. You're his wife. I'm sure he's told you precious little of what he did and saw as an operative. What are the two most important things he's ever shared with you regarding his time of service?"

I recounted the story of his friend John's death. The man had been blown apart by an IED in front of Michael during a mission in the Middle East. According to Michael, John had foreseen his own demise but hadn't told anyone. Michael had known something was wrong but had been unable to prevent the inevitable.

Moving on, I told Brian of the child Michael had inadvertently killed when a mole had ratted him out during a mission. He'd been sent to find and kill a major arms dealer selling weapons to those who would use them against American soldiers. Once Michael's cover had been blown, gunfire erupted. Michael had aimed and fired his gun at the man, but the five-year-old child had run through the room and was struck in the chest by the bullet. Her father hadn't hesitated and had shot at Michael, who'd shot back and killed him. Then, Michael had held the girl in his arms until she died.

"Jadranka was the child's name, wasn't it?"

"Yes. How did you know?"

Michael's father asked me to be patient for a few minutes then left the room. At loose ends and full of nervous energy, I rose and wandered around. As I paced, I tried not to think of Michael screaming as some unknown assailant tortured him.

I ended up sitting in the desk chair, staring at the framed photos that rested on a shelf along the wall. One was a recent formal portrait of Elizabeth wearing her red velvet dress. Another was of the father and daughter together when she was perhaps five. There was a portrait of a younger Brian and a young woman with long brown hair and dark eyes. In a more casual snapshot, the young mother proudly held her toddler. There was a picture of Brian and his personal assistant, James, at some formal function. There was also a picture of a rather plain woman with brown hair dressed in a chef's uniform.

I lifted a framed photo of an adult Michael. He was laughing at something, and so were his contemporaries in the picture. One of them was Rob. I didn't recognize the other man.

John, I thought. *This must be John.*

The final picture in the family gallery was a recent one taken of me, Michael, Hadeel, and Hani standing on the sidewalk in Charleston, South Carolina. We were all smiling and watching a street performer. Tears rolled down my cheeks and onto my satin gown.

"We *will* find him," Brian said as he appeared beside me and handed me some tissues. "I have unlimited resources and quite a reputation. It's only a matter of time."

"But will he still be alive by then?" I asked softly as Brian took the photo from my hands. "And how long have you been spying on us and having people taking secret pictures?"

He led me back to the oversized chairs, and we resumed our seats before he said, "I'm about to do something I've never done with anyone since my wife died. I'm about to be completely honest. I must warn you that if you share any of what I say with others, then I may be forced to protect myself and Elizabeth."

"By having me killed," I stated flatly.

"I've no wish to do that. Quite the contrary."

"But you would." I blew my nose as delicately as I could and said, "Tell me everything."

Chapter Fourteen

Brian settled back with his brandy snifter in hand and began, "It's 2008. I was born in London in 1943 to my Italian banker father and socialite mother. I have it upon good authority that they were wonderful, loving parents. Unfortunately, they were killed in a bombing during World War II. I was left in the care of my maternal grandfather. He was wealthy, bright, and cruel. I had nannies until I was five. That's when he sent me to the best boarding school in England. When it was determined that I was more intelligent than any of my peers, he was greatly pleased. However, he didn't tell me he was proud of me; he told me that my gifts had to be used to further our status and wealth. If he felt I was slacking in my studies or wasting time by socializing with the wrong types of fellows, then I was caned. I despised him."

"I can see why."

"Quite. I was the youngest person to enroll in Oxford University where I read mathematics, science, and history. According to my fellow students, I had everything a young man could want – good looks, money, genius, and force of will. I had everything except love." Sipping his brandy, he said, "I was twenty when I met my future wife."

"What was she like?"

"Hermione was a beautiful creature with superior intellect who came from a life of extreme poverty. It's an interesting parallel that my son should marry a woman with virtually identical attributes and a similar background. There are many of these parallels in our lives, as you'll see during my discourse."

"How did you meet your wife?"

"She was serving pastries, tea, and coffee at a local shop. I began to frequent it and often went there several times daily simply to have the opportunity to talk with her. She was the most loving, kind-hearted person I had ever met. I eventually asked her out for dinner. That was when I found out about Elizabeth."

"Elizabeth? You mean…you mean Elizabeth isn't actually your daughter?"

He smiled indulgently at me and said, "Elizabeth has been my daughter since she was a baby. She's not my biological child."

My head spinning, I asked, "But how? Why?"

"Because she's the living embodiment of her mother's heart." Brian clasped his hands across his flat stomach and said, "As I told you, I asked Hermione to dine with me. She told me she'd love to but would have to decline. I pressed her for a reason, and she explained that she had an infant daughter. She paid a nice older woman to care for the child when she was at work but didn't have enough funds to pay for her in the evenings. Plus, she didn't want to leave her baby all day long. I suggested we have dinner at my rooms and include the child."

"It didn't bother you that she had a baby out of wedlock? That was a different time period and…."

"Hermione could have told me she was a prostitute, and it wouldn't have mattered a bit to me. I recognized the genuine article in her. I needed her more than I had ever needed anything in my life, and all else was secondary. I knew my world could not go on without her in it."

"So, she accepted your dinner offer?"

"She did. When she arrived with Elizabeth, I was taken aback. I'd never met a person with Down Syndrome, and I didn't understand why the child wasn't institutionalized at birth. When I later found out the circumstances of her conception, it only made me feel greater love and admiration for Hermione."

"Why?"

"Because Elizabeth was a product of rape. Hermione had beaten the odds and had surmounted her poverty by getting accepted to university on scholarship, as you would say. Before she could begin her first term, a boy she knew forced himself on her. He was very violent, and she had never been with a man before. She was hospitalized, and her family was notified. As with today, the shame was often on the victim. Fortunately, the boy was prosecuted and sentenced to some time in prison.

"When it was evident that she'd become pregnant as a result of the rape, Hermione's family urged her to go away to a home for unwed mothers and abandon her baby there once it was born. She refused, even after Elizabeth was delivered and her disability was revealed. She said God had sent her the baby for a reason and that an innocent child shouldn't pay for the sins of its father.

"Therefore, Hermione left her family, moved away, and worked hard to support herself and her baby. I saw the Divine in both mother and daughter and soon asked Hermione to marry me. She told me she would have to consider my offer, that she didn't want me to marry her out of pity. I explained that I had nothing but love for her and had never experienced love in my entire existence after my parents' deaths. She began to cry and told me she'd never felt any love as deeply as the one she felt for me with the exception of love for her child. She accepted my proposal despite our brief acquaintance, and I was touched by the wings of an angel that day. We were married within a month, and I adopted Elizabeth as soon as possible. My grandfather was outraged, had a stroke, and died. I didn't grieve for him and took over his empire."

"So, you were happy."

"Very happy, despite some obstacles early on in my marriage.

"Obstacles?"

"I didn't make love to my wife until six months after our wedding. She wanted to and tried to for both our sakes, but being the victim of a brutal rape had left her terrified of sex. We took things slowly and were finally able to have normal sexual relations. Once we did, it was as if another blessing had been bestowed upon me. Until then, I'd only known sex without love. I found it quite a change to enjoy passion and love combined.

"Over the next two years I led a double life. I was the doting, young husband and father at home and a ruthless businessman at work. I did whatever it took to succeed and made friends and enemies, both personal and public. Hermione only knew me as I was with her and had no idea what kind of man I was in the business world." He laughed bitterly and said, "There, I became my grandfather. He taught me well enough how to be cruel, but all of that fell away the moment I walked into my home and saw my wife and daughter.

"When Elizabeth was two, Hermione became pregnant with our first child. She was four months pregnant when she miscarried." He looked contemplative and said, "An unfortunate similarity between you and her. The only difference – and it is a large one – is that I was with her when it happened. She didn't suffer alone." Taking another sip of brandy, he said, "We were devastated and were cautiously optimistic when she became pregnant again two months later." Bowing his head, he said quietly, "She was five months pregnant when she was shot and killed during a visit we made to Israel. If it hadn't been for Elizabeth, I would have become a very evil man. I may not be a saint, but I believe Elizabeth has helped to keep me humane."

"How did you meet Tom?"

"A year after Hermione's murder, an assassination attempt was made against myself and Elizabeth. That was when Tom saved us."

Brian got up and refilled his glass then returned to his seat as I asked, "Why were you so generous with Tom?"

"Because I saw in Tom a combination of myself and Hermione, and I was truly grateful. He single-handedly prevented the murder of my child. That meant more to me than all of my money and power. I asked him to work for me, but he refused. There were no hard feelings, and I gave him the jewelry I'd given Hermione on our first anniversary for Tom to give as a gift to someone just as phenomenal as she'd been. I also gave him my ring as proof of identification should he need my help. All of the jewelry had been custom-made, so I knew I'd recognize it immediately. I also gave Tom a life-long promise of assistance should he ever need it."

"How does Michael fit into all of this? How did you…do it?"

"Become Michael's father?" He laughed darkly and said, "That was quite easy. Michael's mother and her husband were trained assassins in a special task force. I became a target of one of their operations, although I didn't know it at first. Michael's mother was to seduce me, gather information for as long as she could then kill me when I least expected it. She was extremely alluring. I had no problem taking her to bed or keeping her there. I planned on keeping her there as long as possible. I fell in love for the first time since my Hermione but for different reasons. All of that changed when I received information uncovering her true intentions.

"I toyed with having her eliminated, just as she'd planned to eliminate me. That didn't seem like enough. I wanted revenge."

"I don't understand."

"You're too pure of heart and too naïve to think the way people like me think."

I swallowed hard and said, "What did you do?"

There was a sinister smile on his lips as he said, "I had her birth control pills switched with placebos. I took her to the south of France on holiday for a month and made love to her every chance I got. She loved sex and was good at it. Over the course of the month, I was able to make her fall in love with me and asked her to stay four more weeks. She agreed and our marathon lovemaking sessions continued whenever I could draw myself away from my work."

"And Elizabeth?"

"Was safe in England with her nanny and protection. I talked to her on the telephone every day."

"But what was your motive in getting Michael's mother pregnant?"

"I told you. I wanted revenge. What better revenge than one that would last a lifetime?"

"She could have had an abortion."

"She was an assassin, but I knew from my dealings with her that she was narcissistic enough never to abort her own child." Putting his glass down on the table to his right, he said, "I derived great satisfaction from the whole experience. I'm certain you find that horrifying, but I told you I would be honest." When I didn't comment, he went on. "I felt such power when Michael's mother and I were in bed because I knew that each time we made love, there was a chance I was going to put my child in her. I knew she would want that child and that her husband would know it wasn't his. And I was right.

"After the two months had passed, she came to me and told me she was pregnant. I confessed that I knew everything about her and then told her to leave. She tried to apologize for her plans to kill me. I did not accept her apology."

"So, that's why Michael's father called him a burden," I muttered. "He knew Michael wasn't his son."

"Exactly."

"But that was so cruel for Michael!" I exclaimed. "You created life out of a need for vengeance without taking into consideration what you were doing to that innocent child!"

"Yes, I did realize that later. That was when I decided I would take my child from its mother the moment it was born."

"But that would be horrible, too!" I cried. "You were just going to go into the delivery room and take her baby?"

"I was."

I was disbelieving and furious. Brian laughed and said, "I've succeeded in enraging you. I didn't think that was possible."

"You bastard!" I hissed.

"And I've gotten you to swear," he chuckled. "Perhaps I'm the Devil Incarnate after all."

"That's not funny," I snapped.

"Ah, the irony of my self-deprecation is lost on your untainted soul. *That* is funny."

"Finish your story," I demanded. "You obviously didn't take Michael because he was left with his cruel mother and her husband."

"In the short term, it was my mistake not to take him. I did actually witness his birth and was prepared to spirit him away."

"You were there? Did Michael's mother know?"

"No. I wore scrubs, a gown, cap, and mask and was mistaken by her as a member of the hospital staff. In the throes of childbirth, she was not aware of much except her pain. I watched in awe as my son was born and realized as he was placed on her belly afterward that I couldn't take him from her. I remembered my Hermione's words that an innocent child shouldn't have to suffer because of the sins of its father."

"But he did suffer."

"Yes, and I regret that greatly. I'd thought his mother would love him enough to leave her husband, but I miscalculated. I vacillated between taking him and leaving him for the next four years. I was kept awake many nights by my indecision, something that never usually troubles me.

"I finally made up my mind to take Michael, and then his mother and her husband were killed in the subway accident, and Alfredo and Maria Benedetto got custody of the boy who they thought was their grandson. I had, of course, been following the Benedettos for four years and had nothing but respect and admiration for Al and his wife. They were smart, hard-working, loving people, as were all of their children, save for that one son, the one who knew that he wasn't Michael's father. I decided that Michael was better off having a normal life with them rather than becoming part of my dangerous world. So, I kept tabs on him but stayed away. It was difficult, especially since he looked exactly like me and had genius, drive, and eidetic memory. The fact that he and Al were alike in many ways was serendipitous."

"What about when Michael became an adult? Were you tempted to contact him?"

"Tempted would be putting it mildly. However, the fact that we looked so alike made casual contact impossible. I reveled in his every success from a distance and was ecstatic that he showed the same propensity for business know-how that I possessed. Luckily, Al was there to promote and develop that in his daily life."

"And when he joined the Navy?"

"I was very disheartened. I wanted him to avoid the world as I knew it. I wanted him to become the businessman extraordinaire whom I knew he was destined to become. Yet, there was nothing I could do. He was his own man and had his own destiny to follow. I left him to it although I did monitor his overall service. He was an excellent spy, but he had the deep feelings Al and Maria had nurtured in him, those that I might not have promoted. However, those feelings eventually became his undoing and caused his PTSD and his departure from the Navy."

"What about afterwards?"

"I continued to observe. I watched you meet him at the café on Anna Maria Island the first time you had dinner and knew that the two of you were destined to be together."

"You watched us?"

He laughed heartily and said, "I made inconspicuous visits to Michael from the time of his birth. They weren't frequent, but I wanted to see my son and acknowledge him, even though I knew he could never know about me. When he was growing up, I attended baseball games, his First Communion, his high school graduation and the like. I happened to be in town on a 'visit' the day you met him at the beach and went to John's Place for the first time. I attended your wedding although I stayed hidden. You gave me quite a scare when you almost died in the weeks after your marriage. I wondered if Michael would give up living if he lost you since he didn't have his own version of Elizabeth to keep him going."

"Since you had someone checking on him his whole life, then you knew that he was sterile."

"Yes."

"And you knew about my miscarriage."

"I had someone investigate every detail of your life the moment I saw the two of you together. I had to make certain you were as genuine as you appeared."

"You knew we wanted children and couldn't have any. Did you have Adiba and Rakeem murdered, so we'd get their children?"

"No. They were your friends, and I would never, ever have a pregnant woman murdered as my Hermione was. Actually, I had their murderers killed out of revenge for the pain they caused my son and his family. The assassins refused to give up the name of their employer to the end. I was displeased about that and feared for Michael, you, the children, and your friends and family. The government gave you protection, but my people were also on alert."

"Did you kill our protection at the house Wednesday?"

"The man was already dead when I got there."

Rubbing tiredly at my eyes, I asked, "Who do you think has Michael?"

"Jadranka's uncle although I doubt if it has anything to do with the dead child. He's a wicked man who would want revenge for Michael's interference in his arms trade and for the death of his brother. I doubt if he gave his niece much thought."

"What are you doing to find Michael?"

"Everything I possibly can. Even if we had never met, I would do that. I love him and want to see him live and be happy and good. I want him to be the man I was never given the opportunity to become when my parents died. I want him to love and be loved and to be able to forgive himself for any wrongs he thinks he's committed." Leaning forward and touching my hand, Brian said, "Elizabeth forgives me my sins every moment of her precious life, but I worry that once she's gone, I'll have nothing but darkness. I've no wish to become a soulless tyrant who gains no comfort except in the arms of the women I take to bed. They mean little to me and offer me no real peace."

"Are you asking me to *sleep* with you?!?"

"I would never dream of doing that. You're my son's wife, and I've inadvertently done enough to damage him without doing it purposefully. Had you never met and married Michael, then I would have pursued you myself. You, like Hermione, have the power to save great men like me through your own greatness."

"I don't have to sleep with you to save you."

"You're spot on there. Perhaps there's hope for me, yet." Patting my hand, he said, "You look exhausted, and I'm sure you haven't slept much since Michael was taken. Why don't you try to get some rest while my people continue to work on this? Tomorrow, we'll see where things stand. You can have your tea party with Elizabeth, and we shall go to the park unless there's news of Michael first."

"I have so many questions and so much to say, but I can't focus on any more of them tonight. Will you still be honest with me tomorrow and in the future, or was this a one-time event?"

"I told you I couldn't deny your requests. I won't renege on my promise."

As I slowly got to my feet, I said, "Thank you for this. I don't quite know what to do with all of it, but I appreciate your candor."

Brian stood and escorted me through the apartment to the door of the guest quarters. As I reached for the door handle, I said, "I have one final question for tonight."

"I probably have the answer."

"You investigated me and my parents."

"Your entire family as far back as I could go."

"We were always so desperately poor. I know my parents didn't bring in much, but there should have been enough for the basics. Where did the money go?"

"Do you really want to know, Seneca? Does it matter now?" When I hesitated, he said, "Consider your answer carefully before you commit. If you still want to know about your family when all of this is over, then I'll share what I found out with you and let the chips fall where they may. Think about it."

He kissed the back of my hand and bid me goodnight.

"Sweet dreams, Brian."

The startled look on his face was only visible for a second, but I saw it plainly. He bowed slightly and wished me sweet dreams before returning to his rooms. I put on my teacup pajamas, got ready for bed, and was quickly asleep.

I tossed my Poppy his hat, and he reached for it and fell. I watched him die a gruesome death, but it was Michael's voice I heard as he screamed. I began to scream and ran towards the field. I was crying and suffocating with the heat and the horror. All I wanted to do was find someplace safe to hide.

I woke and thrashed about in the bed as I searched for some sort of refuge from my terror and grief. My crying sounded piteous, even to me. I wanted Michael, Cookie Monster, anyone.

Strong arms were suddenly around my shoulders. I was lifted up and held closely against someone's chest. I clung to the someone and cried hard and long. Eventually, I could cry no more and lay trembling and beyond fatigue in the someone's arms.

"Would you like some water?" Brian asked gently.

"N-no. Just hold me and don't let me go. Please."

"Of course."

"Did I wake Elizabeth?"

"No. She can't hear anything that goes on in your rooms. My woman on duty alerted me that you appeared to be having a nightmare, so I decided I should check on you. I'm glad I did."

"Are there cameras in my rooms?"

"I have persons electronically monitoring this entire floor at all times for security purposes." As he stroked my hair, he asked, "Were you dreaming about your father?"

Reminding myself that this man knew virtually everything about me, I nodded against his chest but said, "The last time I dreamed about my Poppy's death I did so much better."

"You're under a crushing amount of stress. That's bound to trigger your psychological trauma issues."

"Brian?"

"Yes, Seneca?"

"Do you ever have nightmares?"

"Sometimes."

"Who comforts you?"

"Hermione. When I wake from a nightmare, I imagine she's there with me telling me everything will be fine and that she loves me. It takes some time, but it does help me to recover myself."

After a while, I relaxed slightly and asked Brian for the glass of water he'd offered me earlier. As he rose to get it, I folded my arms across my bent knees and laid my head on top of them. Brian returned with the glass and set it on the nightstand then went back to stroking my hair. I found it did help to soothe me and closed my eyes.

"Brian?"

"Yes?"

"Have you ever killed anyone?"

"Personally? No."

"But you've had people killed?"

"Yes."

"How can you do that?"

"One does what one must in order to survive. Tom killed. Your friend, Rob, has killed. Even Michael has killed."

"But that was different. I knew that Tom had been in Intelligence. Michael told me after Tom died that Tom was both a spy and an assassin. He tried to explain why someone like Tom would agree to the latter."

"So, he told you about Tom's childhood abuse?"

"Tom told me although he didn't go into detail. He never told me he was an assassin though."

"Because he feared losing your love and admiration, I'd wager. *Did* he lose any once you knew?"

"He was gone. All the knowledge did was make me feel sad for Tom."

Brian stopped stroking my hair for a moment then resumed.

"Michael and Rob weren't assassins," I continued. "They did kill during their missions but not like premeditated murder." When Brian stayed quiet, I asked, "Or did they? Did Michael lie to me?"

"No, he didn't lie. Michael and Rob were both well-trained on how to kill but never assassinated anyone. There is a difference between spies who occasionally must take life and assassins. However, some can be both."

"As Tom was."

"Yes."

"You've had people killed. Does it excite you to order someone murdered?'

"No. I'm a pragmatist."

"Is that how you justify it?"

He was silent. I decided to try a variation on my current line of questioning. He had promised to be totally honest with me, something he said he hadn't done with anyone in decades. I wanted to give him the opportunity to talk openly and to trust me. Perhaps it would help him and, therefore, every life he touched if I simply pushed him to open up as much as possible.

"What are you going to do when Elizabeth dies? Will you still be able to reach that part of yourself that has goodness in it once she's gone from your life?"

"I don't know."

"If we find Michael, then are you going to show yourself to him? You're certainly aware that I don't lie well to anyone. You've told me so much. What am I supposed to do if Michael asks me about my part in finding him? What do I tell Rob or Al or anyone else?"

"Let's find Michael first; then I'll decide how to proceed. I'll work out a solution we can live with."

He touched my cheek with his fingertips, and I said flatly, "You want to make love to me."

"Very much."

"You know I'd never allow that to happen."

"I do. You're my son's wife, and you love each other in the way Hermione and I loved each other. I would never taint that because of my own carnal desires."

I opened my eyes and remarked, "You're a very odd, interesting man, Brian Maggio."

"And you're a brilliant, lovely woman who doesn't know her own strength." As he held out the glass to me, he urged, "Drink and lie back. I'll stay with you until you fall asleep again."

I drank the glass of water and quickly found my eyelids being forced closed. I realized dully that he'd put something in the water and wondered if I would wake up in the morning. If not, I wondered what awaited me in Heaven.

"Sweet dreams, Seneca."

Chapter Fifteen

I woke that morning feeling revitalized and in control. Wondering what Brian had slipped into my glass of water, I got out of bed and went to the bathroom then padded to the living room to check out the drinks and snacks that were in the cabinet. As I withdrew a bottle of orange juice from the fridge and a box of K bars, I yawned then sat in a chair and turned on the TV. I ate my breakfast and tried to distract myself by watching the first fifteen minutes of one of my favorite episodes of *Mythbusters* on the Discovery Channel. When that didn't work, I made myself turn off the TV and go to the bedroom where I dressed in jeans, a purple V-necked cotton shirt, and Keds. I brushed my teeth and washed my face. Once I'd applied my make-up and slipped on my silver hoop earrings and little diamond studs, I French-braided my hair and left my rooms.

The same Hispanic maid opened the door for me when I approached it. I greeted her in Spanish, and she and I had a brief discussion in that language regarding the schedule of the household and what I should expect. As we spoke, I studied her and understood somehow that she was not simply Brian's maid. She was young, beautiful, and provided pleasant conversation and probably much more for her employer.

I was led to Brian's study and stared out of the window at the Manhattan skyline. When I heard the door open and close behind me, I asked nervously, "Any news?"

"Nothing concrete, but I feel as though we're getting closer," Brian told me as he came to stand beside me at the window. He was wearing jeans, a Tommy Hilfiger shirt, and dock shoes. He looked very fit and striking. "My people and I have reviewed all the evidence and tried to trace that last call Michael made to you in order to locate him. Not surprisingly, whoever took Michael anticipated this. That doesn't mean he's won. I'm hoping to have some definitive location information and a plan of rescue in place by tomorrow night."

I nodded and said, "I'm meant to save Michael. I have to believe that or I'll lose my mind."

"I believe we'll save him together although what comes after that I don't know."

We simply stood side by side for a long time and stared out of the window at the cityscape that lay before us.

"You have a thing for brunettes," I said in Spanish. "She's very attractive."

A grin slowly spread across his face as he confirmed, "My maid is always willing to provide me with any service I need."

"Too much information," I declared.

"You started it," he countered.

"Does she…serve you willingly or do you have her family held hostage somewhere?"

"No hostages," he laughed. "She's more than willing. I saved her from a life on the streets and made certain she got clean. She knows that in order to remain as my maid and mistress, she has to stay off drugs."

"You continue to surprise and confound me."

"I'll take that as a compliment."

Not quite sure how to respond, I said, "It's tough for addicts to stay clean."

"Power is the greatest opiate known to man. Being associated with power comes in a close second."

Recognizing the truth in his words, I nodded then asked, "Has anyone called my cell phone?"

"Al and Diane have called four times this morning. They know something's wrong."

"What do I do?"

"You let me handle it."

"What does that mean?"

"Exactly what it sounds like. You're welcome to sit in the room, but allow me to talk with Al."

"What will you say?"

"I won't know until it's time to say it. I have a knack for this sort of thing."

"I'll bet you do. Please call him now."

"As you wish. After that, I'll check on any progress regarding Michael; then I'll take a walk in Central Park with you and Elizabeth. We can have lunch somewhere special. Tonight, we'll have a tea party with Elizabeth for dinner, so wear the other evening gown you brought." When I glanced anxiously at the phone, he said, "Come, sit in the chair while I call my son's grandfather."

My stomach felt like it was tied in knots as Brian dialed Al's number. He pressed the button for the speakerphone and put his finger to my lips. The look he gave me dared me to speak.

"Michael?" Al said in his familiar Italian accent the moment he answered the phone. "Seneca?"

"Seneca is fine, but she can't speak with you at this time. She asked me to call you."

"Who are you? Where is she? Where is Michael?"

"My name is Brian. Seneca is safe with me. Michael is not. We're trying to locate him so that he can return home to you and his children."

Al paused then said gravely, "Someone has taken him."

"I'm afraid so."

"Do they mean to kill him?"

"I don't know yet. The government is also working to find him, but Seneca has appealed to me for help in hopes of locating him sooner."

"You are a friend of Tom's," Al deduced.

"Yes."

"Is the rest of the family in danger?"

"The government people have been protecting all of you since the murders of Hani and Hadeel's parents. Somehow, Michael's protection was compromised."

"You know Michael?"

Brian rubbed thoughtfully at his chin for a time then said, "I know Michael very well, but he knows nothing of me."

There was such an extended silence that I wondered if Al had accidentally been disconnected. However, he finally said, "I know who you are."

Brian actually looked shocked but said nothing. I held my breath.

"It was at Michael's college graduation," Al went on. "There were so many people. I am sure you did not think you would be seen, but I saw you. I knew the moment I spotted you in the crowd that what I had long suspected was the truth. Michael was not the child of my son."

"Why didn't you approach me then and there?" Brian asked with genuine interest.

"Because I realized you must have known all along and had left him in my care for his sake. I turned before you noticed I had seen you and did not turn back."

"I appreciate that. I appreciate everything you've done for Michael. You gave him the normal life I couldn't."

"What will you do if Michael is found?"

"I haven't made up my mind on that. There are many factors to consider. Whatever I do, I'll do because I believe it's in *Michael's* best interest."

"Do not take him from us," Al said emphatically.

"I would never dream of it." Clearing his throat, he said, "I'll call you if there's news. Seneca will call her children every night, but she can't talk with you until Michael is found."

"Why not?"

"Because she knows not how to deceive, and there are things I've shared with her that she can never share with you. Until I know you won't ask, then she can't talk with you or your wife."

"If that is your only condition, then I will gladly never ask her anything about you or what you may have said to her. My Diane will make the same promise. I give you my word."

"I don't doubt your sincerity. I respect you more than you can know."

"So, please let me speak with her. I need to know that she is safe."

Brian narrowed his eyes and challenged me to talk without giving anything away. I squared my shoulders and shot him a glance that said "I'm up for the challenge. Bring it on."

"Be brief," he told me, as he took a seat behind his desk.

"Hi, Al."

"Oh, my angel. It is so good to hear your voice."

"Same here. You came back early. What happened to Antarctica?"

"I had a bad feeling about the trip and told Diane I wanted to return home. She said she did not care about seeing the penguins and ice and would be happy to return to Florida." Sighing, he said, "You do not know how worried Diane and I have been about the both of you."

"I'm safe."

"You have talked to Michael since he was taken?"

My eyes welled with tears, and I said in an unsteady voice, "Whoever has him called me. I didn't get to talk to him long."

"Was he all right?"

I began to cry and covered my mouth with my hand, so Al couldn't hear. I looked at Brian and shook my head. He stood and put his arms around me then told Al, "Michael was not all right. Seneca is rather overcome at the moment."

Al said something in Italian, and Brian commented in Italian. They then proceeded to have a conversation I couldn't understand for several minutes before Al told me in English that he and Diane loved me, and Brian disconnected the call.

Brian stroked my hair as I continued to cry. I wanted to call Dr. Forrester and talk with him about what was happening and how I was handling things, but I knew I couldn't. So, I allowed Michael's father to stand in for Michael and comfort me.

Once I regained control of my emotions, I pulled back and thanked him for what he'd done for me and for Al.

"The man has great integrity and has been a wonderful role model for my son. I do want to help him through this just as I want to help you."

"Thank you for letting me talk with him."

"You did admirably under these conditions." Passing me the box of tissues, he said, "Dry your eyes, and let's take Elizabeth to the park."

After I'd used several tissues, I laid a hand on his arm and said, "Before we go out, there's something I've been meaning to ask you since last night."

"Then ask."

"If somebody in Naval Special Forces set up Michael's mother's assignment regarding you, then surely the Navy knows about you and has figured out that you fathered her baby. I mean, you and Michael look identical, and…and how could they not know? But if they knew, then how did Michael not know? He said he managed to procure his parents' records. Wouldn't he have found out that you were his father?"

"You forget the tangled web of Intelligence that is constantly evolving. In the 1960s, the military was protecting me. In the 1970s, the military was trying to kill me. Administrations change, as do administrators. I've worked closely with the U.S. military since the 1980s and have many friends there. The records pertaining to me and Michael's mother were…misplaced long ago."

"I see. Do you work with other governments as well?"

"Yes."

"To what end?"

Brian drew the backs of his fingers along my jaw line and said, "I may do things you consider reprehensible, but my intentions are good. I wish for there to be less oppression, less poverty, and less ugliness in this world of ours. Therein lies my hidden credo. Keep in mind that there are casualties in every war, and not all wars are fought in plain sight."

"What will you do when we find Michael?"

"Have everyone involved in his kidnapping and torture executed. That will satisfy my desire for revenge, will stop them from doing it to anybody else, and will send a message to anyone who might try to harm your family or friends in the future. It's horrible but necessary."

Wrapping a hand around his fingers and drawing them away from my face, I said, "It is horrible, but I do understand that it's reality."

He smiled sadly at me and said, "My son is so blessed to have you, just as I was blessed to have Hermione. You are his salvation, just as she will hopefully always be mine."

I released his hand and said, "I think we should go to the park. I want to think about something besides what Michael might be going through."

"Agreed."

We walked across the street with Elizabeth and her nanny. As we wandered through Central Park, Elizabeth pointed out places she liked to play or sit. We fed ducks and squirrels and ended up in Strawberry Fields, the area of the park that had been dedicated to John Lennon after his assassination.

"I like the Beatles!" Elizabeth told me excitedly. "I met them when I was a little girl!"

I looked to Brian, who nodded. I supposed I shouldn't have been surprised and speculated as to which other famous musicians, artists, actors, scientists, and writers he knew.

"What were the Beatles like?" I asked Elizabeth.

"They were very nice. They made good music."

"I love their music," I told her. "They changed the face of music forever."

As Elizabeth went with her nanny to the restroom, Brian confided, "She was six when she met them. They were wonderful with her, very gentle and kind. They took the time to listen to her and make conversation. All four were quite impressive personally and professionally. I enjoyed my conversations with them that night and on other occasions where Elizabeth was not present." Scanning Strawberry Fields, he said, "I wept when I heard of John's murder. Elizabeth found me crying and asked me what was wrong. She had never seen me cry before."

"What did you tell her?"

"I told her that John Lennon had been shot and killed by someone who was not in his right mind. She became quite sad and said that she liked John and the way he danced with her at the party when she was small. Then she kissed my cheek and told me John was in Heaven and would always be happy now." Turning to me, he said wryly, "Imagine."

We ate lunch at a local deli that Brian informed me was the best in Manhattan. My hopes of eating something light were dashed, but I gave myself license to consume the delectable Reuben sandwich presented to me and thoroughly enjoyed it, the chips, and the pickle that were also on my plate. I could worry about my weight again when my husband wasn't missing, imprisoned, and being tortured and when I wasn't with his engaging and dangerous father and sweet and innocent stepsister. I thanked Brian for my meal as we left the deli and went down the street to a building that had a modern design and was only four stories high.

"What is this place?" I asked as we entered.

"It's fun time!" Elizabeth told me. "We're going to play and swim!"

"Oh. I'll be happy to watch but -"

"No, you and I shall be playing and swimming as well. So will the nanny."

"But Brian –"

He took me by the wrist and said imperiously, "This is what we all need, Seneca. My people are working on our business around the clock, and we can do nothing at this moment. Trust me. This will provide both of us with a distraction as well as exercise, which is always good for relieving stress. I've been participating in these activities with my daughter for years and have funded many programs like this all over the world. They benefit the child and the family in a multitude of ways. Now, come."

"But I don't have a swimsuit," I protested.

"Yes, you do. It's waiting for you in Elizabeth's locker."

Amazed at the man's ability to anticipate almost every possibility that might arise, I followed Elizabeth and her nanny into a room filled with other Down Syndrome adults and their family members and caregivers. As I'd expected, the Down Syndrome adults had varying intelligence levels, as did the rest of us who were present. For the next hour we played games with educational toys and listened to an elderly instructor read a book. We then spent another hour molding clay and painting. Finally, it was time to swim.

"How often do you do these things with Elizabeth?" I asked Brian as we headed towards the locker rooms.

"As often as I can. I've always been a very involved parent. The more interaction and stimulation, the more the child realizes his or her potential. As I mentioned, it also helps to distract me from the big, bad world outside when I'm doing these types of things with her. It benefits us both."

The simple black one-piece swimsuit that awaited me in the locker fit me perfectly. When I stepped out of the dressing room, Elizabeth was waiting in a frilly pink one-piece bathing suit. The nanny's suit was black like mine but had a little skirt attached.

Brian emerged from the men's locker room in dark blue swim trunks. He was shirtless. Although he was not as muscular as his son, he obviously worked out and lifted weights to retain his muscle tone. He pulled a gray swim shirt over his head as we went to the pool area.

"It would be inappropriate for me to go into the pool shirtless," he told me as we walked.

I wasn't certain if he meant it would be inappropriate because of me or because of the class. I decided not to ask.

"You hurt yourself," Elizabeth said suddenly. "How did you do that?"

Looking at my exposed flesh, I said, "Where?"

She pointed to the scar on my leg and said, "There."

"Oh. That was a long time ago. I had an accident, and some glass cut me. I have other marks, but that one is one of the biggest." Touching the scar, I said, "I think it's healed pretty well."

"Will it ever go away?" When I replied that it would always be there, she asked, "Does it hurt?"

"No."

"I have a scar," she announced. "Do you want to see?"

"Later, darling," Brian told her. "It's time to swim now."

Once we were in the water, I whispered to Brian, "That wasn't very smooth. What are you trying to hide?"

"Nothing. You're quite welcome to see Elizabeth's scar in the locker room. Feel free to ask her about it there."

After the water exercise and free playtime, we all emerged from the pool and went to shower and dress. I stepped out of a dressing room at the same time Elizabeth and her nanny came out of nearby shower stalls wrapped in towels. I asked Elizabeth if I could see her scar.

The scar was on her chest. I had seen many others like it when I'd worked primarily with elderly patients.

"She's had heart surgery. Does she have a pacemaker?" I asked Brian later when his daughter was taking a nap and he and I were seated on the couch in his living room.

"She's on her second one. The first lasted nine years. She's had this one for five. I don't foresee that she'll be having a third."

"Brian, would you do something for me?"

"If I can."

"Would you let me hold you for a few minutes?"

"I don't believe that would be wise. My lust for you is quite strong, and it's only by sheer willpower that I've managed not to try to seduce you."

"Indulge me. You know I love Michael with all my heart. I just need some comfort for a few minutes."

He sighed and turned to take me in his arms. I stopped him and put my arms around his shoulders and drew him towards me until his head rested against my collarbone. I murmured that it was all right to be sad and to grieve the inevitable loss of his little girl.

Brian put his arms around my waist and held me tightly as he cried. I felt him shaking, and one area of my shirt was wet with his tears. I realized that unless there was someone there to take Elizabeth's place in his life after she died, he could easily lose himself in the realms of the cold and the terrible.

Great, I thought. *This isn't just about saving Michael. Now it's about saving Michael, Brian, and the unsuspecting world over which Brian holds such influence. I feel like I need a cape and some super powers.* As Brian ceased weeping, I ruminated, *If he had Michael, me, the children, Al and Diane, and Krystal and Greg and their baby, would it make all the difference? Could I ever trust that he wouldn't try to corrupt any of them? Would it put everyone in more danger? And how would Michael feel about it?*

"Thank you," Brian said quietly, as he disengaged himself and sat up. He wiped his eyes with some tissues and blew his nose before adding, "I know what you're thinking and wish I could give you a definitive answer. I can't."

Before I could ask him any questions, he rose and left the room. Brian's personal assistant, James, soon appeared and suggested I return to my rooms and prepare for our tea party dinner, which was to be at 6:00. I had an hour.

I went to my bedroom and called Rob, who confirmed that the military had many leads but nothing concrete. He asked me if I had any news, to which I replied that my contact had told me he hoped to have definitive answers by the following day. Rob asked me how I was holding up, and I confided I'd been doing everything I could not to succumb to the looming panic that seemed to hover around me at all times. Before he could press me for more information, I told him I had to hang up and let him know I would call again soon.

I then called my home. Greg answered the phone and said Krystal was having a bad day with pregnancy-related nausea and that he'd been playing Mr. Mom with the kids since the morning. Krystal, Hani, and Hadeel were all currently taking naps. I explained there was no new update but would keep him posted. I promised to call back later and talk to Krystal and the children.

Finally, I called Diane. I could hear the tension in her voice and asked her if Al was nearby.

"He's swimming laps in the infinity pool," she told me. "He said he had to do something to take his mind off things and that swimming allowed him not to think."

I recalled Michael saying almost exactly those same words to me and began to cry. I told Diane I wished she were with me. To my shock, she burst into tears and said she wished she were with me, too. After giving each other mutual assurances that everything would be fine in the end and that we'd be seeing each other soon, we said our goodbyes and hung up.

I went to wash my face and apply fresh make-up. I fixed my hair and slipped into my fanciful orange dress with the blue beaded butterflies and dragonflies and my blue shoes. Suspecting Elizabeth would love the dress I'd worn to the fundraiser at the Dali Museum, I donned my jewelry and went back to the main apartment. This time, it was James who opened the door, not the Hispanic maid.

"Mr. Maggio will be joining you and Miss Elizabeth shortly. He asked that you wait for him in Miss Elizabeth's room until everything is ready."

Until he and the maid are finished, I thought. *Maybe she can give him some comfort of her own.*

"James, have you ever lived in South Florida?"

"No, Mrs. Benedetto. I have visited it several times."

"You look familiar to me. Maybe I saw you somewhere during one of your visits."

"Perhaps...."

I'd been right about my dress; Elizabeth loved it. She herself wore her red velvet dress and had a large red bow pinned at the back of her head. She also wore black patent-leather shoes and black stockings.

We played with Ken and Barbie and various other dolls until James knocked on the door and told us the dining room was ready. Elizabeth hastily got to her feet and told me we had to finish getting dressed. I was perplexed.

"We *are* dressed."

"Not for a tea party," she told me. "You wait here."

She disappeared into her dressing room and emerged with two fancy ladies' hats, two feather boas, and two pairs of gloves. She handed me one pair of black gloves, a black feathered boa, and a blue hat that almost matched the color of my shoes but not quite. Her hat, gloves, and boa were all black.

"Thank you," I told her as I accepted the items. "Will you show me how to put them on? I've never worn anything like this before."

I hadn't but did know how they should be worn. However, I knew it would please her to show me, and it did. Once we were suitably attired, she led me to the dining room.

The table had been draped with a beautiful lace tablecloth. Brian, who was dressed in an expensive-looking gray suit, stood when we entered the room and complimented us on our attire. Elizabeth led me to a sideboard where dozens of teacups and saucers were on display.

"You pick the one you want to start with for the party," she told me. "Which one do you like best?"

I selected one that had roses on it and was informed by my hostess that this was a very famous type of teacup and that I had wonderful taste. I smiled and thanked her and asked which one she was going to use.

"This is my favorite," she told me, as she lifted one with a blue-and-white pattern. "Papa says it was my Mummy's before she died, so I like it best." Looking at me, she asked, "Is your Mummy alive?"

"No. She died when I was eighteen."

"Is your Papa alive?"

"No. He died when I was fourteen."

She frowned and said, "That must have made you very sad." When I nodded, she said, "My Papa could be your Papa, too. Then you could have a Papa again, and you and I could be sisters."

Purposefully avoiding eye contact with Brian, I told her, "That would be lovely, Elizabeth. It would be fun if we were sisters. Maybe you could have a brother, too."

"I'd like a brother. Could I have more than one?"

"I believe it's time for tea, darling," Brian interrupted. "Let me select my cup, so we may begin."

Brian's cup and saucer had an Art Deco pattern on it but had the traditional shape. As we sat at the table, a male server materialized and asked me as the guest what type of tea I would prefer. I looked blankly at Brian and Elizabeth. I had no idea what to do or say.

"What sort of tea do you like?" Elizabeth asked politely.

"I – I never really have tea, except iced tea or tea that comes in a tea bag. What kinds of tea do you have?"

"We have twenty-seven varieties on hand at the moment," the server informed me.

That old feeling of inadequacy I hadn't experienced in a long time resurfaced, and I didn't like it at all. Turning to Elizabeth, I said, "I like cinnamon. Are there any teas with cinnamon?"

"The chi one Papa likes has cinnamon," she said seriously. "There's also a tea we have that has pear and cinnamon in it."

"Perhaps a pot of both," Brian directed. "Elizabeth, what will you have tonight?"

"The apple and plum, please," she told the server, who bowed graciously.

"And I will have the oolong that was bought yesterday," instructed Brian. "Thank you."

The server bowed and returned to the kitchen. We soon had our pots of tea with fancy tea cozies on the tops. We also had delicate lace napkins and ornately patterned china ready to hold our food. I was given a lesson on how to have a proper tea. There was a course consisting of various tiny sandwich triangles with no crusts, one of cranberry and orange scones served with clotted cream, and one comprised of several British desserts.

Brian requested that seven other varieties of tea be served throughout the meal, and I was compelled to sample each one. I enjoyed all but two and eagerly listened as Elizabeth told me how to hold my cup and stir in honey and what to eat first and anything else that came to her mind.

Afterwards, we went out on the balcony and watched the twinkling lights of Manhattan. Elizabeth asked me to tell her a story before it was time for her to get ready for bed. My mind had been on Michael, and I struggled to clear it and come up with an acceptable story. She waited patiently, but I couldn't think of anything. I suggested she pick out her favorite book so that I could read to her before she went to sleep.

"You and Papa can take turns!" she declared. "Is that all right, Papa?"

"Of course. Go with Nanny and get ready, then Seneca and I will read to you before it's time for you to sleep."

Once she'd gone, Brian said angrily to me, "Why did you say that to her about having a brother?"

"Because she has a brother, and she might want to know him before she dies."

He took me by the shoulders and tightened his hold until it was almost painful. My knees got weak, as I realized that perhaps he was angry because he'd had news of Michael and was aware that Elizabeth would never meet her brother. My terror must have registered on my face because he loosened his grip and apologized.

"I've had an update about Michael but still nothing definite. It's damned frustrating. I didn't mean to direct my anger towards you."

"Everything we did today was a help, but Michael's never out of my thoughts. I keep hearing him scream." Looking up at Michael's father, I asked, "Were there any new calls on my cell phone?"

"None."

I sighed and said, "I need to call Hadeel and Hani before we read Elizabeth her book. They were napping when I called earlier."

"Use my study. I'll meet you in Elizabeth's room afterwards."

My conversation with my children was both comforting and disquieting. It was a relief to hear their voices, but both of them asked when Michael and I were coming home. They wanted to speak to Michael, and I stumbled over my words in an effort to explain that he couldn't come to the phone but loved them very much. Hadeel was quick to tell me she was being a good girl but that Hani had thrown several temper tantrums that had forced Greg to put him in Time Out twice. When they both blew me kisses goodnight, I wished them sweet dreams.

"Please, hang on," Krystal told me. "I know it seems like forever, but you really haven't been gone that long. The kids will be fine."

"But you're sick and Hani's acting out."

"I'm pregnant, and Hani's being two. We're okay, Seneca. Hold on. You'll be bringing Michael home soon. Take care."

I went to Elizabeth's room. Brian and I read with her then bade her goodnight. Once he and I were in the corridor, Brian said, "We're close to finding the exact location where Michael's being held. Get some sleep. Tomorrow, we may have to leave suddenly."

"Leave? To go where?"

"I'll explain if it becomes necessary. Just be prepared for the possibility. One never knows what might happen in cases like these. We'll be as prepared as we can be for as many scenarios as we can envision."

Chapter Sixteen

It was nighttime, and Michael and I were walking down a street in a city I didn't recognize. He had an arm around my shoulders, and I had one arm around his waist. We were laughing, talking, and having a great time simply being together.

As we reached a narrow alleyway, Michael pulled me off the street and into it. The alley was pitch-black. I asked him what he thought he was doing, and he replied that he didn't *think* he was doing anything. What he was going to do was make love to me.

"Here? Michael, we can't."

"Oh yes we can," he countered, as he lowered his lips to my throat and wasted no time slipping one hand up under my short skirt. I wasn't wearing any underwear. I gasped and reached for his belt. He laughed and undid my blouse as I unzipped his fly and asked, "What if people hear us?"

"Would it bother you if they did?"

Had there been any light in the alley, I knew I would have glimpsed his smile and would have seen the feral look in his expression. He had me pinned to the wall in no time and was thrusting deep. I screamed as I came then stood trembling with him still hard inside of me afterwards.

I was quickly and inexplicably on my back in a cold puddle of water in the dark alleyway. Michael eased inside of me again, and I shuddered and came beneath him in the cold water as he drove into me. I begged him not to stop, even as I anticipated what he was going to say next. I knew what he needed emotionally as well as physically, and I'd always given him what he needed.

"Tell me you love me," he directed.

"I love you."

"Tell me you want me."

"I want you."

His breathing quickened, and he said, "Tell me you forgive me."

"I forgive you."

He came hard, and I came again, crying out as I did so. And then he was gone, and I was lying alone and empty in a puddle of cold water.

I woke with a start and lay clutching the pillow beside me. I longed to hear Michael's voice, to have him hold me, to feel him in me. I wondered if I would ever experience any of those things again. I also wondered if I had cried out when I'd climaxed in my sleep and if Brian's person on duty had heard me. A more embarrassing thought occurred to me. What if Brian himself had been monitoring my rooms?

Sighing, I turned over and looked at the clock. It was 4:00 a.m. If I went to the main quarters, would they let me in at this time of the morning? Was there a way I could sneak in? I'd only seen the living room, dining room, a bathroom, the study, and Elizabeth's room. What lay in the rest of the apartment?

The kitchen was inconsequential to me as were other bathrooms. However, I would be interested to see Brian's bedroom and the rooms where the "monitoring" took place. What else could there be? Living quarters for the staff? A home gym?

A terrible idea struck me. What if Brian was the perpetrator in all of this, and Michael was being held and tortured in a nearby room? He could be right next door, and I might never hear him.

You know that's ridiculous. Get up; get dressed; and get moving. See what happens.

I went to the bathroom, showered, brushed my teeth, pulled my hair into a ponytail, and dressed in jeans and a red t-shirt. I stepped into my sandals but put on no jewelry or make-up and left my quarters then walked down the hallway.

James Harrison, wearing jeans and a green shirt, opened the door for me and escorted me into the living room. When I looked questioningly at him, he said in his lovely British accent, "The staff member on the monitors told me you were up and might be coming."

"So, you had to get out of bed for me?"

"I wasn't in bed, Mrs. Benedetto. Would you like me to get Mr. Maggio for you?"

"No. I want to talk with you. I want you to promise to be honest with me, just as Mr. Maggio has. I'll understand if you can't answer certain questions."

179

I sat on the couch and requested he join me. He hesitated then sat in a nearby chair.

"How did you come to work for Mr. Maggio?"

"I grew up in his household. My mother was his personal chef. When I was old enough, I went to university. After completing my studies, I decided I wished to serve in Her Majesty's Army. When my service was finished, Mr. Maggio asked me to become his personal assistant. I quickly accepted since I was capable of providing him with aid regarding coordination of business matters and protection for him and for Miss Elizabeth."

"Have you had to protect anyone here?"

"Yes, although I've never had to kill anyone to do it as I did during my service in the Army."

"Do you like your job?"

"Very much. Mr. Maggio and I work well together."

"I see." My brain working in overdrive, I said, "You've known Mr. Maggio your entire life. Do you think he's a good man?"

"Why should it matter what I think about his goodness?"

"Because I suspect you know my husband's father better than anyone else. I get the impression that he trusts you more than he would trust others."

"What gives you that impression?"

"Your facial features and build."

He blinked in surprise and said, "I beg your pardon?"

"You may not have black hair and blue eyes, but you have the same bone structure as Mr. Maggio and my husband. How long have you known you were Brian's son?"

His expression was unreadable. I knew he was calculating how much he could and should say. Folding one leg across the other, I sat with my hands laced together atop one knee while I waited for a response. After a time, I began to swing my dangling foot ever so slightly.

"Tell her, James."

We both turned and saw Brian standing in one of the doorways that led into the living room. He was wearing jeans and a black t-shirt that had the little Nike symbol embroidered near the hemline. He looked as though he hadn't slept at all.

Brian crossed the room and took a seat in a chair near James and repeated his order that James answer my question.

"I've known I was his son since I was fifteen."

"And you are…?"

"Thirty-six."

I looked to Brian and asked, "What made you tell him? And why wait until he was fifteen?"

"That was when his mother was the victim of a drunk driver, and he was…in a bad place in his life. I felt it was best that he finally know the truth."

"What did you think before you knew?" I asked James. "What had your mother told you?"

"She would never answer my questions about my father's identity. I looked quite different as a boy, more like my mother's family. So, the resemblance wasn't noticeable during my childhood. I never suspected, but I suppose I should have."

"Why is that?"

"Because she spent every night in my father's room when he didn't have another woman there with him."

Shaking my head, I asked Brian, "Did you love James's mother?"

"We were good companions for one another, but we didn't love each other. She didn't want marriage but did desire financial security and a child. I enjoyed her company and agreed to provide her with what she wanted in exchange for a lifetime commitment as my companion and chef. I would provide for her and the child; that was never in question. The one stipulation was that the child would never know its true parentage unless I chose to enlighten him. And that was exactly how it worked itself out."

"James, were you upset when he told you the truth?"

"Actually, I was relieved. I finally had an answer and understood the years of vague responses to my questions regarding my paternity from my mother."

"What do you call Brian when you're not acting as his personal assistant?"

"Brian."

"Why not *Father* or *Dad* or something like that?"

"Because it wouldn't do for Elizabeth to know," James replied. "My life is already in danger because of my work. If it were well-known I was also Brian Maggio's son, then that would double the risk and put Elizabeth's life in greater jeopardy."

I stood and began to pace in front of the wall of colorful tile fountains. All of this was giving me a headache and providing more complications and opportunities than I wanted to examine.

"You people are unbelievable. All of this secrecy, plotting, underlying motives...."

"Is necessary," James declared.

"Because you've made it necessary! You've wound yourselves up in this web of...of deceit and power and money because you get off on it! It's what you live for, isn't it?"

"It's how we live," Brian replied calmly. "How our lives have evolved."

"How many other children do you have?"

"To my knowledge, I only have Elizabeth, James, and Michael."

Going back to stand in front of James, I asked, "When Brian dies, will you take over?"

"No. I've no wish to head his business."

"When I die, my business empire dies with me," Brian said. "My estate will be dispersed. Elizabeth's care will be handled by James should I precede her in death. My wealth will be distributed three ways. A third will go to charities of my choosing, such as places like the facility you and I visited with Elizabeth yesterday. The rest will be divided between my two sons. James will receive more should Elizabeth still be alive so that she can be properly cared for in her remaining years."

"But if you weren't ever intending to tell Michael that you were his father –"

"Anonymous donations were to be made to John's Place and to various charities to which Michael contributes."

"You think of everything, don't you?"

"If I thought of everything, then Michael wouldn't have been taken."

Rubbing at my throbbing temples, I asked James, "Do you want to meet Michael or keep your existence hidden?"

"I'd like to know my brother but not at the cost of his safety or happiness." Shooting his father a glance, he said, "Michael is a brilliant, complicated man who has his demons but manages to contain them with the love of his family and friends, the focus on his business, and the consulting work he does with the U.S. government. I personally don't believe we should ever meet. I think that Brian and I would draw him into a place where he'd find it impossible to escape."

I mulled over his words then asked bluntly, "What if Michael were to die before Brian?"

"You mean would I kill my brother to inherit his portion of our father's fortune? No. If Michael were to die before Brian, it would change nothing. Upon Brian's death, Michael's part would still go to John's Place and the charities through an anonymous donation. If I die before Brian, my portion would go to the projects and charities I've designated in my own will."

"What if you both die before Elizabeth?"

"Unlikely, but I do have a contingency plan for that," Brian assured me.

I was feeling sick. I hated this world of Brian's with all of its ruthless intrigue, veil of secrecy, and uncertainty. All I'd ever wanted in my life was stability, security, and love. Michael had provided me with all three, yet had added that improbable element of excitement I'd never anticipated. He gave, and I took. I gave, and he took. It was as close to perfect as I could have ever dreamed.

I returned to my seat on the couch and steeled myself before saying, "I know Michael's running out of time. I know you said we're close to finding him. How do you see things going?"

"I can't tell you. If I do and you're captured, then all will be lost."

"But I can't go with you! I'd be in the way. I can shoot or stab someone if I'm lucky, but the odds are I'd endanger more people than I'd help."

"We're talking about a world with which James and I have grown accustomed. We've been more open with you than we have with any other person on this planet. You're trusting us with Michael's life and with yours. Just keep trusting, and all will work out."

"When?"

"In the next twenty-four hours."

I nodded distractedly and said, "I'll never see either of you again after this, will I?"

James looked away, and Brian seemed sad.

"And Michael? What do I tell him?"

"Whatever you feel he should know," Brian answered. "My son is very wise and will accept the truth without setting out on some quest to find us. Maybe it will give him solace to know that Al's son was not his father. Perhaps not. Either way, you'll be there for him."

"And who'll be there for you?"

"You will be. Even once Elizabeth is gone, you and Hermione will keep me somewhat accountable. James also has influence over me and is an enormous part of my daily world. And I do have my current companion and other women in my life."

I had no response to that and stared at my hands in my lap.

Brian asked, "Would you like to know what I found out about your family?"

"It doesn't matter anymore. I don't care about anything except the family I have now and remembering my parents."

Brian gave me a shrewd look and said, "Very well." As he got to his feet, he said, "I'm going to check on our progress." When he reached the doorway, he paused and said, "I will tell you that you gave your son a very fitting name. Your quick-tempered, brilliant, gun-fighting great-grandfather, John Henry 'Doc' Holliday, would've been pleased, I'm certain."

I smiled to myself. James asked me if I'd like some tea.

"I'd love some tea and something to eat."

Within the hour, James, Brian, Elizabeth, and I were sitting together in the dining room enjoying crepes, home fries, and eggs. It was a lovely breakfast, and I reflected that I would miss the father, son, and daughter despite what I knew of their lives and their often sinister world. I wished with all of my heart that they could walk away from it and join us in the sunshine of Florida, but I sensed it would never happen. The courses of their lives had been set in a certain direction and were highly unlikely to change.

After breakfast, I played for a while with Elizabeth in her room. Brian and James were elsewhere working on Michael's rescue.

"Elizabeth, I need to talk to you about something," I said as we pretended to make plastic horses gallop around a stall we'd constructed of Lincoln Logs. "It's very important."

She stopped her Appaloosa from galloping and waited.

I left my Mustang to graze in the pretend field and said, "I may have to go home soon, and I don't know if we'll get to play anymore."

"You could come visit me again. I love you, Seneca."

I smiled and blinked back tears as I said, "I love you, too. I wish I could come back, but I may not be able to. If I can't, then I'll miss you very much."

"Me, too. We had so much fun."

"Yes, we did."

She hugged me and said, "It will be all right. We'll always be the same, Seneca. Remember? We're like sisters!"

"Just like sisters," I told her.

"Will you tell your little girl and boy about me?"

"Of course. I'll think about you every time I play with them."

"And I'll think of you every time I play or go to the park or go for fun time!" she said excitedly. "It'll be all the time."

"I'd like that."

There was a knock on the door. It was James.

"Miss Elizabeth, it's time for Mrs. Benedetto to meet with your father now."

"Oh, okay." She put her arms around me and said, "Goodbye, Seneca. Sweet dreams."

I hugged her tightly and told her I wanted her to have sweet dreams always then got up from the floor and followed James out. Once he'd shut the door behind us, he grew solemn and said, "We need to move now. Your things –"

"I don't care about any of my things. All I care about is Michael."

He nodded and directed, "Come to the study with me."

Brian was waiting for us there. He looked like a hawk ready to swoop down on its prey. The tension in the room was almost suffocating.

"I've been in contact with your friend, Rob, and his superiors as well as their superiors. I believe I have everything timed appropriately."

"What do you mean?"

"I mean that you should follow my lead and ask me no questions. That way, I'll tell you no lies. You do exactly as I say when I say it. If all goes according to plan, we should have minimal casualties on our side, maximum casualties on their side, and save Michael."

"If something goes wrong, then we could all die."

"Yes."

"But you're willing to take the risk?"

"I literally created Michael. He's my child, and I love him and want to see him live even if it costs me my life. I would do the same for James or for my darling Elizabeth. That's the way a parent should feel, isn't it?"

I couldn't tell if he was being glib or serious. I decided he was asking a rhetorical question and said nothing.

"We'll be leaving in about an hour," James informed me.

"Should I change?"

"Your jeans are fine, but wear a dark, long-sleeved shirt, and black boots."

"I don't own black boots."

"There are some in your rooms."

"What about my wedding ring and earrings?"

"You may wear them," Brian directed. "Actually, I'd recommend it. Also, put on some make-up and leave your hair loose."

I didn't understand the rationale behind that, but then there was a lot I didn't understand. I would do what I was told by those who were far more versed in the sort of activity in which we were about to become engaged. I really had no idea what to expect.

Chapter Seventeen

I returned to my rooms and put on the long-sleeved black shirt I'd brought with me as well as the black socks and soft leather boots I found at the foot of my bed. Going to the bathroom, I applied make-up and released my hair from its band and styled it then slipped on my little diamond studs, silver hoop earrings, and my wedding ring.

As I stared down at the antique ring, I said a prayer, asking God to keep Michael alive a little longer, so we could rescue him. I prayed that both of us would survive the day ahead and live to see our children again. I thought of Al, Diane, Krystal, and Greg. I remembered good times with everyone and recalled Adiba and Rakeem and our lives before their murders.

If all went according to Brian's plan, the person responsible for Michael's kidnapping and torture, as well as Adiba and Rakeem's deaths, would be dead himself very soon. Although I could never wish for someone to die, I wouldn't mourn the loss of such a man.

Is Brian that different? You know he's had people killed. Were they all bad people or were some of them simply in his way? Has he ever had people kidnapped or tortured? If he died, would you still mourn him if you knew that was the case?

Someone knocked on my door. I took one last look around my rooms and went to open it. The young Hispanic maid was standing just outside.

"Take care of your husband's father," she said in Spanish. "I need him as much as he needs me. I want to be with him for many years to come."

"You know what kind of man he is."

"One who has been alone for almost all of his life. He may not love me as he did his beloved Hermione, but he cares for me as he did James's mother. I give him comfort when we talk, touch, and share the same room. He saved me from the streets so that I could

187

be there for him. I want to be there for him as he grows to be an old man."

I nodded and said, "Please take care of him, James, and Elizabeth. Keep him and James as good as they can possibly be."

She smiled and nodded then asked me to accompany her to the main quarters. When we arrived in the living room, Brian and James were waiting. Both were dressed in black jeans and black long-sleeved shirts as well as black boots. Despite the tension and nervousness, I almost burst out laughing. We looked like something out of a Hollywood spy movie.

"I'll meet you downstairs," Brian told me and James. "The limo should be waiting."

As we rode down in the elevator, I asked, "Saying his goodbyes to La Senorita?"

"Yes. He does care for her. It's not only about the sex for him, not when it comes to women like her and my mother. He makes a certain connection with a woman and builds upon it. I've seen it with this one and with one other woman besides my mother."

"What was your mother's story? Was she on the streets, too?"

He shook his head and said, "It would turn your stomach if I told you my mother's story. Let's just say that my father rescued her from a vile predicament and had the man responsible for her abuse killed. Brian got her psychiatric help and sent her to culinary school when she was ready. She was an excellent chef."

"So, I see a pattern here. He finds these women in trouble, saves them, and they feel indebted to him and give themselves to him. He is a genius, so I'm sure he worked that out a long time ago."

"I doubt if that's his primary motive. I'm sure that subconsciously it's part of it, but that's not all."

"How do you know?" I asked, as we stepped out of the elevator and walked towards the doors of the building.

"Brian never told me anything about how he met my mother. I found her diaries after she died. That's how I discovered what had happened to her and what Brian had done. In the diaries, she wrote that he never once asked her for sex or tried to touch her. It was she who approached him a year after he'd hired her as his personal chef. He didn't sleep with her for another year after that. She wrote that they simply enjoyed spending time together although they did enjoy the sex as well."

"Maybe Brian is extremely patient."

"Maybe," he conceded. "Or maybe he's a man capable of doing generally unacceptable things but with noble goals in mind. Only Brian knows. I ceased trying to decipher my father many years ago. I may be smart, but I'm no genius. I love and respect the man regardless."

"When did he tell you about Michael?"

"When he told me he was my father. He said I had a younger brother I could never meet who didn't know Brian was his father either. He said my half-brother's name was Michael, but that was all I was told until I went to work for Brian as his personal assistant."

"You helped with the spying on Michael?"

"I checked on him periodically."

"Were you at our wedding?"

"Yes. It was quite beautiful." As we climbed into the limo, he said, "I was especially envious of Michael that day. I saw the love in his eyes and the passion he had for you. I've never felt love like that for any woman. Someday, I hope."

As I settled back into my seat, I asked, "Do you even have a personal life outside of Brian and Elizabeth?"

"I do. I have days off, take separate vacations as well as ones with the family, and have my own philanthropic endeavors."

"Brunettes or blondes?"

He cracked a smile and admitted, "Lanky redheads with nice breasts and a tight backside."

"I think I see the reason you haven't found the love of your life," I said dryly. "You've sort of limited yourself by being that selective."

"I didn't say I would only be with that one type. It's simply the one I prefer. I travel the world all the time. I'll cross paths with the right woman one of these years."

Brian joined us in the limo at this point, and we were soon on our way to the airport. Once we arrived, we went quickly to the private jet. Not long after, we were flying high above the big, bad world. I speculated as to which part of that world housed Michael's prison.

Brian spoke with me about physics and the intrinsic flaws in the theories relating to time travel for the first two hours of our flight. I found the conversation stimulating and appreciated his efforts to redirect my anxious thoughts, but it was clear that Michael was never out of our minds, no matter how technical we got with our discussion. James, who was not the least bit interested in debating physics with his father or sister-in-law, worked on a laptop in another area of the plane.

A steward interrupted our time travel conversation with refills on our waters and some sandwiches. I tried to refuse the food, but Brian urged me to eat and said I needed the energy provided by the sandwiches. He ate with me then excused himself to talk with James.

I glanced at my watch. It was mid-afternoon Eastern Standard Time. I peered out of the window and recalled the first time I'd ever flown. I thought of that wedding night flight and of the intensity of the lovemaking between me and Michael on his friend's private jet.

"Seneca?"

"How much farther?" I asked James as he took the seat across from me.

"Two more hours."

"Where's Brian?"

"Taking care of business." Studying me, he said, "You should sleep for a while."

"I'm too stressed. I doubt if I could fall asleep. Even if I did, I'd probably have a nightmare and wouldn't be functional for a while afterwards."

"We could help you with that."

"You mean with whatever Brian drugged me with the other night?"

"It helped, didn't it?"

"Yes. What was it?"

"I can't tell you, but I can get you some. It wouldn't knock you out for long, but it would allow you to get some good restorative sleep."

Weighing my options, I said, "Sure. Why not? I need to be as sharp as possible for later, right?"

I accepted the glass from his hands, drank it down, and was quickly unconscious. When I woke, I was ready for anything. Well, that was the way I felt.

We landed at a small airport where a black sedan waited for us. Brian, James, and I climbed into the vehicle and rode in tense silence for an hour. I spent most of that time staring out of the window at the passing trees. The terrain was hilly and the forests thick. I could see mountains in the distance.

The car eventually turned off the main road and wound its way upwards on a narrow, long, and smooth driveway. It finally pulled to a halt in front of an imposing-looking modern home. The concrete and glass building seemed very out of place in the midst of such a natural setting.

Two large men hurried to open the car doors for us, and we each got out and were hustled towards the house by them and the driver. Despite the fact that it was summer, the air outside was quite cool. I wondered whether we were in the northern United States or if we were in Canada.

The inside of the house was humming with activity. The place was crawling with men and women who all seemed to be striding purposefully in various directions. Everyone present was fit, clean-cut, and single-minded. It was as if I was in the middle of a military compound, which I supposed I was.

"Is Rob here?" I asked Brian.

"No. From what I understand, he wanted to be present, but he was ordered to stay in D.C."

"So that if this effort failed the government wouldn't lose two consultants," I inferred.

"That's the decision I would have made. It's the most logical, practical, and cost-effective." He took my hand and said gently, "If we succeed, you and Michael will see Rob soon enough."

I nodded and was intending to speak, but he tightened his grip and I remained silent.

A tall man with huge muscles and close-cropped graying brown hair approached us and introduced himself as the head of the U.S. government operation. I didn't pay attention to his name. It wasn't important. All that was important was that he did a good job and worked with Brian to save Michael.

"This entire enterprise is very unorthodox," he said gruffly. "That doesn't mean my people won't do a damn good job, just as they always do."

"That's what I'm counting on," Brian told him. "This is Michael Benedetto's wife, Seneca, and this is my personal assistant, James Harrison. We'd like to review the plans with you and your staff before we leave."

"Definitely." His gaze flitting to me, he asked curtly, "Is Mrs. Benedetto going to be in on the briefing?"

"No."

I opened my mouth to protest, but Brian squeezed my hand so hard that I had to close it in order to keep from releasing a little cry of pain.

"She can wait in the living area," the government man suggested. "I'll have one of my men escort her there."

Brian let go of my hand and told me in no uncertain terms to do what the man said and not to argue with him or anyone else. I went.

The living room of the house was comfortable enough although the modern furniture was not to my taste. I speculated that the government had either rented or commandeered the place for this mission and wondered if the owner of the house had known what would be going on inside these walls. Perhaps this was a house owned by someone in the military and was often used for such activities. Or maybe the U.S. government itself owned the home.

There was a wall of windows running along one side of the living room. The windows afforded a breathtaking view of the nearby mountains. As I stood staring out at them, I touched the glass with an almost imperceptibly trembling finger. The glass was thick. I suspected it was bulletproof.

Interesting, I thought. *Where are we?*

I stared out at the mountains and tried not to think of Michael. My thoughts wandered to Hadeel, Hani, Al, Diane, Krystal, and Greg. There was no way I could avoid thinking about them or Michael, of course. What would the government people say to our family if we didn't return?

An hour later, James entered the living room and told me we would be leaving within fifteen minutes and asked if I needed to use the restroom.

"Well, I didn't, but I do now that you asked. Where is it?"

192

"I have no idea but would like to use the facilities myself before we depart. I'm certain our hosts will be happy to escort us there."

While James utilized one bathroom, I was taken to another. Once I emerged, my escort, who was waiting outside the door, led me to a sterile room filled with a long steel table and metal chairs. There, Brian and Commander Guy were waiting with impassive looks on their faces.

"I understand you know how to shoot a gun," Commander Guy barked. "Are you any good?"

"I am when I'm at the practice range."

Commander Guy looked extremely displeased and said to Brian, "And you expect me to give her a gun? That's bullshit! She could accidentally shoot one of our people or draw fire upon herself just for having the damn thing in her possession."

"She could. I still want her to have a gun and a knife. It will make our enemy take her more seriously."

"You know how to utilize a knife in order to stab someone?" Commander Guy asked, as he swiveled his head back towards me.

"Michael taught me how, but I've never had to do that in real life either."

"What in the Sam Hill do you really think will be gained by giving this civilian weapons to carry into a hostile environment? If what you're proposing goes off as you anticipate, they're going to remove any weapons you have the moment you walk in the door."

"We're going to walk in the door?" I asked skeptically. "The kidnappers are going to invite us in?"

"What did I tell you about questions?" Brian asked with an edge to his tone. Looking at the military man, he said with a polite sneer, "She *will* be given a gun and a knife, and none of us will wear bullet-proof vests. If they decide to kill us, they'll aim for our heads and will have clean shots."

You were meant to save Michael, I reminded myself. *He's meant to live to be an old man. We were meant to be together for a long time. You're going to make it through this no matter what happens.*

Brian, James, and I were each given a gun and a knife but no bulletproof vest. We were then taken to the back of the house and led outside to a black Hummer. I wanted to ask if other soldiers were hiding somewhere in the trees or secretly following us, but I held my tongue as I buckled my seatbelt. James got into the driver's seat, and Brian rode in the back with me.

I had expected a long car ride, but we arrived at our destination in under forty-five minutes. As James eased the Hummer as close as possible to the wrought-iron gates that blocked a wide driveway, Brian lowered his window and said something in a language I didn't know to a man who was obviously on guard duty. The man spoke into a Walkie Talkie in the same language, and the gates automatically swung open.

James drove very slowly towards the house. The Hummer was barely moving as he pulled into the curved driveway at the front of the mansion that looked more like a Swiss chalet than a home in North America. My heart was hammering in my chest as I waited for direction from Brian or James. Neither said anything as we were "encouraged" to leave the vehicle by big men with guns.

I walked towards the house with Brian and James flanking me. As I climbed each step, I repeated silently, *Michael, I'm here. Michael, I love you. Michael, it won't be long.*

Chapter Eighteen

Once we reached the massive front door of the imposing house, we were unceremoniously frisked. Our guns and knives were taken from us, and the cell phones Brian and James had with them were confiscated before we were allowed inside. The foyer was dark and cold. It was also eerily quiet. I felt as if I were in a mausoleum.

A statuesque woman stepped forward and said something in the same language Brian had spoken to the guard. It sounded Eastern European to me, but I was no linguist. I didn't comprehend a word.

The three of us followed the woman down one narrow dark corridor after another until we reached an open doorway. Brian and James drew closer to me and shielded me with their own bodies as we stepped inside what appeared to be a private office.

A man of perhaps forty was sitting on the edge of an enormous black desk. He had dark hair, dark eyes, and rakish good looks. He smiled when he saw the three of us, but it was a terrifying sort of smile. I flinched, and he laughed.

He and Brian spoke for several minutes in the language I didn't know then the stranger abruptly said, "We will speak in English and not Croatian for the sake of the others."

"As you wish," Brian said stiffly.

"You are probably wondering why you are here," the man began dramatically. "The answer is very simple. You are here because I want my revenge on Michael Benedetto for what he has done to me and my family." Grinning sadistically, he said, "But then you do not even know who I am."

"Of course we know who you are," James told him flatly. "Your name is Goran. Michael accidentally killed your niece and killed your brother in self-defense several years ago."

"He killed our business as well!" the man proclaimed angrily. Pounding his fist on the desk, he demanded, "Do you know what he did? Years of work by my father and then by myself and my brother were destroyed by one agent and his operation! Our enterprise to provide arms to countries and terrorist groups was decimated in an instant! I vowed that day I would avenge my brother and rebuild our father's business!"

"What about your niece?" I asked quietly.

"What about her? It was unfortunate that she distracted my brother. Otherwise, he would have killed Michael Benedetto before he himself was killed, and our family would not have been so dishonored!"

"You son of a bitch," James hissed. "You're a disgrace to your country and your niece."

There was suddenly a gun in the man's hand, and he had that gun pointed directly at James's head. For a moment, I thought he would pull the trigger. Instead, he leered at James and said, "I would not expect someone like you to see things from my perspective. And if my investigators are correct, it is *you* who are the son of a bitch. After all, your mother must have been a bitch. Why else would her own father take her to his bed time and time again?"

My stomach gave a nauseating lurch. So that was what had happened to James's mother. I sensed that James wanted more than anything to lunge across the room at the man, but he stood rooted next to me with his hands clenched beside him. Brian made a low growling noise in his throat.

The man redirected his aim towards Brian, who didn't move. Then the man pointed his gun at me. Surprisingly, I felt no fear, only revulsion for this thing that considered himself to be a human being.

"Goran, we have a deal," Brian said tightly. "If any of us is murdered, that will nullify the terms of our agreement."

"Agreement?" I echoed. "Deal? You made a deal with this monster?"

"Mr. Maggio did not share our plans with you?" the man asked. "He is paying me several hundred million dollars in exchange for the life of your husband. It will be enough to make my business flourish once more."

So, that's what Brian told him, I thought. *Greed is a powerful motivator.*

"I want to see Michael," I announced. "I want to know he's still alive."

196

"And I'd like to know the same before our transaction is complete," Brian said icily.

"Why not? The three of you have been stripped of your weapons and are surrounded by my people. I know you will want proof that Mr. Benedetto remains among the living in order for our exchange to take place."

He tucked the gun in the front of his pants and asked that we follow the woman who had led us to his office. As we stepped out of the room, we were quickly surrounded by armed guards. Goran walked behind our little group as we went downstairs into the basement of the house.

It was even colder down there, but it wasn't quiet. I heard Michael scream, and my breath caught in my throat. I might be in a freezing basement, but the hot field was all around me.

"Seneca, this is not the time," Brian said in Spanish.

When Michael screamed again, I stumbled and fought for breath.

"What is wrong with her?" Goran demanded. "Tell her to get up!"

The room was spinning, and I felt as though I would lose consciousness at any moment. Brian and James knelt beside me, and James urged me to breathe through my nose just as Michael always had. This time, it wasn't working. I became panicked and clung to Brian as blackness tinged the edges of my vision.

"Tell your people to stop torturing her husband," Brian commanded. "She has some emotional problems, and this is not making them any better."

Goran sighed and said grudgingly, "Very well." He muttered something to one of his people who jogged ahead of us. The screaming stopped, and I sagged against Brian and took shallow breaths as he stroked my hair.

"I want to move on with this!" exclaimed Goran. "Is she better or not?"

Brian asked me very softly in Spanish if I could stand. When I nodded against his chest, he whispered that it would all be over soon and to be strong. He and James helped me to my feet, and I stood, shaking but determined to continue on.

"This is my house, and I will have rules about how we are to proceed," Goran announced. "We will go into the room where

Michael Benedetto is being held. He will be facing away from us. No one is to speak until I say it is permitted. I will have his wife brought around to face him. Once she has verified that he is alive, I will give Mr. Maggio a phone he can use to initiate the transaction of funds."

"My people will need confirmation from me that all is well before the transaction is finalized," Brian insisted.

"I will leave with you. We will go to a hospital. There, your personal assistant and Mrs. Benedetto will take Mr. Benedetto inside. You and I will leave and go to a public place. Once there, you will finish the transaction, and I will disappear. The two of us will never meet after today."

Brian agreed, and we moved forward again. I was terrified of what we might see when we were brought into Michael's torture chamber. James put an arm around my shoulders and gave me an encouraging squeeze.

Our entourage halted in front of a metal door. Goran nodded to one of his flunkies, and the door was opened.

"After you," Goran said officiously.

The room was about twenty feet by twenty feet in size. Metal cabinets lined two walls. The wall directly ahead of us was plastered with enlarged photos of me, Hadeel, Hani, Al, Diane, Krystal, Greg, Rob, John, Tom, Adiba, and Rakeem. Michael was seated facing that wall with his wrists shackled and raised high above his head by a chain attached to the ceiling.

"Do you like the photographs of his closest family and friends?" Goran asked with a nasty smile. "Reminders."

Because of the way he was seated, I couldn't see much of Michael. What I could see was a mess. His upper back and arms were covered in bruises, cuts, marks, and what appeared to be electrical burns. The backs of his calves seemed to be similarly affected. The rest was hidden by his position and by the chair.

The air in the room was stale and smelled of sweat and…pain. A man with an emotionless expression stood near the row of cabinets on the right side of the chamber. He seemed bored and didn't acknowledge us as we entered.

"This is one of my best men," Goran said proudly. "He's very good at what he does."

"Which is?" James asked tersely.

"Prolonged torture that does not lead to death. If our little deal had not been worked out so quickly, then he could have continued like this for some time. I was actually somewhat disappointed that you were so willing to work with me. It would have been very gratifying to have Mr. Benedetto suffer for a much longer period for what he's done to my family and business." Making a dismissive gesture, he said, "Some things were not meant to be."

I paled as I listened to this madman and wondered how many other madmen there were like him in the world. I considered how many people had been in Michael's place here or in other torture chambers. I was fighting to stay upright and in control of myself. Michael needed me now, and I couldn't do anything about anyone else.

Goran jerked his head towards Michael and said something in his native tongue to the woman who'd been with us from the time we'd entered the house. She roughly grabbed me by the arm and dragged me across the room until I stood directly behind Michael.

"Go ahead," Goran prodded, his enjoyment of my distress quite evident in his voice. "Do as you were told."

My heart pounding so hard that I could virtually hear the blood rushing through my body, I walked very slowly around the chair. The more I saw, the more frightened and angry I became.

Michael was naked and so badly beaten that he was nearly unrecognizable. The injuries I'd seen on his upper back and arms extended almost entirely across his body. His head hung forward, and there was fresh blood on his torso and legs. I glared at Goran, who told me to go ahead and touch him, talk to him, and do whatever else I wanted to do to him in order to make sure he was alive.

"Michael," I said gently. When he didn't respond, I asked, "Michael, can you hear me?"

He stirred and groaned before gradually lifting his head. I unwittingly let out a small cry of shock and anguish when I saw his face clearly. I reached out to touch him then hesitated. I didn't know where to touch that wouldn't hurt him.

Michael's face was horribly bruised. His upper lip was split. One eye was swollen shut, and the other eye was injured in some way I couldn't readily discern. He had a bloody nose that looked broken to me.

"I ordered him cleaned up earlier, but I'm afraid my man got a little overzealous while we were waiting for you," Goran said with feigned remorse. "Poor Michael Benedetto."

I cursed Goran in Spanish. It was an old curse I'd heard one of the elderly women in my trailer park utter when she'd found out the man who owned one of the farms had forced himself on her seventeen year-old granddaughter. The accursed man was struck and killed by lightning the following day. There hadn't been a cloud in the sky.

I said Michael's name again. He struggled to focus on me with the one eye that was open and managed to ask, "What are you doing?"

"I came to save you."

"How can you? You're not even here."

I realized he thought he was hallucinating and reached forward to touch his forehead, the one area of his face that didn't appear to be injured. When he felt my fingertips on his flesh, he sucked in his breath then choked out my name as he released it. I bent down and kissed him where my fingers had been. Michael became agitated and jerked his shoulders and arms as if to attempt to pull them free of the shackles and chain. I knew this had to be causing him great pain and told him to stop and that everything was under control.

Michael laughed bitterly and asked, "Does it look like things are under control? Seneca, get the fuck out of here! You have no idea whom you're dealing with!"

"I believe I do," I said grimly. "Please, trust me. We'll be gone from this horrible place very soon."

"You should never have come."

He was breathing hard and shivering. I knew he was suffering and cold, and I wanted him in a hospital. I looked to Brian, who nodded and said, "It's time to end this, Goran."

The man agreed, as he walked around to stand facing his favorite torturer near the cabinets. In one fluid movement, Goran withdrew the gun from the waist of his pants, turned, pointed it at Michael's torso, and fired. I screamed as Michael jerked reflexively when the bullet hit him and howled with the pain.

Pandemonium erupted in the room as James launched himself at the closest guard to him, while Brian withdrew a gun from somewhere – where? – and shot Goran in the head. I screamed again as blood spattered the wall behind him. Brian took out another guard before the man had a chance to raise his gun. Then he shot the female guard as she charged him.

James had been well-trained in hand-to-hand combat. As his father had used his gun to kill the three bad guys, James used his body and a knife to dispatch the others.

An alarm sounded in the building, and Brian hurried to shut the door. As he did so, it automatically locked.

Strong arms wrapped around me from behind and threatened to crush my ribcage. I yelled and kicked, but Goran's best inflictor of pain was not deterred. I felt one of his hands reach across my face and knew that he was about to try to break my neck.

"Seneca, relax!" Brian roared. "Do exactly as you're told!"

The man said something in Croatian. It gave me enough time to catch Brian's encoded directions. I suddenly slumped in the man's arms. Startled by my unexpected "fainting" episode, he loosened his grip. I bent forward then was dragged back as the bullet Brian fired into the man's chest pushed him and me backwards. The two of us tumbled to the ground.

Once we stopped moving, I scrambled away from the man, who lay moaning and crying out something in his native tongue. Brian stood over him, said something in Croatian, and shot him again in the chest. His body lifted off the floor as it took the impact of the shot then settled back in death.

"I thought you said you'd never personally killed anybody!" I yelled at Brian, as I hurried towards Michael.

"I never have until tonight!" he yelled back. "James, make certain everyone in this room is dead except the four of us!"

"I already have!" James snarled.

It was obvious our adrenaline levels were running high. When I reached Michael, I asked Brian, "How did you know the door would seal itself like that?"

"Because that's what the schematics of this house indicated," he answered. "We'll be safe from Goran's thugs until your military people eliminate them, find us, and open the door."

"Which would be bloody great if Michael hadn't been shot!" James snapped. "*That* wasn't in the plan!"

"I'm not God, James. I do my best, which is all I've ever expected of myself and others." As James came up beside his father, Brian asked, "You're certain there are no other survivors?"

"None."

"Good." Turning to his younger son, he said, "I have no idea how long it will take the U.S. government's people to secure this place and open the door. There are too many factors to consider. It may be fifteen minutes or fifteen hours."

"We need to get Michael on the ground and see how serious his wounds are," I said as calmly as I could.

James hurried over to the dead torturer and patted him down. He came back with a set of keys and handed them to his father. He then stood behind Michael and put his arms around his brother's chest.

The third key Brian tried unlocked the shackles that held Michael's wrists. Michael moaned as Brian eased his arms down while James supported his weight and lowered him to the concrete floor. His head lolled to one side.

"He's probably going into shock," I explained. "Look through the cabinets and see if you can find any blankets."

"Seneca –" Brian began.

"Don't argue with me!" I interrupted brusquely. "We're all done with the intrigue and secret deals and killings now! You're in my territory, so do as I say! I learned a lot as a social worker in the healthcare industry and have more medical training than either of you, so *you* take orders for once and let me do what I can to help Michael!"

"I have basic medical training that I received in the Royal Army," James informed me. "We were mostly instructed on how to deal with combat wounds."

"Very helpful since Michael's been shot. Brian, go look for blankets!"

Brian stared down at his wounded child then went over to the cabinets to search. I knelt on Michael's left side, and James knelt on his right.

"I'm more familiar with illnesses and injuries than gunshot wounds, "I admitted as James and I started to examine Michael. "You focus on the bullet wound, and I'll check out the rest."

"Agreed."

202

It sickened me to see what Michael had endured in a mere four days. None of the burns, bruises, or cuts looked life-threatening, but I had no idea if my husband had internal injuries from punches or blows with solid objects.

"I've no clue how deeply the bullet penetrated," James muttered. "The shot was at pretty close range. The fact that the bullet went in near his ribcage and didn't exit means it's lodged inside somewhere. Hopefully, it didn't cause extensive damage or shatter anything as it passed through." Glancing up at me, he said, "There's not too much blood coming out through the entry wound. That could be a good sign."

"Or it could be very bad," I said quietly. "The blood could be pooling inside."

"I found a blanket," Brian said as he knelt on the floor next to me. "It's all they had in here besides torture implements, the bastards."

Michael moaned and said my name. I slipped my fingers into his hair and felt a large knot on one side of his head. I asked him about the lump.

"The man...he slammed my head against the floor at least once," Michael mumbled. "I lost track of what he did and when he did it." Fighting to focus, he said, "My retina's detached in the eye that still opens. They have to fix it right away or I'll lose vision forever."

"After they fix the bullet wound," I told him. "Once help arrives, they're going to take good care of you in a hospital. At the moment, we're sort of trapped, but we're safe."

He seemed disoriented and asked, "I've been shot?"

I kissed him on the forehead and gingerly took one of his injured hands in mine. He winced as he tried to curl his fingers around my hand. His skin felt hot to the touch, but he was shivering more violently than before.

"Who's with you?" he asked groggily.

I looked to Brian and James for guidance. Both of them stayed completely immobile and waited. I remembered Brian saying that whatever I decided to tell Michael would be the right thing, but I also knew he hadn't anticipated Michael's ever actually meeting him or James. I debated for a few seconds before saying, "It's complicated."

"I'm not…I'm not going anywhere right now," Michael said with the barest hint of what was surely a painful smile.

"Their names are Brian and James."

Michael laid very still and repeated, "Brian and James. My father and half-brother."

Brian, James, and I were stunned. Michael laughed quietly, or at least he tried to. That led to some coughing and then a groan.

"How did you know?" Brian finally asked.

"Goran. He had four days to tell me the whole story. He thought it would torture me emotionally to hear him talk about the truth behind my parentage and family. What he didn't know was that it actually gave me comfort and hope."

"Comfort and hope?" James echoed questioningly.

"For the first four years of my life my father called me a burden. I used to wish before and after his death that he wasn't really my father, that he really loved me. As Goran talked and talked about Brian and his life and mine, I realized I did have another father, one who loved me enough to leave me with Nonno and Nonnie who would give me a normal, happy life." Tears trickled out of his injured eyes as he added, "I had a *real* father, a brother, and a sister."

"Forgive me," Brian breathed, as he tenderly stroked his son's damp hair. "I was an arrogant fool."

Michael grunted with pain as he reached up and grasped at his father's sleeve. He said earnestly, "I forgive you whatever it is you think you've done to me."

"I gave you life, but I did it for selfish reasons," Brian confided. "I'm sorry, Michael."

"I'm not." Tightening his hold on his father's shirt, he asked, "Where is James?"

"Here," James said, lightly placing a hand on Michael's shoulder.

"Don't disappear," Michael pleaded. "Either of you. I know you want to stay away from me, but I need you and my sister. Don't worry. I won't allow myself or my family to be pulled into those parts of your life that are…that…."

Michael's voice trailed off, and he seemed to lose his train of thought. His fingers loosened their hold on Brian's shirt, and he let his arm drop away from the older man. His weak grip on my hand grew even weaker, and he stopped shivering. For an instant, I thought he'd lost consciousness, but something in my gut told me that this was not the case. Whatever was going on in Michael's body was a precursor to something else.

"Turn him on his left side!" I ordered.

"Why?" Brian asked. "What's wrong with him?"

"Just do it!"

James instantly reacted and asked his father to assist him in easing Michael onto his left side. They had just gotten him into that position when he started to seize.

I'd witnessed seizures during my years working with the sick, injured, and elderly. They were always disconcerting, but I knew they would pass and what to do in the meantime. Watching Michael have a seizure was almost unbearable, but I remembered the first rule of thumb for those witnessing a seizure, which was to remain calm.

It was clear that neither Brian nor James had ever seen someone having a seizure. Both appeared fearful, and James looked as if he was going to pin his brother to the floor while Brian brought his fingers to Michael's mouth.

"Stop!" I quickly commanded. James, if you hold him down you'll hurt him. Brian, if you stick your fingers in his mouth he could bite them."

"But I've heard that people can swallow their tongues!" he said worriedly.

"That's not true, but they can choke on their own saliva or vomit. That's why I had you turn him on his side when I realized what was coming." Looking to James, I said, "Don't hold him, but make sure he doesn't bang his head on the floor." Glancing between the father and son, I said, "Keep calm, and talk reassuringly to him until this passes."

Michael made a noise, and I knew from experience with others that he was trying to speak but had no control over his body, including his vocal cords. The noise sounded unearthly, and Brian shocked me and James by beginning to cry and bending down to kiss Michael's forehead. Then he began to speak to his youngest son in Italian. I couldn't understand all the words, but I could hear the love in them.

Michael eventually stopped seizing and slumped to the floor. I suggested we spread the blanket on the concrete and lay him on top of it then loosely wrap it around him. Once this was accomplished, I checked his mouth and the one eye I was able to open.

"He looks dehydrated," I said. "That, in addition to the beatings, shocking, cutting, and the slamming of his head against the floor probably triggered the seizure."

"So, we should get him to drink something," James concluded.

"No."

"But you just said –"

"Can we trust anything in this room not to be poisoned?"

"No," Brian answered firmly.

Michael moaned and called my name. I touched his neck and assured him I was there. His skin was clammy, and his breathing seemed labored again. He inexplicably cried out, and I kissed his sweat-soaked hair and told him it was going to be fine.

"When they come for us, let them know I didn't say anything," he told me through clenched teeth. "Not one thing. No one was compromised because of me. Not my family, not my operations, not anything."

"I'll tell them," I promised. "I'm sure they won't be long."

He cried out again and writhed in pain on the floor. I feared the onset of another seizure and began to tremble. I had watched my father die. I had watched my mother die. Was I now about to watch my husband die?

The door was suddenly flung open, and Commander Guy and armed troops rushed in. Once they were certain the room was free of all threats, the medical personnel were allowed to enter. Brian and James stepped back as I explained what we knew about Michael's injuries and described the seizure he'd had. As they inserted an I.V. into his arm and began their preliminary examination before moving him, I kissed Michael then walked over to Commander Guy and told him what Michael had relayed to us about no one being compromised during his torture.

"I wasn't concerned about that at all," the man said frankly. "I trained Michael myself. He would have died before giving up any sensitive information to anyone." Shaking his head, he muttered, "This was a helluva strange operation, but it seems to have worked out in our favor. I'll ride with you to the hospital. We'll debrief on the way there."

Michael was rushed to a waiting plane and flown out. My attempts to go with him were ignored, so I eventually gave up and agreed to ride with Commander Guy, Brian, and James in a separate plane. We reviewed everything during the flight as a woman digitally recorded our statements although I was told that this would not be the last time we'd be forced to revisit our ordeal in Goran's fortress.

When we arrived at the hospital where Michael had been taken, I glanced at my watch. It was not yet midnight Eastern Standard Time. It was hard for me to believe that all of the dramatic events of the evening had taken place within a few short hours.

I wanted to call the family in Florida, but I was aware I couldn't until I knew for certain what Michael's prognosis was. Brian, James, Commander Guy, and I sat in a room and waited for news. One hour dragged into another and then another. A soldier brought us coffee and doughnuts, and I forced myself to drink and eat.

Rob walked in after we'd been waiting for four hours. He looked as though he hadn't slept for days, and his brown hair was a mess. I immediately got to my feet and hugged him but told him I couldn't talk to him about anything just then. He assured me I didn't have to and sat beside me. Then he caught sight of Brian and gaped.

"I'm Michael's father," Brian said proudly. "This is his brother, James."

"But –"

"Michael didn't know," Brian hastened to say. "Now he does, and things are going to be different." Before I could ask, he said, "I'll explain later. Don't think about anything except Michael now. What I'm going to do is a very good thing. I promise."

I nodded slightly and asked nothing. Another hour passed before a man and woman in scrubs emerged from the restricted surgery area. The surgeons reviewed what had been going on for the last several hours in the operating room. The bullet that had pierced Michael's side had eventually led to the collapse of one lung. Copious amounts of blood had been lost as the doctors worked to repair the affected areas, and they'd had to use large quantities of blood from the blood bank during surgery.

CT and PET scans had revealed no severe internal damage done by the torture. However, Michael had three cracked ribs and severely sprained fingers on the hand I'd held, the one he'd tried to wrap around mine. There was no bleeding in Michael's brain, although he did have a mild concussion. A retinal specialist had been called in to reattach his retina and had succeeded.

"Will he have more seizures?" Brian asked once the surgeons had completed their review of the case.

"It's possible but doubtful. Since he didn't have epilepsy prior to this episode, we feel it was caused by a combination of the beatings, head trauma, dehydration, and oxygen deprivation."

"What oxygen deprivation?"

The surgeons looked at each other before the woman said uncomfortably, "He told your people on the plane that he was deprived of oxygen by his torturer until he passed out. He said when he came to, his wife was standing in front of him. We'll continue to have a neurologist monitor and test him until we're satisfied that he has no permanent brain damage, but he didn't show any signs of that when he first arrived here and was conscious."

"How did they deprive him of oxygen?" Brian persisted.

"Don't say it!" I cried, my anxiety level skyrocketing. "I don't want to hear. I can't. Please."

"You're welcome to read our report," the male surgeon said to Michael's father. "I know the military will be requesting a copy."

"When can we see him?" I asked.

"He's in Recovery. We're going to be keeping a very close eye on him. At some point this morning, he'll be moved to the Critical Care Unit. He won't be conscious until much later today at the earliest. You can see him in the afternoon."

"No!" I said desperately. "I want to see him now. I have to see him!"

Brian took me in his arms and said in Spanish, "We'll only be in the way at the moment. He's safe and being well-cared for here. We need to rest, and then we can see him after lunch."

"But Brian —"

"No. It's 6:00 a.m., New York time. It's 3:00 a.m. here. Don't worry. He's not going to get up and walk away during the night."

"Will he make a full recovery?" James asked the surgeons.

"Assuming there are no setbacks and no brain damage, he should. We can't give you a timeline, yet."

"I don't care about a timeline as long as he'll be okay," I hastened to say. "Thank you so much." Once the surgeons had left the room, I said, "I have to call Al and Diane and then Krystal and Greg."

"What will you tell them?"

"The truth."

"I'm afraid you can't do that," Commander Guy declared. "None of this happened."

"I didn't say I'd tell them the *whole* truth. You're welcome to stay in the room if you like."

"Believe me, I will."

Chapter Nineteen

Everyone stayed in the room as I used Rob's cell phone to make the calls. I dialed Al's number first. The instant I said his name, he thanked God and asked if Michael and I were both safe.

"We're safe. We're…." I looked to Commander Guy and asked, "Where exactly are we now?"

"Seattle."

"We're in Seattle."

"Are the both of you all right?" Al asked worriedly.

"Physically, I'm fine. Emotionally, not so much. As for Michael, he's in bad shape, but the doctors think he should make a full recovery."

"It is very bad?"

I blinked back tears and said, "Yes, very bad, but they say he should be okay."

"Diane and I are going to be on the next flight to Seattle."

"Al –"

"He may not be my flesh and blood, but Michael is my precious grandson!" Al exclaimed. "I must come, Seneca!"

"But he looks horrible!" I blurted out. "I don't want you to have a heart attack and die on us!"

"Ah, my angel. You are always thinking of everyone else except yourself. Remember what the cardiologist has told me? I have a very strong heart for someone my age. I know it will be upsetting to see Michael if he is badly hurt, but I'm his grandfather. I must come to him and to you, who is equally as precious. Diane will be in complete agreement. We may be old, but we are stalwart. What is the name of the hospital?"

I found out the information and relayed it to him, then I asked him to call me on Rob's phone when he and Diane knew their plane's arrival time. Brian said behind me that he would arrange for a car to pick them up at the airport, and I told Al.

"His father decided to stay then," Al said, but there was no resentment in his tone. "I knew that if he met my Michael face-to-face he would never be able to walk away."

"There's so much more, Al."

"And I will talk with his father about that. You take care of yourself and my Michael and think of nothing else." Pausing, he asked, "Have you called your home, yet?"

"No. Once I hang up with you, then I'll call the house."

"What will you tell the children?"

"That Michael was in a bad accident and is in the hospital but will be fine." Sighing, I said, "I hope they believe me. After that, I don't know what comes next. I can't think that far ahead."

"Then do not. We love you, my angel. We will see you soon."

"I love you, too."

I dialed my home number and prayed that the ringing of the phone wouldn't wake Hani and Hadeel. Krystal answered after the first ring and said, "Seneca? Michael?"

"It's me,"

She paused before asking nervously, "Well?"

"He's alive but is badly injured. They say he'll eventually be all right."

"Just how badly injured *is* he?"

I swallowed hard and said, "Tortured. Shot. He had a seizure before we were rescued."

"Oh, my gosh! Where are you? Should we come?"

"No! There's no way the kids can see him like this. Besides, we're in Seattle right now."

"I wish I could be there with you."

"I know you do. How are you, Greg, and the kids?"

"Fine. The kids didn't understand why you didn't call them to wish them sweet dreams last night. I told them I knew you were going to call and that Greg and I would wake them no matter what time it was. It was the only way we could get them to sleep. Greg's getting them up now."

Hadeel picked up the phone and said, "Hello, Mama!" She sounded wide-awake as she continued, "Why didn't you call?"

"I couldn't."

"Mama, why are you crying?"

"Daddy's been in an accident," I told her, hoping that, for once, I sounded convincing while I lied. "He's going to be all right, but he's hurt and is in a hospital."

"Does he have a lot of ouchies?"

"Yes, a lot. That's why Mama's crying. Nonno and Diane are coming to help me take care of Daddy so he can get better as fast as he can and come home."

"They're going too far away, where you are?"

"Yes, Hadeel. They don't let little girls and boys in the hospital unless they're the ones who are sick or hurt, so I need you to stay with Greg and Krystal and Hani until Daddy's well enough to come home. I promise I'll call you every day, and Daddy will call you as soon as the doctors say he can."

"Okay. I'll keep being a good girl, Mama. I'll take care of Hani with Krystal and Greg. I love you."

"I love you, too."

"Tell Daddy I love him?"

"Of course. Have sweet dreams when you take your nap."

The phone was passed to Hani who said, "Mama! Where you?"

"Still far away, little man. Daddy got hurt in an accident and is in the hospital. Krystal, Greg, and Hadeel will explain it to you."

"You and Daddy home?"

"Not yet. Daddy's hurt. We'll be home as soon as we can get there. Be a good boy for Krystal and Greg until we can come back."

"Love you, Mama!"

"I love you, too. Sweet dreams for your nap, Hani."

When he hung up, Krystal said, "You did it."

"What?"

"You know what. That was believable. Greg and I will reinforce what you said. Know that we're there with you in spirit and that we're taking care of Hadeel and Hani for as long as you need."

"Thank you, Krystal."

"Sweet dreams, sister."

"I doubt it, but we'll see."

I hung up the phone and handed it to Rob with my thanks. Then I excused myself to go to the restroom. Once there, I locked myself in a stall and wept for fifteen minutes then washed my face with soap from the soap dispenser and dried it with paper towels before returning to the waiting room.

"Michael's grandfather called while you were in the bathroom," Rob said when I walked in. "The earliest they can get here is six tonight. Something about a storm somewhere along the way that's delaying flights. They'll call when they land."

"There's a hotel one block over," Brian informed me. "I've already made arrangements for us to stay there and booked a room for Al and Diane as well."

"I want to sleep here. What if something happens? I need to be here."

"We'll be sixty seconds away," James told me. "Seneca, we need to rest or we won't be any good to anyone."

I shook my head and declared that I was staying at the hospital. Commander Guy startled me by gently saying, "You should get some rest. I'm not leaving here. Neither is Rob. We'll call you if there's a problem."

I looked to Rob, who nodded and said, "I'm going to keep watch. I'll keep him safe, Seneca. Get some sleep."

I reluctantly went with Brian and James to the hotel. When we arrived, I discovered that Brian had booked a suite for me, himself, and James. Al and Diane would have the suite beside ours when they arrived.

The two-bedroom suite Brian selected had two queen-sized beds in one bedroom and one king-sized bed in the other. There was a bathroom attached to each bedroom, and both bedrooms shared a large living area. Expensive pajamas and robes had been placed on each bed. However, when I lifted the ones on the king-sized bed I realized they were for a man.

"You're not sleeping in here," Brian told me. "I am."

"What? Brian, that makes no sense!"

"It makes perfect sense." As he headed for the bathroom, he said, "The hotel staff is getting us some new clothing and footwear. It will be delivered when I call the front desk once we've rested. We'll also have food at that time. After we eat, we'll return to the hospital."

He shut the door, and I turned to James and said, "He can't just assume he can take over and…and…"

213

"Seneca, think about it. He *needs* to take over for his own sake, and you're in no shape to be taking care of anything right now."

"I'm fine."

"The bloody hell you are." Taking me by the hand, he led me towards the bedroom and said, "You use the bathroom first, then I'll take my turn. We'll sleep, get our clothes and food then go see Michael."

Too tired to argue, I picked up the pajamas provided for me and went to the bathroom. Once there, I took a quick shower and washed and dried my hair before donning the pajamas and brushing my teeth. I climbed into one of the queen-sized beds as James went to shower and change. I fell asleep realizing that James was now calling me "Seneca" instead of "Mrs. Benedetto" and smiled.

I was screaming, crying, and fighting to break free of the thick arms attempting to drag me out of the field. I couldn't breathe and wanted my captors to let me go and leave me in the hot sun where I belonged. I could hear their voices but couldn't understand what they were saying.

I was suddenly pinned to the ground and clawed at those holding me down. Strong hands had my wrists and someone was putting his weight across my chest and belly. I screamed again and strained to push the man off me. I was desperate to get away from the wood chipper and the screams that still reverberated in my ears.

"Seneca, wake up!"

My eyes flew open. James was the one who had me pinned to the floor, and Brian was holding my wrists. Both men had a few scratches on their necks and faces from my fingernails. When I saw the marks, I immediately stopped struggling and lay still. I couldn't speak.

"Are you fully awake now?" James asked. "If I let you up, will you be all right?"

I nodded, and he slowly eased himself off me and sat beside me. Brian let go of my wrists and sat on the other side. Both were breathing hard, as was I.

"Sorry I hurt you," was all I could manage to say. "I was so scared."

Brian stroked my hair and told me not to worry about it, that he'd known the stress of the day would trigger my PTSD and, therefore, a particularly nasty nightmare. That was why he'd insisted that James sleep in the same room with me.

"It was obviously quite a vivid dream," James remarked.

I nodded, rolled over, and pushed myself up on my hands and knees. I was shaking so badly that I could barely stay in that position. I shut my eyes and wished my Mommy was there with me.

"We can't go to the hospital with her like this," James declared.

"I have to see Michael," I insisted. "Michael –"

"Remains unconscious," Brian told me. "I've been checking on him every hour via your friend, Rob."

"I need to go to him."

"We will once you've recovered yourself, eaten, and dressed."

"Would you...would you help me back to the bed?"

"Of course we will," James said quickly then guided me into a sitting position before he and his father helped me to stand. I almost fell, and James lifted me up and laid me on the bed before taking a seat beside me. Brian came around and sat on the other side of me and began to stroke my hair once more. I curled into a tight ball and closed my eyes before drifting back to sleep.

"I don't understand," James was saying as I came awake. "She's a grown woman with amazing ability."

"James, you're a very smart man with no background in psychology," Brian told his son. "It doesn't matter that she's an adult or that she's got more intelligence than the average person. A part of her will always be that frightened child. She has a two-fold psychological challenge. The most evident is that she witnessed her father's horrific demise when she was fourteen. Every child who witnesses a parent die in a violent manner suffers from PTSD to some extent."

"And the other challenge?"

Intrigued to hear what Brian had to say, I pretended I was still asleep and listened.

"Children who are repeatedly traumatized before the age of thirteen are imprinted with emotional connections to things that they may never be able to overcome rationally."

"Please explain."

"She matured in an environment where she had to conceal her superior intelligence and had parents who vacillated between love and hate for each other. She never knew from one day to the next whether there would be food to eat, a place to live, electricity at home, or suitable clothing to wear. Despite her knowledge that she'll never want for anything material again, she can't help but feel insecure and anxious when she's overwhelmed by emotional trauma." Sighing, he said, "Your mother was the same way for different reasons. Not everything is rational."

"I know that. I remember how Mother had nightmares, even though neither of you ever told me what they were about."

"How could we? Seneca will recover from this latest trauma. She and Michael will both need more intensive psychiatric counseling for a while because of what happened, but that will pass. Both of them are very strong-willed people, just as you and I are."

"Do you love Seneca?"

I held my breath and waited for Brian's answer.

"I'll never love anyone the way I loved Hermione."

I stirred and rolled towards the two men, who were sitting fully dressed beside one another on the bed next to mine.

"How are you feeling?" Brian asked soberly.

"Better. Have you slept at all?"

"Here and there."

"Michael?"

"Has regained consciousness once. Things look promising."

I smiled tiredly and asked when we could go to the hospital.

"As soon as you dress and we've eaten," James told me. "Your clothing is waiting for you in the bathroom."

It felt odd to dress in clothing someone else had selected for me. But everything fit and was comfortable, and I was relieved. I put on the socks and tennis shoes then went out to the living room where James and Brian were waiting for me so we could eat. We quickly polished off the breakfast pizza that was topped with egg, sausage, onions, and peppers then left for the hospital. It was 4:00 p.m. Seattle time.

"Are you up to this?" Brian asked me as we walked down the block.

"Yes, thank you." Turning to James, I said, "Thanks to both of you and not just for helping me after my nightmare."

"Michael's my child," Brian said solemnly.

"And my brother," James added. "We would have both died for him last night, even though we'd never actually met him."

"Brian, what did you tell the torturer in Croatian before you shot him the second time?" I asked.

"That I was giving him a much more merciful death than he deserved."

"And what did you tell Michael in Italian when he was having the seizure?"

He stopped walking and took my face in his hands. Smiling slightly, he said, "I swore to him that if he'd hold on and survive I would leave my dark world and devote my life to doing only good and being the father I should have been to both my sons." He glanced at his older son and said, "I'm sorry, James. It shouldn't have taken me this long."

"You don't owe me any apologies although I do have a favor to ask you."

"Anything."

"Once you…retire, I'd like to call you *Father*. I've always wanted to do that ever since I knew the truth."

Brian released me, walked over to James, and hugged him. James looked startled for a moment but then hugged back. The sight made me want to laugh and cry at the same time.

Rob and Commander Guy were in the Critical Care Unit waiting room drinking coffee and talking when we arrived. Both men got to their feet as we approached, and Commander Guy said something about "complete elimination" of our common threat. I purposefully turned a deaf ear on the conversation and went to find my husband. I didn't follow hospital protocol and wait for visiting hours or permission or for the obligatory lecture on how the patient needed to be kept quiet so he could rest. I had no idea what room Michael was in or what he would look like. I didn't care about anything except being with him. If anyone tried to stop me, then I was planning on ignoring them.

Michael ended up being easy to find. There was an armed guard standing outside his door. I expected the woman to stop me from entering, but she merely nodded at me and said, "He's awake at the moment, ma'am."

"Do they have him sedated most of the time?"

Looking uncomfortable, the soldier said quietly, "I doubt if I'm supposed to be telling you anything, but yes. The doctors and nurses are giving him something to help him sleep and to keep him calm.

At least that's what they're telling each other when they're in there talking about his care."

I thanked the woman for answering my question and for keeping watch over my husband. My heart rate quickened, and I hurried into the room. Michael somehow managed to look both better and worse. Some of the bruising was already fading, and I could see that his exposed injured flesh was almost completely covered by a sheen of ointment, probably antibiotic in nature. His left arm and hand were secured in some sort of splint, and his face looked like something out of a horror show. There were stitches in his upper lip. The eye that had been swollen shut was covered by what I suspected was a cool gel pack that would help to reduce swelling. The other eye, the one that had suffered the detached retina, was hidden by a metal shield in order to protect it from accidental damage. There was another cool gel pack draped across the bridge of his nose. Both cheeks remained swollen and badly bruised.

I walked over to the bed and bent forward to kiss Michael on the forehead. He murmured my name and reached blindly for me with his uninjured fingers. I gently took his hand.

"Are you all right?" he asked in a whisper. "Were you hurt?"

"None of us was hurt. Brian and James kept me safe."

"Are they still here?"

"They're here." Running my fingers through his tangled hair, I said, "Try not to talk. Even whispering is probably not a good thing for you just yet."

Disregarding this, he asked, "Is everyone at home safe?"

"Yes. Al and Diane should be here soon."

"I really wish Nonno didn't have to see me like this. Where are we?"

"Seattle."

"Where was I?"

"I don't know. I think we were in Idaho, but I really couldn't say. Rob will tell you."

"Rob's here?"

"Yes. Commander Guy, too."

"Who?"

"The man who trained you. I never did catch his name. I just call him Commander Guy. It suits him."

Michael chuckled softly then grimaced with the pain. He tightened his hold on my hand and told me he wished he could see me.

"You will when they say you can. You need to be still if your retina's going to stay attached."

"I know. Everything hurts too damn much to move around anyhow."

"You were in a bad way when we got to you, and getting shot made it a lot worse."

"They told me I wiped out the blood bank."

"You did."

"I had a seizure before we were rescued, didn't I?"

I hesitated before admitting, "You did."

"It was…terrifying."

"I'm sure it was."

He paused for a long moment before asking, "What did you tell the children?"

"That you'd been in a bad accident and were hurt but would recover. They believed me. Krystal and Greg are going to take care of them as long as we need them to."

"What happened to Goran?"

"Brian shot him in the head after Goran shot you."

"And the man who tortured me?"

"Brian shot him in the chest just before he tried to break my neck. He shot him again once he was down and told him he was giving him more mercy than he deserved."

"Everyone else?"

"Brian and James killed everybody who was in the room with us. I think the rest are all dead, thanks to Commander Guy."

"Good. There's no one left from there to come after me or my family." He sighed with what sounded like relief and said, "I'm done, Seneca."

"What do you mean?"

"I mean I'm done with consulting. I know that had nothing to do with this. Goran wanted revenge for the past, plain and simple. It doesn't matter. I don't want to live like this anymore. Someone else can save the world. I just want to go back to being with my family, helping vets through John's Place, and making love to you every chance I get. I want to be happy and grow old as John said I would. I'll stick to reviewing old information for the government but nothing new. I can make a difference without sacrificing any more of my soul."

"You most certainly can," I told him. "Now, hush and rest."

"Stay with me."

"I will."

I sat in a chair and loosely held Michael's hand as he slept. Nurses came in and out and performed tasks like switching the cool packs on his face, lifting the metal shield on his eye and inserting drops, and changing the bags of fluids. Medications were given through his I.V. tubes at various intervals. Michael stirred minimally each time a nurse was present but didn't actually wake.

Brian and James entered after I'd been sitting for a couple of hours and told me that Al and Diane's plane had been delayed but would arrive soon. As they stared down at Michael, he mumbled something in what sounded like Croatian. I looked questioningly at Brian, who appeared terribly sad.

"He's asking the little child, Jadranka, to forgive him for taking her life."

I frowned and then said, "I want to try something."

Brian and James looked suspiciously at me and waited. I motioned for them to step into one corner of the room and dropped my voice until it was barely audible.

"Michael's drugged. Maybe if I tell him in Croatian that he's forgiven, it will sink into his subconscious somehow and he can stop being so overwhelmed by guilt. Maybe we can do the same regarding John."

"I think we should attempt it," James volunteered. "It's worth a try."

Brian looked pensive then told me how to say in Croatian, "It's not your fault. I forgive you."

I practiced with him for a few minutes. We moved back to the bed, where Michael was still mumbling. I heard the girl's name again, and Brian nodded.

Bending low, I said softly in Croatian, "It's not your fault. I forgive you."

Michael immediately stopped mumbling and visibly relaxed. Brian leaned close to his son's ear and spoke in Arabic, but he altered his voice slightly. I assumed he'd heard John's voice during his years of "observing" Michael and was trying to emulate Michael's closest friend.

I happened to glance at James, who was intently listening to what his father was saying. Whatever Brian was telling Michael was quite involved, and James's attention never deviated. I decided I was going to have a little talk with James later about this.

Once Brian had finished speaking in Arabic, Michael replied in Arabic then fell back into a deep sleep. Brian, James, and I left the room and returned to the waiting area in order to allow Rob and Commander Guy the opportunity to go in to see Michael, although we advised them not to wake him.

"Wouldn't dream of it," grunted Commander Guy.

"We'll talk at length later," Rob added. "Right now I just need to see my friend. It doesn't matter if he's awake or not."

As they went to Michael's room, James and I sat while Brian excused himself to make some calls. Once he'd been gone for a few minutes, I asked James, "You speak a bunch of languages like Michael and your father?"

"No. I speak English and Arabic. I picked up the latter in the Army during my tour in the Middle East."

"What did Brian say to Michael when he was pretending to be John?"

"That he loved Michael like a brother and that there was nothing Michael could have done to prevent his death or to save him. He also said something about being proud of his work and the way Michael had lived his life before and since his death. He told him he wanted Michael to be happy. That sort of thing. Things that John would have said were he here, I'm certain."

"I hope what we did worked," I muttered. "I hope it was the right thing to do."

"I thought it was a stellar idea."

"Thank you."

"Seneca?"

"Yes?"

"You do know that my father loves you, don't you?"

"Yes, but not like Hermione."

"No, but I do believe he loves you more than he did my mother and definitely more than the other woman and his current paramour."

"I wouldn't ever –"

"Don't worry," he interrupted. "He'll never act on it, not as long as Michael lives."

"So, why are we even talking about this?"

"Because it gives you power over him, which is crucial if he's to follow through with his plan to give up his former life and be a good father to me and Michael and do only good things. It's up to you to keep him accountable. I know my father and the way he thinks. Because you remind him so much of Hermione, he'll want to please you and to make you proud of him. Take advantage of that and use it to everyone's benefit."

I mulled over what James had told me while he went to get us both some coffee. He and Brian returned to the waiting area just as Commander Guy and Rob came back. It was at this opportune moment that Al and Diane appeared in the doorway.

Diane stood stock-still when she saw Brian and said, "Good God! Al was right. Michael does look exactly like him."

"No genetics tests necessary," Brian said with a slight smile.

I hugged Al and Diane then introduced everybody. When I got to Commander Guy, I simply said he was the man who'd coordinated the government's part in the rescue effort. I wasn't certain if he wanted the older couple to know more than that and was embarrassed that I hadn't paid attention to his name. To my relief, he gave me a quick nod that let me know I'd done the right thing.

"I must see my Michael," Al said once the introductions were complete.

"He looks terrible, but he's doing all right," I hastened to tell Al. "He said he wished you didn't have to see him like this."

"I would want to see him no matter the circumstances," Al declared. "He's my grandson." Glancing at Brian, he said, "You and I must talk afterwards."

"Most definitely."

The female guard outside Michael's room nodded to us as I led Al and Diane inside. When they saw Michael, Al muttered something in Italian that sounded like a prayer. Diane straightened and strode over to the bed with that no-nonsense look of hers on her face.

"Michael, it's Diane," she said to him. "Your grandfather and I are here now."

"Diane?" Reaching out with the hand not confined in the splint, he whispered, "It's so good to hear your voice. How were the penguins?"

She smiled, took his hand, and said, "We never made it to Antarctica. Your grandfather said he had a bad feeling about something and felt we should turn around and come home. Since he's never said that on any of our previous trips, I took it very seriously. Obviously, he was right. We'll see the penguins another time."

Al approached the bed and gingerly touched the top of Michael's head with his palm before saying, "My beautiful grandson."

Michael whispered something in Italian that made his grandfather smile.

"He says he is not so handsome today," Al translated. Stooping down, he kissed his grandson on the forehead and began to speak to him in Italian. Diane patted Michael's hand; then she and I left the two men alone.

When Al emerged from the CCU some time later, his eyes were red from crying, but he was composed. He immediately suggested we all get something to eat so he and Brian could meet privately afterwards to talk. Commander Guy declined, and the rest of us left to walk to a nearby vegetarian restaurant we'd noticed on our trek over from the hotel.

We were all exhausted and didn't talk much other than to order our food and make the occasional comment to one another. The cuisine was excellent, and I had to force myself to eat slowly and sip the glass of red wine I'd ordered. Al insisted on paying the bill for all of us, and we left the restaurant feeling worn out but more relaxed.

"I've made arrangements for you to stay at the same hotel with us," Brian told Rob. "Your suite is on the same floor as ours."

Rob thanked him as we walked towards a Starbucks. Al cleared his throat and asked Brian if they could detour into it and talk frankly. Brian agreed as long as they could speak in Italian in a quiet corner somewhere. Diane, James, Rob, and I continued on to the hotel as the two men entered the Starbucks.

I went with Diane to her and Al's rooms. We sat on the sofa in the living area for a while without speaking. Finally, she said calmly, "It's all right to cry, Seneca."

"I don't need to cry," I declared. "I'm too tired."

Diane told me not to say a word about anything unless I wanted to, that Al would fill her in on everything he learned. I admitted I wasn't ready to talk to anyone about what had occurred in the last few days. Then I sprang up as I realized I hadn't called Krystal, Greg, and the children. Diane offered me her cell phone, but I told her I needed to *see* Hani and Hadeel. I intended to go to Rob's room to ask him if I could use the computer that I knew he would certainly have with him in order to Skype with my children. She urged me to go ahead and said she was planning to unpack while she had time to herself. I bid her goodnight and left for Rob's room.

Chapter Twenty

When Rob came to the door, he was wearing a bathrobe and had wet hair. I explained why I'd come to his rooms; then I apologized for showing up without calling first and began to leave. He told me to come in and Skype my family while he dressed. I checked the time and almost dissolved into tears. It was 9:00 p.m. in Seattle, which meant it was midnight in Florida. It was way too late to Skype.

I debated as to what I should do. Finally, I used the hotel phone to call the house. Greg answered and sounded as if he hadn't gone to bed, yet. He confirmed that he hadn't.

"The kids are keeping you up?"

"No, work. Without Michael here I'm holding it all together at John's Place. Don't get me wrong; it's going great. It's just a lot of work without Michael around. He does delegate, but he's got so much of what he does in his head that running the place without him being available at all has been…interesting."

"I'm sure you're doing a tremendous job," I told him truthfully. "Michael really trusts and respects you. He wouldn't leave anyone in charge unless he thought that person could do the job well."

"Thanks, Seneca."

"How are Krystal and the kids?"

"Krystal's nausea was a lot worse today. The kids are fine. Krystal told me Hani said he didn't want diapers anymore and stayed dry all day. She put a Pull-up on him tonight though."

"That's great," I remarked with a mixture of pleasure and regret. I was thrilled that Hani was making strides in his potty-training, but I felt guilty that I wasn't there to share in what I was certain was exciting to him. I reminded myself we were all involved in extenuating circumstances and let go of the guilt.

I heard a little voice in the background and then Greg told me Hadeel was up, asking to talk with me. He told her to wake her brother and Krystal.

225

"Oh, Greg. I hate to do that to all of you. I'll keep it short so you can hopefully get everyone back to sleep easily. I wanted to Skype, but I didn't realize how late it was."

"Tomorrow," he said. "How's Michael?"

"Improving. I'll tell you and Krystal more once the kids are back in bed."

I had a short but sweet conversation with my sleepy children then Greg brought them back to bed while I updated Krystal. I apologized for calling so late and told her I hoped she would be able to go back to sleep quickly. She confided that she had been tossing and turning, waiting for me to call and would now be able to rest. She also informed me she'd relay everything I'd said to Greg and suggested I get some sleep.

Rob came in and sat in a chair across from me as I hung up the phone. He looked refreshed after his shower although I knew he was probably dead tired. I asked him how much he'd slept since I'd notified him of Michael's kidnapping.

"Not much, but we're trained for that. Still, it's been a while since Michael and I've been in the field. I'm ready to crash. I'll sleep tonight." Raising his eyebrows, he asked, "You?"

"I've slept but not well. Maybe tonight."

There was a long, awkward lull in our conversation.

"Seneca, are things really okay between us? I didn't want to make you feel uncomfortable the other night when I told you I didn't think I'd ever find a woman like you for myself."

"Everything's fine as long as you and I can remain science buddies and friends. If you can't do that, then I think we'll have to stop our calls." Rubbing tiredly at my eyes with my knuckles, I muttered, "I'd hate to have to find another science geek like me to chat with about the things most people don't even understand."

He laughed softly and said, "There *aren't* many other people who can have the sorts of scientific discussions you and I get into. You really have no idea how brilliant you are when it comes to physics. I'm sure Michael's told you about how the military people picked his brain and did all sorts of tests to figure out how he remembers things the way he does and how he learns so much so well. They studied me in the same way but for different reasons."

"Science?"

"Amongst other things," he answered enigmatically. "They would *love* getting their hands on you."

"I'm not that smart."

He laughed out loud at this and said, "Like hell you're not. You definitely have above-average intelligence, but when it comes to physics…." Shaking his head, he said, "Your brain works at a far more advanced level than most top-ranking physicists, including myself. I have to struggle to keep up with you sometimes. Yet, you won't even consider working in the field as a physicist. I guess I'll never understand why."

"Maybe I don't understand either," I reluctantly admitted. "I'll keep working through you if that's okay."

"It's okay, and we're okay. I really do find you amazingly appealing, but I know you don't love me. We're just really good friends, and I'll take what I can get and be all right with it."

"You're sure?"

"Yes."

"I'm glad to hear it. I don't want to lose our friendship."

"Me neither."

I stood and said, "Goodnight, friend."

Grinning, he rose, shook my hand, and said, "Goodnight, friend."

"Sweet dreams, Rob."

"You, too."

I returned to the suite I was sharing with James and Brian. When I entered, everything was quiet. I checked Brian's room, but his bed was still made and empty. James was asleep in the room he and I were sharing.

After going to the bathroom and removing my clothing, I donned my pajamas, washed my face, brushed my teeth, and then went to bed. I figured I was so tired I would sleep soundly and wake refreshed. Mercifully, I was right.

When I woke at 9:00 the following morning, I was alone in the bedroom. I showered and dressed in more clothing that I hadn't selected for myself before going out to the living room. That was when I saw the beautifully wrapped box on the coffee table.

The box was larger than a shoe box but not by much. I removed the pink bow and carefully peeled the tape on one end, then along the seam on the back before pulling away the pink-and-purple striped wrapping paper. Curious, I lifted the lid of the gift box and peered inside.

I removed a lovely dark walnut box that had a hinged lid. I raised the top and stared as a beautiful ballerina twirled in front of a mirror to the tinkling strains of *Swan Lake*. I watched the tiny figure go round and round to the sound of the music. A large teardrop fell onto my jeans.

I closed my eyes and listened to the music, remembering myself dancing with abandon in the exquisite costume my teacher had given me. I recalled the joy in those moments, the freedom I'd felt not to have to be afraid of anything.

"Do you like it?"

I opened my eyes and looked at Brian before saying, "Very much."

"Elizabeth was right. You deserve pretty things."

"Every little girl deserves pretty things." As the music box wound down, I asked, "Why didn't we ever have enough money when I was a child?"

"I thought you didn't want to know what I learned about your past."

"I didn't, but now I think I have to."

Brian sat beside me on the couch and closed the box. I picked it up, wound it, and lifted the top again. We watched the ballerina gracefully twirl to the lovely music until the box wound down again.

"Are you sure you want to know about the money?" Brian asked.

"All those years of living hand to mouth were so damaging. I need to know why I had to live like that."

"Even if it tarnishes the images you have of your mother and father?"

"Just tell me."

"From what my people discovered, your father was well-liked by everyone. He was especially popular with women and often gave them money. He knew how to charm his way into their beds, and they seemed to know how to charm him out of what little he earned as a farmhand. With as many women as he took to bed, I'm amazed you don't have quite a few half-brothers and half-sisters. My investigators found none. You were his one magnificent progeny."

"And my mother?"

"Did the best she could with what she had. There were no dirty little secrets uncovered regarding her. She seems to have been a simple, loving woman who developed low self-esteem because of her own abandonment as a baby. She then had the misfortune of falling in love with a charismatic, handsome man who wanted her to remain faithful to him while he slept his way through your backwards little community." Leaning against the couch cushions, he said, "I suppose it's a testament to your father that his fellows were so laissez-faire when it came to their friend's bedding their wives. Perhaps it was because they knew their wives would squeeze whatever money they could from their friend. It's also a testament to your mother that she eventually divorced her husband despite her own insecurities." Touching my cheek with the backs of his fingers, Brian said, "Both of your parents wanted more for you. They met their own tragic ends and left you alone."

"I think I was always alone."

"No," he said firmly. "My people reported that everyone they interviewed told them time and time again how much your parents loved you and how proud they were. They were merely undereducated, hard-working adults who didn't know how to be better parents to their daughter."

"I know they loved me. That doesn't mean I didn't feel alone."

"It's a travesty regardless of how you look at things."

I offered Brian my heartfelt thanks for what he'd said and for the present. Then I told him, "I'm going to wind this up and watch her dance at least once a day every day that we're at home. Reading was my escape, but dancing was what gave me my freedom."

"Perhaps it's time to attend a ballet?"

"Not yet, but maybe soon." I closed the music box and asked, "How did it go with Al?"

"Very well. We're going to keep our lines of communication open at all times. He's Michael's grandfather and always will be. I've no wish to disrupt his relationship with Michael, you, or the children. However, we're in uncharted territory. We've both agreed to voice any concerns we have should they manifest themselves, and I'm certain they will."

Remembering James's words about my power over Brian, I touched his arm and said, "You can do this. I have faith that you'll make it work. Michael wants you and James to be part of our lives, but he won't hesitate to break off ties with you if he knows you haven't really changed. He'd be sad about it, but he would tell you to leave and never come back."

"To protect his family."

"And himself."

"This is going to be extremely difficult for me," Brian admitted.

"I know, but you can do anything you set your mind to. Your capacity, drive, and funds are pretty much unlimited. You'll do what it takes to be a good parent to Michael and James, just as you've been to Elizabeth."

"Yes, I will."

I smiled and said, "Good. I was thinking that once Michael is stable enough to be moved, then we could go to your apartment in Manhattan. The children can't see Michael until he looks much better, and Elizabeth needs to meet her brother."

"And I need to explain to her that James is her brother. She won't understand, but she'll accept it easily. She's always loved James." His eyes bright with tears, he said, "She's always loved everyone."

"Where is James?"

"With Michael."

"Well, I want to be with Michael, too. We all do. Let's get the others and go to him."

I rose from the couch. Brian smiled up at me then stood and walked with me towards what would certainly be the greatest challenge of his life. He was a man who lived for a challenge, and I felt confident that he wouldn't allow this one to defeat him. He, James, and Elizabeth would become part of our world, and that pleased me greatly. I needed the three of them in my life and didn't want them to disappear forever.

What Brian had told James the day before was true. Because of my childhood, I was always at risk of feeling insecure and afraid. The more people I had in my life who loved me, the less likely I was to feel those things. I'd used my separateness as a shield for years. Once Michael had breached my defenses, I couldn't go back and needed people around me who loved me and would take care of me no matter what the circumstances. Now, I would never be alone again.

Three weeks passed before Michael was released from the hospital. Then, he and I flew with Brian and James to Manhattan. Two more weeks passed, and Michael continued to improve steadily.

Michael and I stayed in the master suite of the guest quarters at his father's apartment where he forced himself to follow the doctors' orders. He had been strongly lectured about the need for him to only leave the bed in order to use the restroom, eat, or shower, and it was preferable that he spend at least three-quarters of each day lying prone. During waking hours, he was allowed to wear a soft patch over the eye that had suffered the detached retina, but at night he still had to wear the metal patch.

The bruising, electrical burn marks, and cuts had either already healed or were healing. His face, except for the patch, looked normal that day for the first time since he'd been injured. The doctors assured me his insides were healing as well and that he should make a full recovery. We'd decided to return to Florida within the next week since we felt the children would now be able to see him without being frightened or accidentally hurt him by climbing on him to give him a hug or in play.

I had been Skyping the children each evening, but Michael had insisted he only talk to them on the phone due to his appearance. We had both Skyped Dr. Forrester every day for virtual therapy sessions but were handling things much better than anticipated. Apparently, what Brian and I had done while Michael was drugged seemed to have helped him to release his guilt over killing the little girl and not being able to save his best friend. Dr. Forrester had praised our initiative, but he had cautioned us that none of us should ever tell Michael what we'd done, which was understandable.

Al and Diane had flown back and forth between New York and Florida each week in order to provide Hadeel and Hani with reassurance and to help Greg and Krystal. Although Greg had been doing a wonderful job running the business both alone and in conjunction with Michael via phone, Krystal continued to battle terrible nausea and was on some special medication due to difficulties with her pregnancy. Still, she didn't feel well most of the time and had decided to take an indefinite leave of absence from her job.

Personally, I didn't foresee Krystal's returning to work. With the salary Greg was now making, she didn't have to work and could be a stay-at-home mom like me, which was what I knew she really wanted. She and Greg were already worried about how to be good parents since they'd both had bad parents, and they wanted her to be at home with the baby. I would be thrilled if that happened and looked forward to spending more time with her and her newborn when it eventually arrived.

I sighed. A part of me couldn't stop wishing that I was the one having the baby.

Chapter Twenty-one

"Seneca?"

"Hm?"

"What are you thinking?"

"I'm thinking that I wish we could have sex," I told Michael, as I sat on the edge of the bed. "I'm thinking I want you in me and that Brian's unhooked the monitors in our bedroom so no one could hear or see anything."

"That's not what you were thinking, but I do like that idea." He grinned up at me and said, "Let's make love."

"You're not supposed to move around too much or do anything 'forcefully' for a while or else you could detach your retina again. It's still too soon."

"For me to make love to you as I usually do, but that doesn't mean we can't have sex at all."

"Are you up to it?"

He laughed heartily at this and said, "I think I was up to it the day they let me out of the hospital, pain or no."

"So, what do you propose?"

I was soon straddling him, and he had one nipple in his mouth while he rubbed the other with one thumb. I came quickly and listened to that familiar low growl he made in his chest when he wanted to climax. I sat up and moved my hips as his hands glided over my belly, breasts, and thighs until we came in quick succession. Afterwards, I snuggled next to him on the side where he hadn't been shot.

"God, that felt so good," I murmured, as he stroked my hair.

"It's what kept me going when Goran's minion was torturing me."

"How?"

"When someone is causing you terrible pain, you think of the thing that brings you the most pleasure and hold onto it. When we're together in any way, I feel complete. I tried to remember that when he was hurting me. It actually worked most of the time. I'd think about how beautiful and smart you are, conversations we'd had, the way you look when you sleep, your laugh, the things you do, the way you make love, what a great wife and mother you are, and the way you make everyone around you feel good. You saved me, Seneca."

I was about to tell him that it was he who had saved me when the phone beside the bed rang. I lifted the receiver and listened for a moment before saying, "Let me ask Michael. We'll let you know." Once I'd hung up, I explained, "That was James. He said Elizabeth wanted to know if you felt well enough to have a tea party for dinner tonight. She said you looked like you felt better early this morning when she came to visit with you."

"A tea party sounds like fun. Do we get to dress up?"

"Definitely."

"Then let's do it. I'm tired of lying around in pajamas. What I'd really like to do is have an extended lovemaking session with you, but I doubt if it would be good for my recovery at this point. I think I'll have to settle for a tea party. The only thing is that I don't have a suit to wear."

"I'm sure you do. Brian thinks of everything."

"Yes, he does."

"Are you worried about him?"

"A little, but I'm confident he'll keep his word. He's been working hard on the dissolution of his business empire and has been talking with me and James about expanding his charitable projects. He's also house-hunting in Nonno's neighborhood by working with a realtor in that area. James is looking for a house in the vicinity as well. Soon, we'll all be living in Southwest Florida."

"What are we going to tell the kids about Brian, James, and Elizabeth?"

"I don't know. I don't know how to tell my Benedetto family either. I am and always will be a Benedetto, but will they think of me differently if they know I'm not a blood relation? That worries me more than anything."

"Maybe Brian could stay away when they come for visits."

"We've talked about that, but I'm just not sure. I have to figure it out."

I kissed him and said, "Don't worry about anything except enjoying our tea party tonight. Your sister will be thrilled."

"Yes." Smiling, he said, "She's wonderful, isn't she? The kids are going to love her."

"Michael –"

He placed his hand lightly on my mouth and said, "I know what you told me. I know she may not live for many more years and what might happen. I'm not thinking that far ahead today."

At 7:00, we were seated in Brian's dining room. I was wearing my orange dress with the blue beading, and Michael had on a tuxedo, as did Brian and James. Elizabeth wore a purple dress that had an orange ribbon around the waist.

"Papa had somebody find the same color orange as your dress!" she exclaimed excitedly. "We match!"

"We do," I agreed. "We're the same, remember?"

I had spent part of the afternoon playing with her in her room then we'd taken a walk through Central Park. She'd told me that she was so glad we'd been able to keep being sisters after all and was so happy to have two brothers as well. Now that we were having our tea party, she and I had on our hats, boas, and gloves. The five of us ate, chatted, and laughed. It was a wonderful meal for an extremely unusual family group.

"I have a request," Brian said, once our plates had been removed. "We're all here together and dressed for one of my darling Elizabeth's famous tea parties. I'd like to have a picture taken with all of us in our finery minus the gloves, hats, and boas, so I can add it to my collection in the study."

"As long as I can take off this patch," Michael declared. Knowing I would object, he turned to me and said, "I'll put it back on after the pictures. I don't want to look like something out of a pirate movie in our family portrait."

"Where are we going to take the picture, Papa?" Elizabeth asked.

"I was thinking in the living room in front of the wall of fountains. Would that suit everyone?"

I smiled as we entered the room. The furniture had been cleared from one area and two chairs were positioned in front of the section of the wall where there was purple tiling. A man with a camera was waiting, and special lights and reflectors had been set up to capture the perfect portrait. Brian had definitely not come up with this idea on the spur-of-the-moment.

The photographer took several pictures, some with Elizabeth and me sitting in the chairs with the men behind us and some with all of us standing. Once the man was done, we were able to look at the photos on his laptop and agreed there were two that were our favorites.

In the first one, Elizabeth and I were seated. Michael stood behind me and rested his hand on my shoulder. James stood between his father and brother. Brian had his hand resting on Elizabeth's shoulder. We looked happy and relaxed, despite our formal attire and pose.

The other picture was selected for a different reason. We were all laughing at something and our pleasure was evident in our expressions and positions as we stood in a line with our arms around each other's waists. It was a very human image, and it made us grin to see it.

Brian thanked the photographer and requested that the three sets of photos be printed on a canvas material so they would look more like portraits. One set would be for Brian and Elizabeth, another would go to James, and the last to Michael and me. The man said he would have everything ready within twenty-four hours and collected his gear and left. Men appeared and put the furniture back the way it had been before our not-so-impromptu photo session.

I looked over at Michael, who seemed to be suddenly exhausted. This was the most activity he'd had in over a month. When he began to reach up to casually rub his eye, I stopped him and said, "I think it's time for us to go back to our room, put the drops in your eye, put on the patch, and go to bed."

He nodded and admitted that he was, indeed, worn out. He and I hugged his sister, brother, and father before we left for our quarters. Then we returned to our rooms, undressed, put the drops in Michael's eye before covering it with the metal patch, and went to sleep.

The ringing of the phone woke us the next morning. Michael lifted the receiver and said, "James? Yes. What is it?"

I felt Michael tense beside me and quickly sat up in bed. I stared at him as he spoke to his brother and tears began to stream down his temples. I took his free hand in mine but didn't squeeze, since it had been the one with the sprained fingers and was only recently out of its splint.

When Michael hung up the phone, I sat wide-eyed and waited. When he began to cry harder, I scooted up in the bed and gently ran my fingers through his hair, kissed him, and asked him what was wrong.

"Brian and Elizabeth are dead."

My own eyes instantly filling with tears, I exclaimed, "What?!? How?"

I envisioned assassins and wondered how they'd managed to breach Brian's security measures. When I asked about this, Michael said there had been no killers in the apartment.

"How then?"

"James said Brian went to wake Elizabeth, as he does every morning when he's not away on business. She...she had died in her sleep. He called to James, who verified that she had no pulse. Then he asked James to leave him alone with Elizabeth for an hour and not to wake us, yet. James said he went to his own room to grieve. When he returned to the bedroom, he found Brian on the floor. It looks like he died not long after James left the room. He said Brian must have had a heart attack or an aneurysm, but he's leaning towards the former because of the circumstances. A coroner will have to determine the actual cause of death, but I agree with James. Brian probably had a heart attack."

A heart attack, I thought. *More like a broken heart.*

Michael and I rose and dressed then went to the main quarters. I refused to go into Elizabeth's room and see the father and daughter, but Michael didn't hesitate. I sat in the hallway and listened to the brothers talk, then cry as I quietly shed my own tears. They eventually emerged, and 911 was called.

I asked James if he'd told Brian's lover about his death. He nodded and said she'd run from the apartment in tears. He'd sent someone out to search for her. I nodded but feared that her life was over. Without Brian, she would most likely be back on the streets trying to escape her pain through drugs. She could be the third victim in the day's tragedy.

Brian and Elizabeth were buried side-by-side three days later. Brian, who'd suffered a massive coronary, had left instructions that he have no funeral service when he died. He merely wanted anyone who cared about him to say their goodbyes and see him buried with a simple headstone. Al and Diane were the only other people present at the gravesite besides James, Michael, and me.

"What now?" Diane asked as we ate dinner at the apartment that evening.

"My father had his will revised after last month," James admitted. "Since Michael knew of his existence, everything was kept the same with the exception that his portion would go directly to Michael and not to his business and charities through anonymous donations. Elizabeth preceded Brian in death. Therefore, a third of the estate will go to the charities our father supported, a third will go to me, and a third will go to Michael. All the properties will be sold, and the monies from them will be included in the dispersal of funds."

"Will you still move to Florida?" Michael asked seriously. "I want you to. You're my brother, and I want you to be part of our family."

James nodded soberly and said, "I have no one else. Most of my life was spent living with and then working with our father. My mother's been gone for twenty-one years. My father and sister are now gone as well. I believe it's time for me to start living my life for myself, but I've no wish to live it alone."

Al, Diane, Michael, and I returned to Florida the Saturday after the funeral. Our ecstatic children greeted us at the door and almost knocked us down with their enthusiastic embraces and excited chatter. We hugged Greg and Krystal then sat in the living room and simply *were* with Hadeel, Hani, and the others. Michael and I petted Buttons, who purred and rubbed against us. It felt fantastic to be home.

"Hani Superman!" our son declared then proceeded to show us how long he could "fly" on the living room floor. Once we'd applauded and hugged him, Hadeel showed us the dance she'd learned in ballet class while we'd been gone. We all clapped again and hugged her as well.

"Mama and I missed you and Hani so much," Michael said, as he kissed Hadeel on one temple. "I'm so sorry we had to be away for so long."

"You didn't mean to have an accident," Hadeel pointed out. "Are you all right now, Daddy? When can you not look like a pirate?"

He grinned and said, "Soon. I'm not quite well, but I'm getting there. Being with you, Mama, Hani, Nonno, Diane, Krystal, and Greg will help me finish getting better, because it makes me so happy." Looking to me, he said, "There's someone else who's going to help, too."

"Who?" she asked curiously.

"His name is James. I found out when I was…in the accident that he was my brother. I never knew I had a brother. He's going to come live near us."

"Cool!" she said and practically jumped out of his lap with her excitement. "What does he look like?"

"We have a couple of pictures," I offered. "Wait here, and I'll get them."

I went to our room and retrieved the two carefully packaged portraits taken the night before Elizabeth and Brian's deaths. I brought them back to the living room and showed them to the children, Krystal, and Greg. Hadeel pointed to Brian and said, "That's the man I saw the day before you had to go to Daddy! He really does look like Daddy. Who is he?"

Michael started to speak, swallowed hard, and said, "He was my Daddy, but I didn't know it until I had my accident. The woman in the picture was my sister. I didn't know about her either. She and my Daddy were going to move here with James, but they died earlier this week."

Hadeel appeared frightened and asked if they had had accidents, too. We all hastened to reassure her that they hadn't and that it was just their time to go to Heaven.

"So, they're up in Heaven with our first Mama, Daddy, brother, and your baby, Mama?"

It was difficult for me to breathe, but I managed to nod as Michael told her that yes, his father and sister were in Heaven with the others. She said something to Michael in Arabic, and he nodded and replied in Arabic. Hani looked up from where he was playing on the floor and said something in Arabic, and Michael smiled.

As the two children went to get a toy that they wanted to show us, Greg asked, "What was that about?"

239

"Hadeel told me no one is ever sad in Heaven and that everyone goes there someday. Hani said there were dogs in Heaven, and he liked dogs."

"Rumi's poem," I muttered. "*Love Dogs*. I read it to them sometimes, since it was the last thing Adiba referenced before she died. I never thought they were actually paying attention that closely."

"Little minds absorb more than we can know," Al remarked with a slight smile. Looking to Krystal and Greg, he said, "They absorb love, too. Your baby will be very happy."

Both of them thanked him, then Krystal excused herself to use the restroom. I brought the framed pictures back to the master bedroom and laid them on the bed. Then I removed the music box Brian had given me from my suitcase, wound it, and watched the ballerina twirl.

"That's so pretty," Krystal said from the doorway.

"Michael's father gave it to me when Michael was in CCU. Michael's sister had a different one that I brought back for Hadeel."

"Are you okay?"

I looked at her, the small swell of her lower abdomen more pronounced since the last time I'd seen her. I shook my head but assured her I would be fine. She looked doubtful but merely smiled and came over to give me a hug.

"I wish Tom was here," I told her, my head resting on her shoulder. "I miss Tom."

"I know. Maybe you should go to his grave and talk to him."

"But he's not really there."

"No, but you might try it anyway. You need to talk to him, no matter where you are. You have a bunch of stuff to say to him, I'm sure. You've been through a lot."

That night while Michael and the children slept, I went to the living room and retrieved Tom's childhood teddy bear and the illuminated piece of glass that Salvador Dali had given him years earlier. I placed the artwork next to one of the framed photos of me and Tom and held the bear as I began to speak. I told Tom about everything that had happened. I talked of how scared I'd been, of how thankful I was Tom had led me to Brian, and of how grateful Michael and I were that we'd gotten to know the man and his daughter even if it was only for a brief time. I told Tom I loved and missed him and that I hoped he was happy in Heaven with Adiba, Rakeem, John Henry, Brian, Elizabeth, and my parents. I asked him to keep watch over me and my family. Then I put everything back where it had been, checked on my children, and returned to the bed I shared with my husband. I had to admit that I did feel better having spoken to my dead friend. I supposed every person had his or her own idea of where deceased loved ones were. I was glad I didn't have to go to the cemetery to talk to Tom. I could do it any time I wanted right in my own house, and that was a very comforting thought.

"Did you and Tom have a nice chat?" Michael asked me, his eyes still closed.

"Michael, how –"

"I had a talk with Brian while you were in the living room."

I placed my head against his chest and felt his arm encircle my shoulders. It felt so nice and normal to have him be able to hold me in our bed again. I fell asleep listening to the soothing sound of his breathing and the feel of him stroking my hair.

Chapter Twenty-two

"She's beautiful, isn't she?" Greg asked, as he stared down at his newborn daughter. "I hope to God I can do right by her and be a good dad."

"You'll be a great dad," Michael told him. "And Krystal will be a great mom."

"Thanks, Michael," Krystal said tiredly. "I think you're right."

I smiled down at the baby girl in my arms and asked, "Okay, so now that she's here, what's her name?"

Greg and Krystal looked at one another before Greg said, "We wanted to name her after our two closest friends. So, her name will be Michelle Seneca. We're going to call her Mick."

I grinned and repeated, "Mick. I like that. It's so cute." Kissing the baby's soft head, I said, "Welcome to the world, Mick."

"You guys didn't have to do that," Michael protested.

"We wanted to," Krystal told him. "Greg and I never would've met if it hadn't been for Seneca, and the two of you have been there for us ever since."

"And you've been there for us," I reminded them. "We love you."

"And we love you," Krystal said firmly. "Mick is going to be very lucky to have the two of you in her life, just like we are."

I knew Krystal was exhausted and in pain and that we should leave the new parents alone with their daughter. I told Michael as much and handed Mick to her mother before kissing Krystal on the cheek and telling her how proud I was of her for making it through what had turned out to be an extremely difficult pregnancy, labor, and delivery. She thanked me for being there with her every step of the way, even though she knew it had been rough for me emotionally. I gave Greg a brief hug, and he and Michael gave each other a quick, manly hug before Michael put an arm around Krystal's shoulders and told her to try to get some sleep. He touched

Mick's cheek with one fingertip. Then, we left the room and went downstairs and out of the hospital into the cool January night.

"Let's go out," Michael said impulsively. "It's Friday evening. Why don't we go to Ceviche and meet up with the gang and dance for a while?"

"Okay."

He was about to turn the key in the ignition of the SUV, when he paused and asked, "Do you want to cry now or later?"

"Now would be good."

We unbuckled our seatbelts, and he held me tightly against him as we cried. After a while, we quieted and simply held one another. Eventually, I pulled some fresh tissues from my purse and we wiped our cheeks and blew our noses.

"I guess we're never going to quite get over not being able to have our own babies," Michael said.

"No, but you have to admit we've gotten a lot better about it since we adopted Hadeel and Hani."

"We have, but that doesn't make the wanting go away completely, does it?"

"No, but it'll be okay. I think now that Mick's here we can get on with our lives and not think about it so much."

"Until Krystal gets pregnant again."

"She won't."

"How can you be so certain?"

"Because she told me when you and Greg were out of the room that her doctor advised her she shouldn't ever try to have another baby. I think after everything she went through carrying and having Mick, she and Greg will be all right with that."

"I'm sorry for them but kind of relieved for us." Shaking his head, he said, "That sounds terrible, but it's true."

I kissed him and said, "Let's go out like you suggested. Al and Diane agreed to watch Hani and Hadeel for as long as we wanted. We should go. Why don't you call James and see if he wants to meet us there?"

The restaurant was packed, and we used the valet parking and went inside and upstairs. James arrived shortly thereafter and asked how Krystal and the baby were.

"Both doing well, thank goodness," I told him. "Her name's Michelle Seneca, and they're going to call her Mick."

He smiled and said, "Mick. I like it. I'll have to drop in on them when you tell me they're up to it. How's Greg taking to fatherhood?"

"He's scared to death, but he and Krystal will do fine," Michael told him. "He's taking a two-month family medical leave from John's Place to be with Krystal and Mick. You want a temporary job?"

"You know, I'd love one," James grinned. "I worked with our father for so long. It'll be nice to work with my brother now." Turning to me, he asked, "Could I have this dance, Seneca?"

I did a little curtsy, kissed Michael, and went out onto the dance floor with James, who was almost as good a dancer as his brother.

"The kids were wondering if you're still coming over to the house for dinner tomorrow night," I told James. "Hadeel says she has something special to read to you in Arabic, and Hani wants you to play Legos with him as you did last time. Al and Diane will be there as usual."

"I wouldn't dream of missing the family time at the Benedetto household."

Someone tapped me on the shoulder. I turned around and looked up at an attractive, tall, lanky red-head. She smiled pleasantly at me and asked in a lilting Georgia accent, "May I cut in?"

I immediately stepped away from James and said, "Certainly. This is my brother-in-law, James."

"James. That's very nice. I'm January."

"January?" James echoed in his lovely British voice.

"Yes, I know," she said with a roll of her eyes. "My parents weren't very clever. I was born January thirty-first. I'm just glad I wasn't born later. It can be hard enough for people in the collegiate world where I teach to take me seriously with a name like January, but if my name were February…?"

James laughed and grinned madly at me. I smiled and nodded then went back to where Michael was waiting for me.

"Who's that?" he asked as I took a sip of red wine.

"I think that may be the future Mrs. James Harrison."

"What?"

"Call it a hunch. James told me once that he has a thing for tall, lanky redheads with nice breasts and a tight backside. She fits the bill and seems to have brains and wit as well. Plus, she has a charming Southern accent."

"Then maybe she's the one," he said with a smile. "I hope so. He deserves a family of his own and wants to find love." Kissing the side of my neck, he murmured, "Speaking of love, have you talked to Rob, lately?"

I did a double take and said, "Just our usual weekly science geek chats. Why?"

"Because he called me at lunch and said he thinks he's in love. She's an M.D. he met at a fundraiser last night. I've never heard him sound so bowled over by anyone, excluding you."

"Michael, we never –"

He kissed me in order to silence me and placed a hand at my waist. When he drew back, he said, "Rob told me a long time ago how he felt about you but swore he'd never pursue you. I felt badly for him because he told me he didn't think he'd ever find a woman like you to fill the void in his life. Well, from the way he was talking about this doctor, I think he might have changed his tune. I have a feeling they won't leave his place or hers all weekend long. He seems totally smitten."

"Good for him. Rob's a great friend, and I want to see him find someone he can share his life with."

"As long as you can continue your physics dialogues."

"You and I could talk physics."

"Unlikely. I'm nowhere near your level."

"And I couldn't run a business to save my life, so there you are. We are unique, just like everybody else."

He gave me that engaging grin of his, took my hand, and then led me out on the dance floor. We danced for a while then decided it was time to head for Al and Diane's. I excused myself to freshen up while he ordered us each a glass of water.

On our way to the elevator, Michael pulled me into a dark corner and kissed me passionately. I felt the usual electric charge between us and moaned softly as he pressed against me. I could feel the hardness of him and wrapped my arms around his waist. When he drew back, the animal look was in his eyes.

"I have to run by the office for a minute," he told me. "It won't take long. I just have to grab some papers I need to review with James tomorrow."

Unable to speak, I merely nodded and walked with him towards the elevator. He put an arm around my waist in that all-too-male "mine" gesture that I so appreciated. Within minutes, we were in the SUV on our way to John's Place.

I went inside with him, wondering if he intended to have sex with me there. However, the cleaning crew happened to be in attendance, so that wasn't going to happen even if it had been his intention. I walked to his office with him, leaned against the corner of his desk, and admired the Frida Kahlo print while he withdrew the papers he needed from a file drawer. Then he strode over to me, slipped a hand under my skirt, and slid his fingers through the side of my panties. I threw my arms around him and automatically spread my legs slightly. When I gasped, he kissed me, covering my mouth and concealing my cries as I climaxed.

"Michael, what are you doing?" I breathed when he removed his hand and gathered his papers.

"What I've been wanting to do since I was tortured last summer."

"But we've had sex since then," I pointed out. "Lots and lots of times. Sometimes, it's quick. Sometimes, we're at it for hours."

"But it's not quite like before. I don't know why, but I haven't been able to be as spontaneous as I used to."

"Dangerous," I said with a slight smile.

He smiled back and said, "Dangerous. Between finding out about my real father and all of it...I think I was questioning my limits. I believe I've figured it out now. I'm ready to be dangerous again, at least when it comes to sex. Are you ready for that?"

"Anytime."

He gave me such a wicked grin that I felt like climaxing on the spot.

We drove to Al and Diane's house. It was 9:00, and I'd expected the children to be ready for bed. Instead, Hadeel and Hani were sitting at the kitchen table having bowls of cereal along with Al and Diane.

"We have been having great fun," Al said. "They have used up much energy and were hungry."

"So were we," Diane admitted. "Although we've had a wonderful evening. We watched a Disney movie, and then Hadeel showed us her new dance. She's very good, especially for someone who's not even four, yet."

"And Hani is teaching us how to build things with Legos," Al told us. "The things he makes are intricate, and he's not quite three!"

"I want to spend the night at Nonno and Diane's!" Hani declared.

"Please, Mama!" Hadeel pleaded. "Daddy?"

"I don't know," Michael said uncertainly. "You've been here all day since Mama and I went to the hospital with Krystal and Greg. Nonno and Diane might be tired."

"Oh, let them stay," Diane told us. "We'll go to bed soon. We have some of their things here. It will be fine."

Hani said something to Michael in Arabic, and Michael answered back with firmness in his tone. Both children nodded then went back to eating their cereal.

"I said they can stay if they do exactly as you tell them."

"*Bellisimo!*" Al said enthusiastically. "Now, sit for a moment and tell us about the baby and how the new parents are faring."

We left the house at 10:00 and drove home. The night air had gotten cold, at least to me. Michael, of course, seemed unaffected. He probably would have gone for a swim if he hadn't wanted to make love to me so badly. We went into the house, which was blessedly warm, and began to undress one another.

Michael's cell phone rang, and he checked the caller I.D. and groaned with aggravation, but told me he had to take the call. As he did so, I fed Buttons and petted him then went to the bathroom and brushed my teeth. As I finished, Michael came in and apologized but said the call had come from the new director of the Detroit location of John's Place, and the man was having problems that required Michael's attention.

"Are you going to Detroit?"

"I think this can be worked out remotely, but we'll see. If the issues persist, then I'll head for Michigan to handle things. I'd rather not at this time with Greg out and James unfamiliar with the business."

Coming up behind me, Michael pressed against me and brought his hands to the front of my sweater. He deftly undid the buttons and pulled it off then undid my bra and let that drop to the floor. I brought my hands up and wove my fingers into his hair as he caressed my breasts then slid his hands down and undid my skirt. It fell to the floor, and my underwear soon lay on top of it.

I turned and slipped my hands under his sweater, then pulled it over his head. I quickly undid his pants and pulled them and his boxers down. He stepped out of them. I had expected him to lead me to the bed, but instead he picked me up and carried me through the backdoor and across the lanai.

"Michael, it's freezing! I'm cold!"

"You won't be for long," he told me with a mischievous smile. "I want to make love to you on the beach. It's a beautiful night, and the moon is full."

"Hel-*lo!* It's also freezing."

He laid me down on a blanket that he'd obviously spread out on the beach while I was in the bathroom. Before I could object, he covered my mouth with his and positioned his body on top of mine. Although still shivering, I stopped arguing with him and gripped his broad shoulders. I looked up at Michael with his powerful, muscular body poised over me and moved my hands across his naked flesh. I opened myself to him and pulled him towards me. He suddenly appeared ferocious, and I wanted to feel the animal unleashed.

I unleashed a ferocity of my own and completely forgot about being cold. I lost track of time and of how often I came and reveled in being one with Michael. We eventually collapsed into each other's arms and held onto the magic of that night. I became aware of the cold again and of the biting winds coming in off the Gulf of Mexico.

Michael rose, wrapped me in the blanket, and carried me back into the lanai. He put me down and shook off the sand on the blanket but let the thing fall to the ground before taking my hand and returning to the warmth of the house.

"One more time tonight," I murmured, as he kissed me when we got to the bedroom. "Come in me, Michael."

So, we made love one more time that night. I screamed my release; he roared his. Then we spooned our bodies together under the comforter and slept peacefully until dawn.

I woke to the feel of Michael's lips on my neck. He stroked my hair and whispered that he loved me more than anything in the world. I twisted around until I was facing him and told him the same thing. We kissed; then he asked me if I would do something for him.

"Anything I can."

"I want to take you to the ballet next weekend. Would you be able to handle it?"

I thought about this for a while then smiled at him and said, "Attending a ballet would be wonderful."

Grinning, Michael said, "You're beautiful, you know that?"

"I do, thanks to you."

"Don't thank me. You've been beautiful since you were born."

"But you were the one who made me see it." Running my fingers along his jaw, I asked, "Do you know how much I love you?"

"I've never doubted that from the first time we met. You and I were meant to be together. I told you that you make me complete. I meant every word."

Settling into his embrace, I repeated, "Complete. What a perfect way to describe what we have and what we are. That used to be a lovely dream for me. I'm so happy it's become our lovely reality."

ABOUT THE AUTHOR

Lauren Cutrera, who also writes under the name Barbara Cutrera, has published over 20 contemporary romance, romantic suspense, paranormal romance, mystery, and fiction novels. Diverse people and plots highlight her works, drawing readers into the characters' unique journeys as they navigate their way through their struggles and triumphs. Lauren and her husband, Budge, are the proud parents of a grown son. They live in southwest Florida and have a cute and naughty Yorkie, Hadrian, who sleeps next to Lauren as she writes each day.

Explore other published works by the author at amazon.com and goodreads.com

Check out all things Lauren (and Barbara) at www.laurencutrera.com

And connect with her there or on

Facebook: https://www.facebook.com/profile.php?id=100063631654302

Instagram: https://www.instagram.com/laurencutrera/

Pinterest: https://www.pinterest.com/laurencutrera/_saved/

OTHER BOOKS BY THE AUTHOR:

The Essential Elements Series

Kindred Spirits
Scorched Creek
Spirits Corner
Memory Lane
Homeward Bound

The Limitless Series

Sight Unseen
Better Left Unsaid
Unheard Of
Under Her Skin
Brain Storm
Out On A Limb

The Seneca & Michael Duet

A Lovely Dream
A Lovely Reality

The Gift Series

The Healer's Gift
Jordan's Way
Bound by Grace
The Nameless

The Real World Series

Over, Under, Across & Through
A Good Man's Life
Mercy
Unfinished Business (Final Chapter)

<u>Standalone Novels/Short Stories</u>

In A Manner of Speaking
Prim & Proper
Lucky
Compromising Positions
True: 3 Short Stories

www.ingramcontent.com/pod-product-compliance
Lightning Source LLC
Chambersburg PA
CBHW061610170626
46811CB00001B/376